John Roy Musick

Estevan

A Story of the Spanish Conquests

John Roy Musick

Estevan

A Story of the Spanish Conquests

ISBN/EAN: 9783743399471

Manufactured in Europe, USA, Canada, Australia, Japa

Cover: Foto ©Andreas Hilbeck / pixelio.de

Manufactured and distributed by brebook publishing software (www.brebook.com)

John Roy Musick

Estevan

"THEY GAZED ON A STRANGE VALLEY AND A WONDERFUL CITY."

COLUMBIAN HISTORICAL NOVELS.   VOLUME II.

ESTEVAN

A STORY OF THE SPANISH CONQUESTS

BY

JOHN R. MUSICK

Author of "Columbia, a Story of the Discovery of America."

Illustrations by

FREELAND A. CARTER

New York
FUNK & WAGNALLS COMPANY
LONDON AND TORONTO

PREFACE.

THE first volume of this series, covering the age of discovery, concluded with the death of Columbus. This volume, designed to cover the period known as the age of conquests, begins with the sailing of Ojeda and Nicuesa to Darien, and concludes with the discovery of the Mississippi. As in the former work, historical events are narrated with great regard for accuracy. There is so much romance in the Spanish conquests in America, that one has only to select incidents, and, by the exercise of a little skill in weaving them together, an entertaining novel is made. Hernando Estevan, one of the leading characters in "Columbia," appears in the beginning of this volume: but the romance centres about his son, Christopher, and the daughter of Vasco Nuñez de Balboa.

JOHN R. MUSICK.

Kirksville, Mo., February 1, 1892.

TABLE OF CONTENTS.

CHAPTER I.

PAGE

AN INFANT WORLD, ... 1

CHAPTER II.

THE MAN IN THE CASK, ... 16

CHAPTER III.

AN UNKNOWN SEA, ... 35

CHAPTER IV.

A FICKLE LOVER, ... 55

CHAPTER V.

LOVE AND DEATH, ... 71

CHAPTER VI.

THE OPPORTUNITY, ... 92

CHAPTER VII.

THE YOUNG HUMANITARIAN, ... 107

CHAPTER VIII.

DOÑA MARINA, ... 121

CHAPTER IX.

THE BLOODHOUND'S VICTIM, ... 136

CHAPTER X.

THE GOLDEN CONQUEST, ... 148

CHAPTER XI.

MATCHLOCKS IN THE AIR, ... 165

v

CHAPTER XII.

OFF FOR SPAIN, ... 183

CHAPTER XIII.

INEZ OVIEDO, ... 195

CHAPTER XIV.

LOVE AND HATE, ... 210

CHAPTER XV.

PIZARRO AND CORTEZ. 224

CHAPTER XVI.

RETURN TO THE NEW WORLD, . 237

CHAPTER XVII.

A MYSTERIOUS FRIEND, . . . 250

CHAPTER XVIII.

THE CITY OF GOLD, ... 266

CHAPTER XIX

SEIZING A KING, ... 282

CHAPTER XX.

A BANQUET OF DEATH, ... 300

CHAPTER XXI.

THE SECRET MARRIAGE, . . . 318

CHAPTER XXII.

AN INDIAN GIRL'S LOVE, . . . 334

CHAPTER XXIII.

THE FATHER OF WATERS, ... 350

CHAPTER XXIV.

THE WANDERER FINDS REST, . . 366

CHAPTER XXV.

CONCLUSION, ... 382

HISTORICAL INDEX, ... 391

CHRONOLOGY, ... 401

LIST OF ILLUSTRATIONS.

PAGE

They gazed on a strange valley and a wonderful city
    (see page 152), ... *Frontispiece*
Caravel at sea, ... 1
Balboa's strategy, ... 19
"Will you take me?" 33
Leoncico, ... 36
"Santiago! And at them!" 39
A vast ocean glittered in the morning sun, . 52
"Don't you see how happy I am?" . . . 97
"Hold, lieutenant, would you kill your slave?" . 113
"From what country did you come?" . . 128
"Santa Maria! I am slain!" 181
Madly he leaped toward the frightened steed, . . 202
Side by side they floated down the narrow stream, . 217
With a glad cry she was in his arms, . . . 235
"You are going away to Peru," 241
Nicosia advanced toward the beast, ... 259
"Follow all who can," 306
"She comes!" 351
De Soto, ... 363
Then came long weary months of wandering over
    the plains, ... 368
"Estevan, farewell!" 380
"Behold your son!" 388
Map of the period, ... 156

ESTEVAN.

CHAPTER I.

AN INFANT WORLD.

THE evening of November 9, 1509, the little town of San Domingo was in a fever of excitement. It had been a busy day, and the confusion and hubbub continued until late in the night. Ships were lying in the harbor ready to sail with the rising sun. It was their object to explore and conquer the then unknown "Castilla del Oro," or what was supposed to be the "Aurea Chersonesus" of the ancients, whence King Solomon procured the gold used for building his temple.

A question which but a short time before had threatened to plunge the colonies into a civil war had been amicably settled. Ojeda and Nicuesa, two

1

bold, enterprising cavaliers, claimed the governor
ship of Jamaica and Darien.   Juan de la Cosa induced the rival governors to allow the river Darien
to be the boundary line between their respective
jurisdictions at that point.   Don Diego Columbus,
son of Christopher Columbus, and hereditary admiral and viceroy-general, settled the dispute over
Jamaica himself.   He already felt aggrieved at the
distribution of governments without his consent
and even his knowledge, contrary to the privileges
inherited from his father the discoverer.   Jamaica
lay almost at his own door, and he would not brook
its being made a matter of dispute between these
brawling governors; so, without awaiting the slow
and uncertain course of remonstrating with the
king, who had already shown little regard for his
wishes and rights, he took the matter in his own
hands, and offered the governorship of Jamaica to
his stanch friend and brave officer Juan de Esquibel, who with seventy men took command of the
island and held it subject to Don Diego Columbus,
notwithstanding that the fiery Ojeda swore he would
strike off his rival's head if he did so.

The above stirring incidents formed live topics
for conversation among the inhabitants of San
Domingo.   Ojeda had become somewhat reconciled
to the act of Diego Columbus, and was, on the next
morning, to sail with his vessels to the conquest of

his possessions in Darien, which were rumored to contain fabulous wealth.

Long after the darkness of a tropical night had settled over the little town, people were busy either making arrangements for their departure, or, in knots and clusters, on the streets and in the houses, were discussing the wonders which the expedition was to unfold.

We invite the reader's attention to a group of four men assembled in one of the apartments of Hernando Estevan's house, a substantial dwelling, standing on an eminence in the suburbs of the town, with a fine view of the bay and ships riding at anchor. The best-known man of the group at this time was Hernando Estevan himself, who had come with Columbus on his first voyage, and was among the first to touch the soil of the infant world. Hernando loved the great admiral, whom he had served since boyhood, and who on more than one occasion had saved his life. When he became cognizant of the intrigues of Bovadilla to deprive Christopher Columbus of his rights, he was loud in his denunciation of the admiral's enemies, thereby bringing down upon his own head some of the thunderbolts which ruined Columbus.

The three companions of Estevan on this evening were Hernando Cortez, Vasco Nuñez de Balboa, and Francisco Pizarro, three men since known to

fame as explorers and soldiers. Of the four,
Cortez, although by no means diminutive in size,
was the smallest. He was slender, graceful and
handsome, a native of Medellin, of an ancient
and respectable family, but of dissolute habits, and
the last person one would expect to engage in the
desperate enterprises which later in life marked his
career and placed his name first among the Spanish
conquerors. He was gallant, kind-hearted and
jovial, and in the old world as well as in the new
was continually involved in some love scrape. He
had fought a score of duels, and on this evening
was suffering from a sword thrust in the hip which
compelled him to go on crutches. Vasco Nuñez
de Balboa was a native of Xeres de los Caballeros,
of a noble though impoverished family. He was a
soldier of fortune, of loose, prodigal habits, and,
like Cortez, a libertine. At present he was as
badly crippled with debts as was Cortez with a
sword thrust.

The fourth man, all things considered, was, perhaps, the most remarkable of the group. Francisco
Pizarro was a modern Romulus. Instead, however,
of building up an empire, as did Romulus, he destroyed a kingdom. He was born about the year
1472, at Truxillo, a city of Estremadura, in Spain,
being an illegitimate son of Gonzalo Pizarro, a colo-
nel of infantry, who was an uncle to Hernando

Cortez. Pizarro was abandoned by his mother, Francisca Gonzalez, when a child, and his early life was very obscure. He never received any education, and tradition says that in infancy he was suckled by a sow, a story quite as plausible as that Romulus in early life drew his nourishment from a wolf. In boyhood he was a common swincherd and was kicked up into the world until he became old enough to kick back. He inherited his military ability from his father. Pizarro was moody, taciturn, and at times sullen. There was a natural ferocity about him, strangely in contrast with his cousin Hernando Cortez. The latter was always friendly with Pizarro, regardless of their difference in rank, station and birth, and even acknowledged him as his cousin.

The four men whom we have thus introduced sat about a table on which was a jar of wine and some drinking cups, for Estevan, the host, was noted for his hospitality.

"So a truce has been patched up between the rival governors," said Balboa, sipping his wine.

"A truce which will be permanent," answered Estevan. "The admiral has disposed of Jamaica."

"To the dissatisfaction of Ojeda," put in Cortez. "Ha, ha, ha! the fiery little fellow has had many drawbacks of late. It was worth seeing him when he proposed to settle the dispute in single combat."

"Would not Nicuesa accept his challenge?" asked Pizarro, in his deep orotund voice.

"Accept! ha, ha, ha, ha! He did accept," laughed Cortez; "but that was the joke. Nicuesa proposed, as a preliminary to the duel, that they have something worth fighting for, and that each should deposit five thousand castillanos, to be the prize of the victor."

"Such a swordsman as Ojeda need not long hesitate at such a proposition," remarked Balboa.

"Nor would he, had he possessed the money. The cunning Nicuesa knew he had not a single pistole in his treasury when he made the proposition." Cortez laughed loudly, Estevan and Balboa smiled, while Pizarro sat gazing sullenly at the wall.

"Ojeda will make his fortune now," sighed Balboa, after a short silence. "I would that I could go with him."

"Why can't you?" Pizarro asked.

"Creditors!" sighed Balboa. "They are on every side. There is gold for the idiots at Castilla del Oro. I have a strong arm and a keen sword to earn it, and why won't they let me go?"

"Do they object?" asked Estevan.

"Yes. To-day a delegation of my creditors paid me an unwelcome visit, and gave me to understand if I made any effort to leave the island without first having satisfied their demands, I would be arrested and thrown into prison."

"Then you are in reality a prisoner at San Domingo?" remarked Estevan.

"I am going to escape and carve out an empire for myself," answered Balboa. "Ojeda would have been in the same plight as I, had not Bachelor Encisco loaned him the money."

"Try a loan yourself?" laughingly suggested Cortez.

"Where, pray, could I secure one?"

"Not from me, I swear," answered the merry Cortez; then, with a sudden contortion of the muscles of his face, he added: "Ah! that wound pains me! The devil drove his sword well nigh to the hip joint."

"How did you receive this last wound?" Estevan asked.

"It's another lady affair. Alonzo Bestiadez became mortally jealous of his pretty wife because she deigned to smile on me, and forthwith challenged me. It adds one more scar to my list," and Cortez laughed as if it were a joke.

"Could you swear he was jealous without a cause, Cortez?" asked Hernando.

"Nay, nay, my good friend, do not press me too close. Alonzo has his wife, I have my wound, so let the matter end, though the wound is unlucky for me."

"Why so, friend!" asked Hernando. "Perchance it may keep you out of some worse scrape."

"I was to go with Ojeda on this expedition."

"I thought he excluded friends of the late admiral."

"Not so, he is hard pressed for men and will take any who can go. Even Pizarro goes with him."

Pizarro nodded his head in silence.

"And Balboa would go if he could escape the embraces of his creditors."

"So I would," and Balboa laughed as recklessly as did the merry Cortez.

"This ugly wound is all that detains me. Our friend Estevan, here, is in love with adventure; why don't you make one of the party?" asked Cortez, directing the last part of his speech to Estevan.

"I have a wife," answered Estevan.

"So you have, the beautiful Christina, though I have not seen much of her of late," continued the rollicking Cortez. "You must be madly in love with her, indeed, to forego the pleasure of this conquest for her society."

"I am soon to be a father," added Estevan.

"Aha!" cried his three convivial companions,

starting to their feet. Cortez, with a spasm of pain, clutched his wounded leg and sat down. As soon as he could speak he said:

"You are a lucky dog, Estevan, to be the father of the first white child born in the New World. You will have richer treasures than Castilla del Oro can furnish."

"I would not care to sail with Ojeda, anyway," added Estevan.

"Why not?"

"He is an enemy of the admiral, and I am Don Diego's friend."

"That is a truth," said Cortez, "and woe is the man under Ojeda who is friendly to Columbus."

"Of all of us, Francisco Pizarro, alone, will accompany the expedition," put in Balboa.

Pizarro answered with a silent nod.

These men were typical of the great explorers and cavaliers of the age. They were men whom nothing discouraged or dismayed. In the fervor of their belief, they seemed to be inspired and to inspire.

Pizarro, foundling and swineherd as he had been, was one of the class of daring enthusiasts. He was a man of brain as well as brawn. Reason first kindled his passion, but passion was the instrument he used. While appearing to appeal to men's judgments, he forced himself into their hearts.

Nothing is more contagious than enthusiasm; it moves stones and charms brutes. It is the genius of sincerity, and truth accomplishes no victories without it. Though gloomy and taciturn as he usually was, Pizarro could become loquacious, and even eloquent at will. When he became roused at last and told his companions of the golden conquests which awaited those brave and daring enough to secure them, Cortez, for the time being, forgot his wound, Balboa his creditors, and Estevan his wife and prospective heir.

"Before us is a vast unknown world, with treasures that would outrival a Crœsus," said Pizarro. "The season is ripe for wealth and fame. Both await the man who has the courage to draw his sword and carve out his fortune."

"I will go!" cried Balboa, enthusiastically.

"But your creditors," interposed Cortez, with a smile.

"My creditors may wait until I have amassed a fortune, when I will return and satisfy them in full."

It was late when the little party broke up that night. Cortez with his crutch and cane hobbled away to his humble abode, regretting that he could not be one of the crew to sail on the morrow. Estevan, fired by the oratory of Pizarro, wished that his affairs were so arranged that he could embark in the dangerous enterprise of conquering Darien.

At early dawn he was awakened by the tumult of embarcation. Hurriedly dressing, he hastened toward the bay, which presented a scene of unusual excitement. The horses, which had been left until the last, were being taken on shipboard. Cavaliers in glittering helmets and shining armor were hurrying here and there. Crossbow-men, arquebusiers, halberdiers and sailors were embarking. The morning air resounded with music. The departing soldiers and adventurers indulged in song and jest, as though they were going on a mere holiday excursion. The Spanish imagination was easily quickened, and the Spaniards, naturally enthusiastic, caught the contagion of conquest, while their fancies wove triumphs and treasures exceeding the most marvellous dreams.

"You have come to witness the departure," said a familiar voice at Estevan's side, and turning, he beheld Cortez leaning on his crutch. "It is a glorious sight, Cortez, and I feel a desire to go myself," answered Estevan.

"This accursed wound holds me here; but I will bide my time. God ordains us for different fields of action, and, perchance, it is best that we do not go to Darien."

"Poor fellows! Many of them who march so

proudly to board the vessels may never return," thought Estevan. Little did he dream how few would return.

In shining harness, glittering helmet and clanking sword, Ojeda rode his prancing steed to the water's edge. Dismounting, his horse was driven into a scow to be taken on board, while the governor waited on the sands to oversee the embarcation. As a boat was about to pull from shore, a man darted forward and entered it.

"Pull away—pull away!" he shouted to the oarsman.

But ere an oar could be dipped in the water to speed the boat forward, several harpies of the law rushed forward, and, seizing Balboa, dragged him from the boat.

"Unhand me!" he cried, drawing his sword.

"What have we here?" demanded Ojeda, hurrying to the scene.

"This is Balboa, a fellow who owes us, and takes this means of escaping his just obligations," answered one of the creditors. "We intend to drag him before the alcalde mayor and send him to prison."

Francisco Pizarro, in the hope of aiding his friend, quitted the boat, and, with his hand on his sword, was advancing toward the officers. Knowing it would not do to interfere with the rights of

Balboa's creditors, Ojeda turned toward Pizarro and said:

"Back to your boat, fellow; if he owes debts, let him pay them."

"Unless he can induce Bachelor Encisco to do it for him!" put in a jester who was on the beach. This remark being a direct thrust at Ojeda, who had been helped out of a financial strait by the lawyer Encisco, so enraged the governor that he drew his sword and chased the young knave for two hundred paces, but the jester was swift on foot and Ojeda heavily encumbered with his armor, so the culprit escaped. Ojeda returned, and, entering his boat, was pulled away to his vessel. Anchor was weighed, sails spread, and amid the thundering of cannon and glad huzzas, that portion of the fleet which Ojeda was to take with him sailed. Some of the vessels under Bachelor Encisco, who had borne the expenses of the expedition, remained behind for recruits and supplies, to follow a few months later.

Estevan and Cortez watched the sails until the fleet disappeared, never to return. Cortez, cursing the ill luck which prevented his enlisting in the expedition, hobbled back to his house, where he was soon joined by Balboa.

"Did they release you so soon?" asked Cortez.

"They only detained me until the fleet was gone;

but I will join Ojeda yet.   I will be an explorer, Cortez, and carve a name for myself among the conquerors of the New World."

Cortez winced, as he tried to move his wounded hip.

"I wonder whose sword it will be next to pierce my flesh?" he coolly remarked.

Months rolled on, and only the wildest rumors of the expedition reached San Domingo.   Those who had friends and relatives with Ojeda strained their eyes, gazing seaward in the hope of seeing a sail.   None dreamed of the dangers, trials and sufferings from the ocean, treacherous reefs, unhealthy morasses, and poisonous arrows of revengeful enemies, which menaced the adventurers at Darien.   The winter passed, ushering in the year 1510, a year memorable in the history of the New World.   Bachelor Encisco was beating up recruits and loading his ships with supplies for San Sebastian, and expected soon to weigh anchor and go in search of Ojeda.

One bright morning, early in the new year, the feeble wail of an infant was heard in the house of Estevan.   No sooner was the glad news spread over the town, than old and young flocked to gaze on the first white child born in the New World. The admiral, Don Diego Columbus, who had always been Estevan's warmest friend, was among the first to congratulate him over the birth of a son.

The babe grew strong, and as he lay on his bed, gazing with great blue eyes at Balboa, Cortez, and Diego Columbus, he seemed to be reading in their faces his own stormy future. What a wild career was marked out for that child! Well for the peace and joy of his parents that they were not permitted to read the future of their son. At the proper age the child was christened by the bishop of San Domingo. His parents gave him the name of Christopher Rodrigo Estevan, and appointed Don Diego Columbus as his godfather. Those who saw the child thought its bright face foretold a grand destiny. The good bishop declared that it was no ordinary child. It was seldom ailing, and still more seldom gave evidence of grief. It seemed quietly concentrating all its energies for a wonderful future. Those little feet were to tread great mountain systems then unknown, to thread deep and almost impenetrable forests in far-off lands, and those deep blue eyes were to behold golden cities, witness kings hurled from their thrones, and see dynasties overturned.

CHAPTER II.

THE MAN IN THE CASK.

BACHELOR ENCISCO had almost received his complement of men and supplies, and was busily engaged loading his ship. Neither Ojeda nor Nicuesa had been heard from since their departure, and there were various conjectures as to their fate. But new adventurers had arrived from Spain and the island, ready to engage in new and dangerous enterprises.

On the day before the vessel sailed, Balboa met Estevan on the street, and led him apart from the crowd.

"Estevan, I want to talk with you."

"Do you wish to negotiate a loan?" Estevan asked with a smile.

"No, I prefer running away from old debts to contracting new ones. I want to tell you that I intend to go in the ship which is about to sail."

"Will not your creditors interpose an objection?" asked Estevan.

"No doubt, if they know it," Balboa answered.

16

"I propose to sail without their knowledge and thus spare the public another scene. I have sold the Bachelor some casks of provisions from my farm, and they are coming to-night to take them on board. I want you to superintend the shipping of the casks."

"Where will you be?"

"In one of them."

Then he explained that Estevan was to nail him up in a cask, that he might be taken aboard, and his presence be kept secret until the ship was well out at sea. While they were discussing the wild scheme, Cortez, still limping from his sword thrust, was discovered coming down the street.

"There comes our friend Cortez, who has some judgment, if he is a gallant, devil-may-care fellow," said Balboa. "Let us take him into our counsel."

Estevan assented and called to Cortez.

"What mischief are you twain concocting now?" he asked, as he approached them.

"I am in distress, Cortez, and want the aid of both of you," answered Balboa.

"If it is a loan you wish, my friend, I swear, by St. Anthony, I am unable to aid you. When I shall have settled with my surgeon I will not have a pistole left. I, who came to the New World in search of gold, have so far found nothing but steel."

"I do not want a loan."

"Not want a loan; then your nature has experienced a complete revolution, for I thought you wanted nothing but loans? What do you wish."

"I want you to help me in a strategy."

Cortez was always ready for any wild harem-scarem enterprise, and when the scheme had been explained to him he laughingly answered:

"Certainly, I will assist to ship you as pork to Terra Firma."

Estevan and Cortez went to Balboa's farm, and headed him up in a cask. An armed escort was sent to convey the provisions which had been sold to Encisco. The cask containing the stowaway was placed on a cart and hauled to the harbor, where it was taken on ship-board. Cortez, whose wits were always at his command, formed a valid excuse for the absence of Balboa.

Before midnight all were safely on board, and the stowaway, who was to make the expedition among the most famous of Spanish conquests, crouched dozing in the cask, wishing they were well out at sea. At sunrise anchor was weighed, sails unfurled, and amid salutes from the fort, answered by cannon from the ship, Bachelor Encisco began the voyage.

The shore grew fainter and fainter as the vessel bounded over the billowy way until at last it faded from view. Encisco was walking the quarter deck when his attention was attracted by a noise in a large cask which was supposed to contain salt pork.

BALBOA'S STRATEGY.

He paused for a moment, listening, and hardly able to credit his senses.

"Let me out!" he heard a voice calling.

At once suspecting that he had a stowaway on board, the enraged Bachelor called for a hammer and knocked in the head, when Vasco Nuñez de Balboa, to the great surprise of master and crew, emerged like an apparition from the cask. Encisco was highly indignant at being thus outwitted, although he had gained a valuable recruit by the deception; and in the first ebullition of his wrath, he gave the fugitive debtor a rough reception.

"This is Balboa, whom Ojeda refused to take with him!" he cried, seizing him by the shoulder. "Why have you come in this manner?"

At a glance, Balboa saw that the armed escort, which had piloted them some distance from land, had returned, and he felt little fear of the enraged Bachelor. He calmly surveyed the scene before answering.

"I took this means to come," he said, "because my creditors would allow me to come no other way."

"You think to impose on me," the irate Bachelor returned. "But I will have nothing to do with you, and shall set you ashore on the first uninhabited island we reach."

"Surely not; that would be murder."

"It will be justifiable. I will have no worthless vagabonds to breed dissensions in my colony."

Balboa possessed as haughty a spirit as any noble

in Castile, and those cruel words cut his pride.
Gnashing his teeth he laid his hand on his sword.
Encisco was also a spirited man, and a fatal encounter might have resulted, had not the pilot
interfered. He persuaded the Bachelor to be reconciled, assuring him that Balboa, though poor and
in debt, was a gentleman of good family, and, being
in the prime and vigor of his days, tall and muscular, seasoned to hardships and of intrepid spirit,
was an acquisition to their forces to be desired.
Thus a truce was patched up between them, though
the spirited Balboa never fully recovered from the
cruel words of Encisco. At first he was morose
and sullen, but after a few days he began to mingle
among the men, with whom he became very popular. Having been to the coast on a former voyage, his knowledge was valuable to the commander
of the expedition.

Arriving at mainland, they touched at the fatal
harbor of Carthagena, the scene of the sanguinary
conflicts of Ojeda and Nicuesa with the natives.
They were alarmed, while working on a boat, by the
appearance of a body of armed Indians, threatening
to give battle. A few days later, two Spaniards
while on shore were surrounded by savages, and
threatened with death. One of the Spaniards,
speaking the Indian language, communicated with
them and terms of peace were made. From them

Encisco learned something of the terrible fate of the colonists who had preceded them, though he could learn little of Ojeda and Nicuesa.

One day a cry of, "Sail! sail!" rang out from the harbor, and Encisco was amazed to see a brigantine come to anchor in the bay. Ordering a boat he was rowed to the side of the strange vessel. Balboa, who was one of the crew to row the Bachelor to the vessel, was astonished to find the brigantine under command of Francisco Pizarro, who had left San Domingo a few months before as a common sailor.

"The brigantine is manned by men who sailed with Ojeda," cried Bachelor Encisco. "The villains have mutinied against their commander and deserted with the vessel. I will arrest them and inflict on them the severity of the law."

Hurriedly ascending to the deck, followed by Balboa and five or six men, he beheld a sight which might have shocked even the most desperate of Spanish conquerors. The men who, but a few months before, had sailed away full of vigor and buoyant with hope, had dwindled to a single ship's crew of ragged, miserable, half-starved wretches, who, wild-eyed and savage as the men and beasts with whom they battled for existence, glared at Encisco with a fury that might have made even his dauntless spirit quail.

"Who is your commander?" demanded the Bachelor.

"I am," Pizarro haughtily returned.

"By whose authority?"

"Governor Ojeda, whose lieutenant I am."

Pizarro's naked sword was in his hand, his eyes flashed, and his manner was so ferocious that Encisco became more civil.

"Where is your authority?" he asked.

Pizarro produced his letter patent signed by the unfortunate Ojeda, showing that he left Pizarro as his *locum tenens* at San Sebastian.

"Where is Ojeda?" asked the Bachelor.

"Some time ago he sailed for San Domingo for reinforcements and supplies, as we were starving."

"What vessel did he sail in?"

"With Bernardino de Talavera, who joined us with a crew of desperadoes and cutpurses."

"I fear, then, he is lost," said Encisco. "Bernardino de Talavera is a pirate and stole the ship in which he and his desperate crew sailed. Where are you going, and why have you deserted the colony?"

"We were starving," replied Pizarro," dying by sickness, famine and poisoned arrows. If we received no news in fifty days, we were to embark in the ships left with us for Hispaniola. We waited fifty days, and, not hearing from Ojeda, were going to embark in the two brigantines left us, but having seventy men and only two small vessels, all could not go. We decided to wait until sickness, famine and poisoned arrows had reduced our num- bers, so that we could all go in the two vessels. It did not take long; we were soon sufficiently re- duced. Then we killed the four horses left with us, and salted them away to supply us with food. The other brigantine, commanded by Valenzuela, was foundered at sea, and all on board perished."

One of Pizarro's sailors added: "I saw a great whale or some other monster of the deep, strike the vessel with its tail and stave in its side as well as shatter the rudder, and it sank so near to us that we could hear the cries of our friends, but could not aid them."

"Why did you come here?" asked Encisco.

"We put in for provisions?" Pizarro answered.

Encisco being of a sanguine temperament, not- withstanding this melancholy story, determined to proceed to the conquest of Darien, and establish the government at San Sebastian. Expeditions made into the country were productive of rumors of gold in the interior, which raised the cupidity of the Spaniards. Gold was said to be so plentiful at a place called Zenu that it was taken in fishing nets.

It was no easy task to induce Pizarro and his

starving crew to return. Balboa, burning with ambition, secretly urged Pizarro to do so.

"Come back with us, Pizarro, and we will rule the colony. Ojeda will return no more, no one knows where Nicuesa is, and this wild life will not long suit the Bachelor."

Pizarro's ambitious spirit at last took fire again, and, with his crew, he returned to San Sebastian to battle once more with the natives and explore the wonders of the New World.

Bachelor Encisco was unsuited for governor of the colony. The good generalship early displayed by Balboa soon placed him at the head of every successful expedition. He grew in favor so rapidly with the men, that Encisco became alarmed lest this man whom he had brought away in a cask should depose him. At Balboa's suggestion they landed at the village of a powerful cacique named Zemaco. After a skirmish, the natives abandoned their town, and a Spanish colony, under the name of Santa Maria de la Antigua del Darien, was formed.

Encisco had not long entered upon his duties as alcalde mayor and lieutenant governor, when there arose dissensions and disputes, in which Balboa and the Bachelor were arrayed against each other. In one of their discussions, Balboa openly defied Encisco's authority.

"Then you defy the power of the king," cried Encisco. "Ojeda's commission is from the crown, and I hold under him."

"You are not in Ojeda's domain," Balboa answered. "The boundary line which separates the jurisdiction of Ojeda from Nicuesa runs through the centre of the gulf of Uraba. Darien lies on the western side, allotted to Nicuesa. As lieutenant of Ojeda your authority here is an usurpation."

This bold speech being uttered in the hearing of the colonists, most of whom were already opposed to Encisco, sounded the death knell of the Bachelor's power. His authority was set at defiance, and a few weeks later he yielded up the reins of government, returned to San Domingo and thence sailed for Spain.

To depose Encisco was an easy matter, for most men are ready to assist in pulling down, but to choose a successor was a task far more difficult. The time had come for Balboa to act, and he was not slow to avail himself of the opportunity. Some of the people were in favor of Nicuesa, as they were within his province, and while the discussion was running high, Colmenares, who was searching for Nicuesa, appeared on the scene. Balboa was willing to do what was fair among the men, and favored an equal division of gold. He ruled as governor *de facto* until Nicuesa was found, at the port of Nombre de Dios, in a miserable starving condition. From Colmenares, Nicuesa learned of the rich and prosperous settlement at Darien in his own domain, and set out to take possession of it. But he proved as injudicious as was Encisco. Scarce had he taken possession, when he said to Balboa:

"Your men have gold taken in their conquests?"

"They have," admitted Balboa.

"Where is it?"

"It is theirs, won by hardships and perils, and will but ill requite them for what they have undergone."

Upon this, Nicuesa flew into a rage and swore the gold belonged to the crown, and that he would punish all private individuals for retaining it. Pizarro heard the remark, and as soon as he was alone with Balboa, asked:

"Are we compelled to yield up our private possessions?"

"Inform the men of the governor's demands," was the answer he received.

The cunning Balboa knew that this decision of Nicuesa would prove his ruin. An influential lawyer, Bachelor Carrol, was in favor of dispossessing Nicuesa and selecting Balboa in his stead. He became bold in his denunciation of Nicuesa.

"A blessed change we have made," he said.

"In summoning this Nicuesa to the command, we have called in the stork to rule who will not be satisfied until he has devoured us."

Two parties immediately arose in the colony, and Nicuesa was forced to fly for his life to the woods, and then to his brigantine in the harbor. The life of the unfortunate governor was in danger, and Balboa began to relent.

"Men and Spaniards!" he cried. "Deal not so harshly with Nicuesa. Remember he is a gentleman and our governor."

"No, no, no! We will receive no such a fellow among us as Nicuesa," interrupted a brawling rascal named Francisco Benitez.

"Take out that brawling jester and reward him with a hundred lashes on his bare shoulders for the remark he has made against his governor," cried Balboa.

In a few moments the howling of Benitez was evidence that the order was being obeyed. The colonists were outspoken in their determination not to permit Nicuesa to rule over them. Balboa, a gentleman by birth, repented what he had done. He had not anticipated the popular fury which, in his ambition for power, he had helped to kindle. But Darien had rejected Nicuesa and would not have him under any consideration.

In vain Nicuesa reminded them that he was

governor of the territory, and that they were guilty of treason to the crown in thus opposing him; in vain he appealed to their humanity, and protested before God against their cruelty and persecution. The Spaniards were in that state of tumult when they were ready to add cruelty to injustice. Not content with expelling the discarded governor from their shores, they allotted to him the worst vessel in the harbor, an old, crazy brigantine, totally unfit to encounter the perils of the sea.

Seventeen followers embarked with him, and the frail bark set sail March 1, 1511, for the island of Hispaniola, but was never seen or heard from again.

In less than one year from the time he left San Domingo in a cask, an absconding debtor, we find Balboa governor *de facto* of Darien, with nations of untold wealth all about him. He exhibited wonderful ability, both as a conqueror and as a ruler. While he dealt the most terrible vengeance on the warlike and rebellious natives, he conciliated the conquered, and made them his friends. From Indian captives he heard wonderful stories of vast countries beyond the mountains, where gold was found in great abundance. Pizarro, returning from a cruise along the shores of the Isthmus, brought with him two Spaniards, clad in painted skins, like Indians, whom he took to Balboa.

"From whence come you?" asked the governor.

"We escaped from Nicuesa about a year ago, and took refuge with Careta the chief of Coyba," one answered.

"Has he much gold and provisions?"

"He has more gold than you have ever seen, but it and his provisions are concealed."

The stories they related roused Balboa's cupidity and he resolved on the conquest of Coyba at once. With one hundred and thirty well-armed men and several bloodhounds, he set out for Careta's dominions. The difficult and dangerous march was made in three days. Learning of their approach, the cacique received them kindly just without his town. Through interpreters, Balboa informed Careta that they were hungry and thirsty.

"If you are hungry and thirsty I will soon satisfy your wants," said the cacique, and he ordered food and drink to be brought them. When their wants were satisfied, Balboa explained:

"I am governor of Darien, and my people are in want of food. Will you give me food for the colony?"

"I am sorry, I cannot," answered Careta. "I have no corn nor meat to spare. We have long been at war with Ponca, a neighboring cacique, and my people were prevented from cultivating the fields."

One of the ungrateful spies, who had been so kindly cared for by Careta, spoke up:

"The old wretch speaks falsely, Governor Balboa. He has an abundance of provisions stored away in secret places."

"How can we get at them?" asked Balboa.

"Pretend to depart for Darien, but return in the night with your troops and take the village by surprise."

Balboa complied with the suggestion. Taking a cordial leave of Careta, he set off for the settlement. In the dead of night, when the entire village was buried in deep slumber, he led his men back into the midst of it. Slow matches were lighted, arquebuses loaded, crossbows strung, and lances couched for deadly work. Before the inhabitants could be roused for resistance, the cacique and many of his people were captives. All was accomplished without the shedding of a drop of blood. Secreted provisions were discovered, and two brigantines were filled with food and provisions, and Balboa set out for Darien.

Careta was separated from his people and taken by Balboa himself to Darien. Not until he was brought into the governor's house did he discover that his wife and children were prisoners also. A cry was heard on the morning air, and an Indian princess, all glittering with ornaments of gold and pearls, burst into the apartment and fell weeping on the neck of her captive father. The new-comer was Careta's beautiful daughter, the most lovely aborigine the Spanish governor had ever seen. Her costume was wild, but becoming. It consisted of a skirt of tinted doe-skin, and moccasins ornamented with precious jewels. Her abundant black hair was gathered from her forehead and fell in a glossy flood over her shoulders. Escaping the general captivity of her family, she had followed the Spaniards to Darien to learn the fate of her parents.

At sight of his favorite child, the stoicism of the old chieftain forsook him, and, giving way to a flood of tears, he turned on Balboa a look of reproach.

"What have I done that you should treat me so cruelly?" he asked. "None of your people ever came to my land that were not fed and sheltered, and treated with loving kindness. When you came to my dwelling, did I meet you with a javelin in my hand? Did I not set meat and drink before you and welcome you as a brother? Set me free, therefore, with my family and people, and we will remain your friends. We will supply you with provisions and reveal to you the riches of the land. Do you doubt my faith? Behold my daughter, I give her to you as a pledge of friendship. Take her for a wife, and be assured of the fidelity of her family and people."

"WILL YOU TAKE ME?"

Then the forest queen rose, turned from an appealing father to the stern-browed conqueror, and, smiling through her tears, took one timid step toward Balboa. Each graceful action and hope-lighted smile seemed to say:

"Will you take me?"

What would not society's queen give for that simple grace, that appealing action, natural to the untutored maiden? Her marvellous beauty melted the heart of the stern Spanish conqueror, and, clasping her in his arms, he exclaimed:

"Your father is saved, and you are mine!"

Careta remained three days at Darien, during which time he was treated with the utmost kindness. Balboa took him on his ships and showed him every part of them. He had the war-horses displayed before him with their armor and rich caparisons, and awed him with the thunder of his artillery. Fulvia, the Indian maiden, was almost constantly at his side, evincing a fondness for her lord, which soon become a passion. Balboa caused his musicians to perform a harmonious concert on their instruments, at which the natives were lost in admiration. Having thus impressed Careta with the idea of his wonderful power and endowments, he loaded the cacique with presents and permitted him to depart.

Careta joyfully returned to his territories, and

3

his daughter remained with Balboa, willingly, for his sake, giving up her family and native home. Though never married according to the forms of the Catholic religion, she regarded herself as his wife, as she was in sight of Heaven and according to the usages of her country. He treated her with great fondness, and she gradually gained great influence over him. Fulvia became a chief character in the great tragedy enacted at Darien early in the six- teenth century. To his love for her, Balboa owed his ultimate ruin.

CHAPTER III.

FULVIA'S wild, strange beauty was in harmony with the new world in which she lived. Balboa, the gallant, who had never been smitten, though assailed by the fairest of Spain, yielded to the power of this strange being. She studied his every want, and seemed to live only to make him happy. His comfortable home was daily decorated and festooned with rare tropical flowers. All her trinkets and golden treasures were brought to adorn their little temple, in which she worshipped her lord as a god. Being intellectually bright, she soon learned to speak his language, and her mellow voice was heard every evening breathing soft Spanish words of love.

"You are a treasure, indeed, Fulvia," said Balboa one evening on entering his home, made fragrant with rare exotics. "I regret to leave you, even for a few days."

"Must you leave me?" she asked, her face growing sad.

He was about to answer, when a howl, issuing from the kennel in which he kept his bloodhounds, interrupted him.

"Leoncico scents battle afar off," he said.

"Leoncico, the bloodhound!" exclaimed Fulvia, pressing her hand to her heart as if she felt a pain there. "Does it mean another conquest?"

"It does."

"Against whom?"

LEONCICO.

"Ponca, your father's enemy. To-morrow I set out with Colmenares and eighty picked men to aid your father in his war against Ponca!" He paused to mark the effect of his words, but her face was still sad, and Balboa added: "In return for you, I agreed to help your father fight his enemies."

"I want father's enemies conquered, but I shall tremble for my lord."

The governor embraced his wife, assured her that he was invulnerable to Indian arrows, and sought to calm her fears.

At early dawn next morning, eighty picked men were mustered on the plaza. They were fine-looking fellows, with their steel helmets and nodding plumes, arquebuses, swords, lances, pikes, **and** shields of wood, to ward off the poisoned arrows of the enemy.

More terrible than any steel-clad knight, at that grand review, was Leoncico, Balboa's famous blood-hound. Old Spanish chroniclers describe Leoncico as minutely as if he had been a favorite warrior. He was of middle size, but immensely strong, of a dull yellow or reddish color, with a black muzzle. His body was scarred all over from wounds received in innumerable battles with the Indians. The dog surveyed the line of steel-clad men, heard the clank of armor, and set up a howl more terrible than any war-whoop of savage, or thunder of artillery.

"Be quiet, Leoncico!" commanded the governor. "You shall have your fill before we return."

"A wonderful animal," remarked Colmenares. "They dread him more than ten mounted knights."

"With good cause."

The brigantines were ready for the voyage to the country of Careta, and the embarkation had commenced when Pizarro approached Balboa.

"Am I to be left?" he asked. "On all your former invasions I have been your companion. Do not leave me on this."

Balboa was a man of a generous spirit, and he smiled good-naturedly.

"You shall not be forsaken, Francisco; you may accompany us."

The expedition landed at Coyba, where they were met by Careta and his generals with a cordial welcome, and arrangements were at once made for the conquest.   The war-like cacique Ponca, having heard of the powerful alliance which his enemy Careta had made with the white men, felt from the first that there was but little hope for him.   However, he mustered his army, and, with the best grace possible, met them on the plain.

A thundering volley of arquebuses and artillery was followed by the old Spanish war cry, "Santiago! and at them!"

Pizarro led the charge of the horse, and Balboa of the foot soldiers and bloodhounds.   Leoncico, with the howl of a devil, leaped at the throat of an Indian general, brought him to the earth, and crushed out his life.   The fearful hounds, war-horses, and thundering guns were too much for the Indians, and they fled to the mountains.   Balboa followed up his signal victory by ravaging the country of the conquered cacique and sacking his towns, in which he found considerable gold and provisions.

On returning to Coyba, Balboa was pleased to meet his wife, who had followed him.   Through Careta, friendly negotiations were entered into with Comagre, who ruled a large mountain country and had three thousand warriors at his command.   In

company with Careta, the
Spanish army set out for
the province of Comagre,
which was situat-
ed at the foot of a

"SANTIAGO! AND AT THEM!"

lofty mountain, in a beautiful plain twelve leagues
in extent.

The cacique and his seven sons, followed by a
numerous train, met the strangers and welcomed
them to his province. The Spaniards were conducted with great ceremony to the village, where
quarters were assigned them, and an abundance
of provisions and attendants furnished.

The dwelling of the cacique, in magnitude,
solidity, and architecture, surpassed anything the

Spaniards had yet seen. It was one hundred and fifty paces in length, eighty wide, founded on great logs and surrounded by a stone wall. Balboa and his followers were made subjects of special attention by the cacique's eldest son, a tall fine-looking fellow, who evinced intelligence superior to his brothers. He had travelled much in the interior, seen many strange people and wonderful countries, but regarded the Spaniards as the greatest people he had ever met. He gave Balboa a large quantity of gold wrought in various ornaments, and sixty slaves taken in war. With his usual generosity, Balboa set aside a fifth part for the crown and divided the remainder among his followers.

The announcement that a division of gold was to be made on the porch of Comagre's dwelling brought every Spaniard to the great piazza. The gold weighed four thousand ounces, and in the division a violent quarrel arose between some of the soldiers and Pizarro, who, having forced himself on the expedition, they denied the right to share the profits. The noble young donor, disgusted at this sordid brawl among beings whom he had regarded with reverence, struck the scales with his fist, scattering the glittering gold about the porch.

"Why should you quarrel for such a trifle?" he cried. "If this gold is so precious to your eyes, that for it alone you abandon your homes, invade peaceful lands, and expose yourselves to such sufferings and perils, I will tell you of a region where you may gratify your wishes to the uttermost."

Balboa, who had been at the other end of the porch when the quarrel commenced, came up just as Fulvia was interpreting his speech.

"Behold those lofty mountains," continued the young savage, pointing to the south. "Beyond them lies a mighty sea, which may be discerned from their summit. It is navigated by people who have vessels almost as large as yours, and like yours furnished with sails and oars. All the streams which flow down the southern side of those mountains into the sea, abound in gold; and kings who reign upon its borders eat and drink out of golden vessels. Indeed, gold is as common among these people of the south as iron is among you."

Deeply interested in what he heard, Balboa quieted his companions, and turned to the young cacique.

"Where is this unknown sea," he asked, "and how can we penetrate the opulent regions on its shores?"

After a moment of hesitation the young prince answered:

"The task is difficult and dangerous. You must pass through the territories of many powerful ca-

ciques, who will oppose you with hosts of warriors.
Some parts of the mountains are infested by fierce
and cruel cannibals, a wandering, lawless race; but
above all, you will have to encounter Tubanamá,
whose territories are at a distance of six days'
journey, and more rich in gold than any other
province. This cacique will be sure to come forth
against you with a mighty force. To accomplish
the enterprise, you will require a thousand men
armed like those who follow you."

"How have you gained your information?" Balboa asked.

"From captives taken in battle, and from one of
our own people who was for a long time in captivity
to Tubanama, the powerful cacique of the golden
realm."

Having some doubts of the marvellous story he
had heard, Balboa asked: "Are you manufactur-
ing this story of the South Sea, or is what you are
telling true?"

"It is true," replied the young prince, "and I
will establish the truth of it by going with you at
the head of my father's warriors."

This was the first intimation white men received
of the Pacific Ocean. As religion and avarice went
hand in hand with the Spaniards, their priest baptized the cacique and his sons, giving to the former
the name of Don Carlos; then Balboa and his men

set out on their return for Darien to make arrangements for the expedition to the new ocean.

On his arrival home, Balboa found Regidor Valdivia returned with only a limited amount of recruits and supplies. The pseudo-governor again sent him to Hispaniola with a letter to Don Diego Columbus, giving an account of the wonderful ocean, and asking him to use his influence with the king to engage a thousand men for the enterprise. The royal fifth which he remitted equalled fifteen thousand crowns in gold; he also sent presents in curiously wrought golden ornaments to Don Diego Columbus, Cortez, and Estevan's baby boy.

Balboa was not one to remain inactive, and while awaiting the result of Valdivia's mission he projected many expeditions into the interior.

"There is the great country of Dobayba, which your people have not yet seen," said Fulvia one day to her liege, while she sat at his feet. "It is a land of wonders, and while you wait, you would be well repaid for making a visit to it."

This was the first time he had heard of a region called Dobayba.

"Where is this region?" he asked.

"It is forty leagues distant, on the banks of a great river which empties into the Gulf of Uraba. Dobayba derived its name from a mighty woman of the olden time, the mother of the god who created the sun, moon, and all good things. She has power over the elements, sending thunder and lightning to lay waste the lands of those who displease her, but bestowing fertility and abundance upon the possessions of her faithful worshippers. They have erected a great temple for her worship. Here the natives repair with their gifts of gold and pearls and precious stones. Once, when they failed to bring her share of treasure, the goddess caused a drought upon the land, and many perished. For generations, golden offerings have been hoarded up in this temple, until it is said that it is filled with treasure, and its walls covered with golden gifts."

In rapt attention, Balboa listened to the narration of the wonderful legend. The Spaniards who had come to erect temples to the worship of the true God, had no hesitancy in desecrating the temples of the heathen, and, having implicit faith in Fulvia's story, which was corroborated by others, Balboa determined to go in search of the Golden Temple.

Selecting one hundred and seventy of his bravest men, he set out on the expedition in two brigantines. His old enemy, Zemaco, the cacique of Darien, hastened to Dobayba, and, informing the cacique of the advance of the Spaniards, persuaded him to retire at their approach. Bleak coasts, interminable wildernesses, deep morasses, and deserted towns greeted the Spanish conquerors. Only a few miserable people living in houses constructed in tree-tops and reached by ladders could be found, until they had gone farther inland, where they were greeted by ambuscades with poisoned arrows.

Balboa, assured that he would find the temple of gold, would have continued his search, had not Fulvia, who with only one attendant had followed him from Darien, traversing leagues of unknown wilderness, brought him the alarming intelligence that his old enemy Zemaco, the cacique of Darien, had induced several other powerful caciques to join him for the purpose of making a general attack on the Spanish colony.

"How did you learn this, Fulvia?" he asked, on receiving the startling news. She hesitated a moment, and then, with tears in her eyes, answered:

"A brother, in an evil hour, was induced to enter into the conspiracy. He tells me that on the tenth night from last night, the town of Darien is to be attacked and every Spaniard put to death. My brother told me to hide myself in a certain place until he came for me, lest I should be slain in the confusion of the massacre."

Balboa's brow grew dark as he said: "Zemaco is my evil genius and must die. Hasten back to Darien, Fulvia, and I will follow you and make arrangements for defence. Send for your brother, I must see him."

"Will you slay him?"

"No; for though he has proven himself a traitor and my enemy, he is your brother."

The joy of Fulvia knew no bounds. She hastened back to Darien and summoned her brother to come and aid her to escape.

One of the essential qualities of a great general is rapid movement, and Balboa, to an excellent degree, possessed this qualification. On the same evening Fulvia's brother was to come to consult with her on means of escape, he secretly returned to Darien and warned every man to be on his guard.

Fulvia's brother came, was put under arrest, and confessed everything, admitting a deep-laid plot to assassinate all the Spaniards.

"The chiefs are three leagues to the west, in a valley," he added, "with five thousand armed warriors and a host of canoes."

With a large force Balboa surprised the army and captured all the chiefs save Zemaco, who was shot to death with arrows. The leaders were hanged in the presence of their fellow-captives, and this put an end to the conspiracy.

Considerable time had elapsed since the departure of Valdivia for Hispaniola, and Balboa became uneasy lest Bachelor Encisco should reach Spain and prejudice the sovereign against him. He concluded it was best to repair at once to Spain in person, to communicate to his sovereign concerning the South Sea, and ask for troops and funds sufficient for its discovery.

His friends opposed the plan, and most determined of all in the opposition was Fulvia, who feared to part with him lest she should never see him more. After much debate and contention, it was decided that Juan de Cayzedo and Rodrigo Enriquez de Colmenares should be sent in his place, instructed to make all necessary representations to the king.

Being only a pseudo-commander, clothed with no authority, Balboa had no sooner ended the Indian war than internal factions arose among the restless colonists, threatening the utter destruction of Darien. How long he might have been able to manage the unsteady populace, it is impossible to say, had not an event transpired which diverted the minds of the Spaniards from their internal quarrels. At the moment when the little government seemed about to engage in civil war, two ships from Hispaniola, freighted with supplies and one hundred and fifty men, arrived, bringing a commission for Balboa, from an official who probably had no authority to issue it, constituting him captain-general of the colony. This shadow of a title to authority was a godsend to Balboa, for he could not have held his people together much longer without it.

As if to counterbalance this good fortune, a letter from a friend in Spain was received a few days later, containing the alarming information that the deposed Bachelor Encisco had carried his complaints to the foot of the throne and had succeeded in rousing the indignation of the king to such an extent as to obtain a sentence in his favor, condemning Balboa in costs and damages. Balboa knew that ere long he would be summoned to appear in Spain in person, but having as yet received no legal notice of the king's displeasure, he determined to push out at once, and by one brilliant achievement atone for all the past and fix himself firmly in the favor of the monarch. It was a desperate undertaking for a mere handful of men, but fame, fortune, life itself depended on the prompt execution of the enterprise. To hesitate was to be lost.

Choosing one hundred and ninety of his most resolute men, and taking in addition a number of bloodhounds, which he had found to be formidable allies in Indian warfare, he set out on the perilous undertaking.

With the faithful Fulvia, who determined to accompany him, he embarked the force in nine pi-

rogues on the first day of September, 1513, and
sailed to Coyba, where he rested a short time, and,
leaving his wife and half his men, on September 6th
struck boldly out for the mountains. Then commenced a journey which for trial and danger has
never been surpassed. Death in a thousand forms
faced the invaders at almost every step. On the
second day's march from Coyba they came to the
village of Ponca, which they found deserted. The
retreat of the cacique was discovered, and Balboa,
with his peculiar faculty for winning the confidence
and friendship of the natives, easily persuaded him
to make terms of peace, even procuring guides
from him. Captivated by the kindness of his conqueror, Ponca confided to Balboa the richness of
the country and assured him that on gaining the
summit of that lofty ridge, which seemed to rise up
to the skies, he would behold the sea all spread
out before him. In high hopes, the Spaniards set
out through a broken rocky country, covered with
matted forests, and intersected by deep, dark, and
turbulent streams, many of which it was necessary
to cross on rafts.

After days of toil and hardship the province of
Quaraqua, an enemy of Ponca, was reached. The
very fact that the white men were coming, guided
by subjects of his enemy, was sufficient to incite
Quaraqua to take the field against them. The In-

4

dians were armed with bows, arrows, spears and double-headed maces of palm wood.

In the middle of the afternoon the Spanish invaders came on this formidable army. It seemed as if the very heavens would crack from blowing of conchs and yelling of Indians.

"Remember you are Spaniards fighting for your king and the Cross!" shouted Balboa.

He placed the arquebusiers and bowmen in the front rank, while the lancers remained in the rear to follow up with the bloodhounds, which were to be let loose after the first volley. The Indians came with terrific yells until quite close, when Balboa gave the command:

"Open pans! Apply matches!"

Peals of thunder and flashes of lightning, accompanied by strange missiles whizzing through the air, followed the command, and the natives saw their companions fall dead and dying on every hand.

Then came the dread cry, "St. Jago, and at them!"

With terrible cries, the bloodhounds, led by Leoncico, plunged through the smoke at the enemy, men following the dogs. Some of the enemy were transfixed with lances, others hewn down with swords, while many were torn to pieces by the dogs, and all who survived the slaughter were put to flight.

"The Cross conquers all!" cried Balboa. At the village, where they found considerable booty, the Spaniards paused to rest. The village was at the foot of the last mountain which remained for them to climb, but some of the Spaniards were wounded and others so fatigued that they could not proceed farther that day. Here Balboa was forced to wait within sight of the mountain top commanding the long-sought prospect. Only sixty-seven able-bodied men were left for duty.

As the sun descended behind the mountain, Balboa, sitting on a large stone, gazed off on the bold peak and asked himself if he would on the morrow behold the unknown sea. His heart beat impatiently and at times his faith was shaken. If a great ocean lay beyond the mountain, then Columbus and all previous navigators had been mistaken in believing this country to be a part of the Indies. If it **was** not a part of the Indies, what strange land was it?

Next morning, September 26, 1513, with his remaining followers, he set out from the Indian village and began to climb the height. It was rugged and steep, but with indomitable courage they pushed on. About ten o'clock they emerged from a dense forest, and arrived at a lofty and airy region of the mountain. The last summit remained **to** be ascended, and the guides, pointing to the emi-

nence, said that from the top of it the southern sea
was visible.

"Remain here!" commanded Balboa to his followers. "I must be first to gaze on the ocean."
With palpitating heart he began the ascent of the
lone mountain top. Would he behold the un-

"A VAST OCEAN GLITTERED IN THE MORNING SUN."

known sea; or was it all a delusion of the Indians?
He climbed on, the summit was gained, and O
joy! he was saved! he had carved his name forever

on the tablet of fame; for a glorious sea burst on his view. Below extended a vast chaos of rock and forest, green savannas and wandering streams, while afar the waters of a vast, unknown ocean glittered in the morning sun.

Enraptured, the grim warrior fell on his knees and thanked God that to himself was given the glory of this discovery. He called his followers to his side, and pointed to the ocean.

"Friends," he said, "behold that glorious sight, so long the desire of our hearts. Give thanks to God that to us is given this favor and advantage. Pray Him to guide us and aid us to conquer the sea and land which we have discovered, and which Christian man has never entered to preach the holy doctrines of the Evangelists. As to yourselves, be as you have hitherto been, faithful and true to me, and by the favor of Christ, you shall be the richest Spaniards that have come to the Indies; you will render the greatest service to your king that vassal ever did to his lord, and you will have the eternal glory and advantage of all that is here discovered, conquered, and converted to our holy Catholic faith."

Followed by his men he descended the mountain, waded into the ocean up to his waist, and took possession of it in the name of his sovereign. What a change had come to Vasco Nuñez de Balboa in three

years! From a rash roister, a gambler and libertine, he was converted into a discreet, politic captain. He who had fled his creditors but a short
time ago, was now the possessor of seas and lands.
Thus it is that men are often made by their fortunes; their latent qualities are brought out, shaped
and strengthened by the necessity of every exertion
to cope with the greatness of their destiny.

CHAPTER IV.

A FICKLE LOVER.

For the present we must take leave of Balboa, in the flush of his glory, and return to San Domingo. Many incidents worthy of mention have transpired since Balboa's departure. Ojeda, who left Darien, landed at Cuba, at that time uncolonized, and finally arrived at San Domingo to die in poverty and neglect. In 1512, an event transpired which caused some comment and amusement. An old knight, called Ponce de Leon, deceived by Indian stories of a fabulous fountain which had the power of restoring youth to the aged, set out to find it. He failed in the object of his expedition, but discovered a beautiful land, which, from its flowers and the fact that it was discovered on Easter Sunday, he called Florida. As neither populous cities nor gold had been discovered, the land was thought to be too poor and insignificant to colonize.

A Florentine, who had accompanied Ojeda to the New World in 1507, returned to Europe and published a book on the discoveries of Columbus, himself, and others. English, Spaniards, Germans, French, and Portuguese all read the wonderful book with avidity, and, by some uncontrollable law of circumstances, christened the New World by the first name of the author, Amerigo, or America, adding one more proof to the time-honored adage that the pen is more powerful than the sword.

Asking pardon for this digression, we will return to old friends and acquaintances. Estevan lived quietly at San Domingo with his wife and child. The boy grew strong and healthy. Cortez, the same rollicking, devil-may-care fellow, was a frequent visitor at his house, and became a great favorite with little Christopher Estevan. Before the baby was able to toddle about the house, he used to sit on the knee of Cortez, pull his whiskers, and crow with delight at the grimaces made by the young cavalier.

One day Don Diego Columbus, the admiral, came to Estevan's house and in course of conversation said:

"Estevan, I have determined on the conquest of Fernandina.* Our mines are almost exhausted, and we need more territory for these restless spirits. Besides, the royal party, always at enmity with the

---

* The name originally given Cuba by the Spaniards.

Columbus party, is growing strong, and it would be well for the peace of Hispaniola to transplant them. Will you accept a commission to subjugate the island?"

"Most willingly," answered Hernando Estevan; "but in order to conciliate the royalists, would it not be better to commission some of them?"

"It would be wise."

"Then do it. Who among them is most competent to undertake the enterprise?"

"Would Don Diego Velasquez answer?"

"Yes, and make the Castilian, Hidalgo Pánfilo de Narvaez, his lieutenant."

"I thought to offer that to you or Cortez."

"No, for sake of harmony we will surrender our claims."

This was in the year 1511, one year before Ponce de Leon discovered Florida. Velasquez was commissioned governor of Cuba, and, preparing a small force under his lieutenant Narvaez, landed and proceeded to the subjugation of the island. That noble old priest, Las Casas, having the good of the natives at heart, accompanied the army and prevented as much bloodshed as was in his power.

Hatuey, a chief who had fled from San Domingo, finding the Spaniards still pursuing him, retired with his followers into the interior of the island where he made a most desperate resistance, but was

overpowered, captured, and sentenced by Velasquez to be burned alive. At the stake he was
urged by the priest to embrace Christianity, that his
soul might find admission into Heaven.

"Will white men go there?" he asked.

"They will," answered the priest.

"Then I will not be a Christian; for I would not
go to a place where I must find men so cruel."

It evidently never occurred to the Spaniards
that, in the name of Christ, they were guilty of
acts more becoming devils than men.

Velasquez diligently occupied himself with
measures for promoting the prosperity of the island.
Settlements were formed, towns laid out, and St.
Jago, the seat of government on the southeast
corner of the island, rapidly grew into a city of
importance. The governor invited settlers and
made them liberal grants of lands and slaves. He
encouraged them to cultivate the soil, giving par-
ticular attention to sugar-cane. Above all, he was
intent on working the gold mines, which promised
better returns than those of Hispaniola.

Hernando Estevan removed with his family to
Cuba among the first settlers of the island. His
emigration was the year after the old knight Ponce
de Leon failed to find the fabulous fountain of
youth, and the same year in which Balboa discovered the unknown sea. He built him a neat

little home at St. Jago, and entered into a prosperous business as a planter and trader. At times he felt a keen desire to embark in some of those golden enterprises, but his business and family duties required his presence at home. Years rolled on and two more children came to bless his home, and with such domestic ties, he was contented and happy.

Christopher Estevan was a strange child. At four or five years of age he seemed to possess the knowledge of a lad of ten. His great blue eyes and thoughtful manner indicated the student and philosopher. His quaint humor, grave demeanor, and solemn, unchild-like manner was noticed by all. He seemed to take great pleasure in wandering alone in the deep solitudes of the forest. For hours at a time he would watch a bird build her nest, or the smaller animals of the woods skip and play before him. He was happy at all times, occasionally boisterous, but usually quiet, loving solitude.

His fondness for Hernando Cortez, who had also emigrated to Cuba, increased with his years.

Cortez was the same rollicking, dashing fellow as of old. Although a libertine, he made pretensions to being a gentleman. His own affairs as usual were not progressing well, for he was in another love scrape.

A family named Xuarez had settled on the

island. They were poor but proud, and made some pretensions to gentility, even claiming noble birth. There were four sisters in the Xuarez family, and Cortez was not long in forming their acquaintance, and in turn making love to each.

"Cortez," said Estevan to his friend one day, "you will get into trouble again if you are not careful."

"I suppose I will," sighed Cortez, "but I am used to it."

"Do you love Catalina Xuarez?" Estevan asked, and with a light laugh the merry fellow answered:

"I really don't know; sometimes I think I do, and sometimes I think I don't."

"Governor Velasquez seems very much concerned."

"Have you seen the governor?"

"Yes—only this morning he told me if Hernando Cortez jilted Catalina Xuarez he would regret it."

The brow of Cortez grew dark, and striking his fist upon the table at which he was sitting, he said:

"Governor Velasquez shall not drive me to matrimony. If he wishes to be my patron, why don't he commission me to some conquest?"

"The governor fears you, Cortez."

Cortez laughed lightly, but there was a flash in

the young man's eyes which denoted latent ambition.

"We have both been ill used," he said. "Because I have been gay and frivolous the governor has set his seal of displeasure upon me. But I will lead armies to victory yet. We live in an age fruitful in opportunites, and I am going to avail myself of them despite all Governor Velasquez may do. My name shall be remembered when that of Velasquez is forgotten."

With impatient eagerness Cortez rose and paced the room, while his brow contracted with thought. Estevan, amazed to find his friend capable of a serious thought, watched him in silence. The mood was gone in a moment, and his mind recurring to his love affair with the Xuarez sisters, Cortez resumed his seat and burst into a peal of merry laughter. Estevan regarded this as his normal condition, and, with a smile, asked the cause of his merriment.

"I was just thinking what a time the Xuarez sisters had, determining which should capture me," he laughingly answered.

"I dare say you made love to all?"

"That I did, and right well, too."

"Cortez, though you are my beloved friend, you are a scamp, and I am ashamed of you."

Cortez laughingly answered:

"By St. Anthony, such a declaration from any other man would necessitate my calling him out; but, Estevan, your tongue may wag at will—I forgive you."

The child Christopher, who had been playing about the door, at this moment entered. He was now five years of age, and a child of much more than ordinary intelligence. On seeing Cortez, a glad smile lighted his face, and, with a cry of joy, he rushed into his arms.

"My little friend, where have you been?" asked Cortez, taking the child on his knee.

"Watching men beat slaves."

"Beat slaves; they deserve it, no doubt."

"No they don't," the child answered. "The men are bad to be so cruel to the poor Indians. I found a dead Indian in the woods, yesterday, when I was watching the birds."

"That is not an uncommon discovery nowadays," said Cortez. "It was some native who had escaped his master."

"Yes, and the body had such cruel stripes upon it," resumed the child. "Then it had been torn by dogs."

"The lazy vagabonds won't work, they must die."

"Would you want to work for others?" asked the child. "Would you want men to chain you, beat you, and make you work in their sugar-cane, or mines?"

"Estevan, we have a young priest here," said Cortez, keenly feeling the reproof. "From whom learned you this lesson of humanity?"

"The good Las Casas says you do wrong to beat and kill slaves."

"I warrant that it is the argument of Las Casas. He seems to espouse the cause of the natives."

Cortez, who did not care to hear any more reproof from the child, put Christopher from his knee and took his departure. Cortez lived as a genteel bachelor in a very nice house, with both Indian and negro slaves cultivating his plantations and mines. Negroes had been brought from Spain during Isabella's time to ameliorate the condition of the Indians, who died rapidly under the galling yoke of slavery, while the black race seemed to flourish in bondage.

On reaching his house, he found an Indian boy awaiting his return.

"Do you come from the governor?" asked Cortez, for by his costume he discovered that he was an attaché of the hidalgo's household.

"Yes, señor, I have a letter from the governor," he answered, and he gave Cortez a sealed missive. Hastily opening it, the youthful cavalier read:

"St. Jago, March 30, 1515.

"Señor Cortez:—Your conduct is very unseemly. You have given Catalina Xuarez to believe you loved her; you have even asked her hand in marriage, and now you have disappointed her. You must comply with your promise."

"Velasquez."

The look of indignation on the face of Cortez was quite marked. He hastily wrote across the bottom of the page:

"It is your business to govern Fernandina, and not to meddle with the private affairs of your subjects."

With this reply he returned the missive to the governor.

Velasquez next day met Cortez on the street and openly rebuked him for his unfaithfulness.

"Why should you care, governor? What are the Xuarez sisters to you?" demanded Cortez, turning on his heel and leaving the governor to fume and swear.

There was a disaffected party in the island who were opposed to Velasquez, and Cortez, soon after, connected himself with them. They met at his house to talk over their causes of discontent, among which was the partial distribution of land to the friends of Velasquez. It was no easy task for a ruler, however discreet and well meaning he might be, to satisfy the indefinite cravings of speculators and adventurers, who swarmed like so many harpies in the track of discovery of the New World.

Gerund, the jester of Velasquez, a sort of privileged character, coming suddenly on the conspirators at the house of Cortez one evening, overheard the following speeches:

"Friends, let us no longer endure the ill treatment and partiality of Velasquez," said Cortez.

"How can we help ourselves?" asked Estevan, one of the party.

"I propose to lay our grievances before Don Diego Columbus, at Hispaniola."

"The voyage will be hazardous," answered Estevan. "One will have to make it in an open boat across an arm of the sea eighteen leagues wide."

"I will do it," declared the impetuous Cortez. "I will be your embassador, and will, myself, lay our grievances before the admiral."

All were well acquainted with his fearless spirit and knew he was well fitted for the expedition. The conference lasted late into the night, and just before dawn of day the intrepid Cortez was to set sail for Hispaniola. Estevan had risen to go home, the assemblage was about breaking up, when there came a sudden summons for admittance. Cortez went to open the door, when he espied an officer with a score of soldiers.

"Betrayed," he cried, drawing his sword.

"Hold!" interposed Estevan, seizing the arm of Cortez. "We can't afford to resist the king's officers."

"You are right, but Velasquez is revengeful and may hang me," Cortez answered, thrusting his sword back into his scabbard.

The officer had a warrant for the arrest of Cortez and two or three others, but Estevan, who expected to share a like fate, was permitted to go free. Had it not been for the intercession of influential friends, Cortez probably would have been hanged before the first torrent of the governor's rage had an opportunity to subside. He loaded the captive with fetters and placed him in prison. The second night of his confinement, the fickle lover forced open the window of his prison and escaped. Although lodged on the second floor he managed, without injury, to let himself unobserved down to the pavement. He then made the best of his way to a neighboring church, where he claimed the privilege of sanctuary.

Next morning, as Velasquez was passing the church, Cortez called out from the portals to him, with a good-morning greeting.

"What are you doing there, you rascal?" the governor demanded.

"Claiming the privilege of sanctuary."

"I will have you yet; you can't always remain there!" thundered the enraged governor.

He hurried to the town, where an alguacil named Juan Escudero was found.

"Juan, do you want to earn a hundred pistoles?" the irate governor asked.

With a smile, Juan answered that nothing would suit him better. "You can do so," continued the governor. "Hernando Cortez, a vagabond who has been breeding dissensions and hatching conspiracies, escaped from prison last night and is hiding at the church. Watch your opportunity, and when he comes out from the wall of the church, seize him."

Eager to earn the reward Juan began at once to spy upon the church. Little Christopher Estevan carried food to Cortez at the church, for the child was permitted to go and come as he pleased. On the third day of his forced confinement in the sanctuary, Cortez, enticed by the silver laughter of some señoritas on the street, ventured beyond the walls, and Juan Escudero suddenly sprang on him from behind, pinioning his arms, while others rushed to his aid and the escaped prisoner was secured.

"I will hang you for this," cried Cortez, trembling with rage and exertion.

A second time Cortez was put in irons. This time he was placed on board a vessel which was to sail for Hispaniola next morning, where he was to be tried for treason. Though the charge was of a serious nature, Cortez knew that the Xuarez family were at the bottom of his persecutions, and that he could put an end to the trouble at any time by becoming reconciled to Catalina. It was an odd courtship, but the period of Spanish conquests was noted for oddities. During the night, Cortez slipped his irons, crept to the deck of the ship anchored in the harbor of St. Jago, and climbing down into a boat, pulled ashore. Next morning, looking from the window of the self-same church, he saw the governor riding by, and called to him:

"Good-morning, governor, do you wish me to remember you in my prayers?"

Velasquez, amazed and enraged at the fellow's impudence, answered:

"I have a mind to hang you!"

"You might save me for a better purpose, governor. I am coming to see you soon."

The governor, overcome with exasperation, rode away and Cortez sent for Estevan. On his arrival, the jolly, good-natured prisoner took his hand and said:

"I am in a devil of a fix. Here I am cooped up like a monk in a cloister, passing the days in studying the carvings of the altar. I have resolved to arrange matters."

"How?"

"I will marry Catalina, and that will assuage the grief and anger of the governor."

"Do you love Catalina, Cortez?"

"Love her, my friend? Why, a poor devil like me loves all pretty women alike. But I must make a choice at last. I am done with this roystering life, and, when I am married, I will become a man. Go to Catalina and give her this letter; then bring my sword, buckler, and daggers."

Estevan complied with his friend's wishes, and that same evening the fair Catalina paid her fickle lover a visit in the church. It is evident that matters were satisfactorily arranged, for she quitted the sanctuary with a smile on her face.

"It is all settled," Cortez said, next day, when Estevan presented himself to his friend. "Catalina and I have made up our quarrel, and I am going to call on the governor."

"Call on the governor! Are you mad?"

"No. I will beard the lion in his den, and within twenty-four hours we will be the best of friends."

The governor was on a military excursion some distance from the capital that evening, and Cortez left the sanctuary, and, hastening to the camp, presented himself unexpectedly before Velasquez. The governor was startled by the sudden apparition of his enemy, completely armed, before him.

"What does this visit mean?" he asked, with some dismay.

"I came to make an explanation of my conduct, governor," said Cortez, coolly, but courteously.

"You have? Don't you know I can have your head cut off?"

"Yes, but you won't."

"Won't I?" cried Velasquez, his anger rising.

"Sit down, governor, calm yourself; pray don't allow yourself to become excited."

So great was the magnetic power of Cortez, that the governor, without knowing why, obeyed.

Then Cortez coolly drew a chair to his side, and, seating himself, told the governor of his reconciliation with Catalina, that it was his intention to marry, settle down, and become a good citizen. The governor, charmed with the boldness of the young scapegrace, and overjoyed to know that there was a prospect of his becoming a worthy and respectable citizen, embraced him.

"My friend, we will now have a bottle of wine, and you shall spend the night with me," said the governor. They drank until both became merry, and retired. When the messenger arrived to announce the escape of Cortez, he found him in the apartments of his excellency, where both were actually sleeping in the same bed.

CHAPTER V.

AGAIN we find ourselves in Darien. It is evening, and beautiful is the moonlight of the tropics.
In those salubrious climes the day so quickly glides
into the night that twilight seems scarce a bridge
between them. One moment of darker purple in
the sky, of a thousand rose hues in the bay, of
shade half victorious over light, and then burst
forth at once the countless thousands of stars—the
moon is up, night has resumed her sway.

There is a great bustle in the little village, and
on the soft sounds of early night break the rude
clank of arms and tread of tired men. The rem-
nant of the little army which set out but a short
time ago has returned, bringing back the news of
the discovery of an ocean. Never Castilian maid
met conquering knight with more joyous affection,
than did Fulvia, who flew down the sandy beach to
greet her lord as he disembarked, and lead him
back to the home in which she so long and so
anxiously had waited for him. With her own

71

hands she prepared his evening meal, poured his wine for him, and placing him in bed soothed him to repose.

Next morning Balboa despatched a ship and caravel to Coyba for the companions and treasures which had been left behind. Fulvia, knowing something of the importance of the success of the expedition, asked if he need now fear his enemies at court.

"No," he answered. "The discovery of that sea will silence them, and elevate me to the highest favor with my sovereign."

He wrote letters to the king, setting forth all he had heard and seen of the southern sea, and of the rich countries upon its border. Beside the royal fifths of the expedition, he prepared a present for the sovereign, in the name of himself and his companions, consisting of the largest and most precious pearls they had collected. As an intelligent and trusty envoy on so delicate a mission, Pedro de Arbolancha, a true and well-tried friend, who had shared his toils and dangers and was fully informed of all the circumstances, was chosen.

The delays of his ambassador proved fatal to Balboa. Bachelor Encisco pursued the usurping governor with such relentless fury that, before the arrival of his friend, Don Pedrarias Davila was appointed governor of Darien, and sent to explore

the unknown ocean, a rumor of which had reached
the king.

Before his arrival, Balboa enjoyed a period of
tranquillity and happiness. He devoted his time
and attention to the improvement of his colony, and
Darien was soon the most prosperous of all the
Spanish settlements in the New World. If he entertained fears that affairs were not going right in
Spain, these fears were lulled to repose by lapse of
time. One evening, while reclining on a cot, Francisco Pizarro called to inform him that a fleet of
vessels had just come in sight.

"Perhaps it comes from Spain," said Balboa, his
hopes alternately rising and falling as he reflected
that the news might be good or bad.

The ships belonged to the newly appointed governor, who fearing the redoubtable Balboa, anchored
a league from the settlement, and sent a messenger
on shore to announce his arrival. The envoy, having heard so much in Spain of the powers and ex-
ploits of Balboa, and the riches of Golden Castile, expected to find a blustering warrior maintaining barbaric state in the government which he had usurped.
Great was his astonishment, therefore, to find this
redoubtable hero a plain unassuming man, clad in
cotton frock and drawers, with hempen sandals on
his feet, directing and aiding the labor of several
Indians who were thatching his cottage. The mes-

senger cautiously and respectfully approached the conqueror, who, ceasing in his labors, turned anxiously to hear him, for already he had misgivings.

"Señor Balboa," he said, "I am a messenger sent to announce the arrival of Don Pedrarias Davila, governor of Darien."

Whatever might have been Balboa's feelings at this intelligence, his features were too well schooled to exhibit any emotion.

"Tell Don Pedrarias he is welcome, and I congratulate him on his safe arrival, and am ready with all who are here to obey his orders," was his discreet answer.

The envoy had scarce taken his departure with Balboa's answer, when all Darien was in an uproar. Francisco Pizarro and other warm adherents of Balboa were loud in their protestations and declared in favor of resisting the new governor with force.

"No, it will not do to resist a governor sent by the king," said Balboa. "We must submit and trust to time to right our wrongs."

Next day (June 30) Pedrarias landed and at once assumed control of the colony. He went first to Balboa's house accompanied by his public notary, Oviedo, the historian.

"I am directed by our king," he said, "to treat

you with great favor and distinction, to consult you
about the affairs of the colony, and apply to you
for information."

Balboa, innocent and unsuspecting, gave him all
the information he required. During the interview
Fulvia remained in an adjoining apartment trembling with dread.

"I am sorry that you gave him the information
he required," she said, when they were alone.

"Why?"

"Having gained it, he will now have no further
use for you, and may take it into his head to dispose of you, for he is a bad man."

Fulvia proved correct, for in a few days Pedrarias dropped the mask and proclaimed a judicial
scrutiny into the conduct of Balboa and his officers.

The examination was conducted by the licentiate
who had come as alcalde mayor, but Balboa's
shrewdness again came to his relief. He procured
as witnesses none but his friends, who described his
heroism in such highly colored terms that Pedrarias,
becoming alarmed lest the examination should elevate the man he had designed to crush, stopped it.

At this time a fearful epidemic seized the town.
Every one was more or less affected, even the veterans of the colonies, but to none was the epidemic
more fatal than the crowd of youthful cavaliers,
who had once flitted so gayly about the streets of

Seville, and had come to the New World filled with the most sanguine expectations. The governor himself was attacked, and for days lay at death's door.

On his recovery, Pedrarias, finding his colony reduced to the most straitened circumstances, despatched a ship-load of starving people to Cuba, and sent an expedition into the country to forage among the natives for provisions. Fearing to increase the popularity of Balboa, should he appoint him to the command of the expedition, he entrusted it to a favorite, and the only man competent for such leadership remained idle in the colony.

Thinking to pursue his explorations at his own risk, Balboa despatched a friend to Cuba for ships, men, and supplies for that purpose. This was all done secretly, however, for he did not care to trust the governor. The weary weeks that followed were passed in idleness by him who was capable of making Darien prosperous.

One evening, as Balboa sat dejected and broken in spirit in his hut, Fulvia, who ever remained his good angel, came to report a vessel loaded with armed men off the coast who wished to consult with him. It proved to be his agent, Andres Garabita, from Cuba, where he had procured a vessel and recruits for exploring the South Sea.

"I must communicate with him at once," said

Balboa on ascertaining who it was, and he rose with the intention of going to his boat; but at that moment the tread of mailed warriors was heard without, and next moment an officer of the governor entered, and seized the explorer's shoulder.

"I arrest you, señor," he said.

"Away!" and Balboa shook him off and laid his hand on his sword. Realizing how dangerous it would be to resist one of the governor's officers, Fulvia seized his arm and implored him in the name of her love to make no resistance. Putting up his sword, Balboa asked: "On what charge do you arrest me?"

"Treason. You are in communication with a strange ship of armed men, and it means treason to the governor."

Although Balboa denied any treasonable designs, Governor Pedrarias had him dragged away and confined in a wooden cage, the only prison the town could boast of at that time. The quick-witted Fulvia was not slow in devising some means for the rescue of her lord. She hastened to the bishop of Darien, told him what had been done, and implored him to intercede for Balboa.

"I will see about it at once," answered the bishop. He accordingly went to Pedrarias, and in a short time proved to the satisfaction of the governor that, although the ship's crew were friends of Balboa, they entertained no treasonable designs, and the prisoner was released. The bishop urged the governor to permit Balboa to resume his expedition to the South Sea, but his jealousy was too strong to listen to such counsel.

Pedrarias determined to conquer the South Sea, especially the Island of Pearls, himself, so he despatched Gaspar Morales and Francisco Pizarro on the expedition with an army of sixty men. Balboa was left behind disconsolate and discouraged, and passed the time in his cabin comforted only by his wife, who remained his good angel in his darkest hours.

Morales and Pizarro, after many hardships and conflicts, reached the South Sea, and with four large canoes set out for the Island of Pearls. They were resisted by the warlike cacique with maddened desperation, but with flashing guns and the terrible dogs they conquered, and the cacique made a treaty of peace. He gave them a basket of pearls, two of which were the finest that had ever been known, for some hawk's-bells and hatchets.

"These things I can turn to some purpose," said the cacique, "but of what value are pearls to me?"

On discovering that these baubles were precious to the Spaniards, he led Pizarro to the summit of a tower, commanding an unbounded prospect, and pointed to the west.

"Behold before you the infinite sea, which ex-
tends even beyond the sunbeams. As to these
islands which lie to the right and left, they are all
subject to my sway. They possess little gold, but
in the deep places of the sea around them are to be
found a great many pearls. Continue to be my
friends, and you shall have as many as you desire, for I value your friendship more than pearls,
and as far as in me lies, I will try never to for-
feit it."

He then pointed to the mainland which stretched
away toward the east, mountain beyond mountain,
until the summit of the last faded in the distance,
and was scarcely seen above the watery horizon.
Then he told them of a strange, far-off land of in-
exhaustible riches, inhabited by a mighty people.
As he went on repeating the vague but wonderful
rumors of wealth and splendor which the Spaniards
had so often heard of the kingdom of Peru, Pizarro's
cupidity was roused and he greedily listened, while
his dark, flashing eye followed the finger of the
cacique along the line of shadowy coast, and his
daring mind kindled with the thought of conquering this golden empire.

The expedition, though fruitful in rumors of
Peruvian splendor, was, beyond a few pearls, of no
practical results. Pedrarias set on foot various
other expeditions, all of which failed to meet with

the success desired, and the people began to murmur at his neglect of Balboa, who alone led to victory.

"Why not give us our leader, and then we can
conquer these rich countries," they declared.
The politic bishop, becoming alarmed at the uneasy
state of the public mind, sought to bring about a
reconciliation.

"Governor Pedrarias," said he, one day, on calling at his house, "your treatment of Balboa is
odious to the people, and must eventually draw upon
you the displeasure of the king."

"Balboa is a dangerous man," Pedrarias answered. "He usurped one governorship and might
another."

"But why persist in forcing a man to become
your deadliest enemy, whom you may grapple to
your side as your firmest friend?" added the
bishop. "You have several daughters—give him
one in marriage; you will then have for a son-in-
law a man of merit and popularity, who is a hidalgo
by birth, and a favorite of the king. You are in-
firm and well advanced in life, while he is in the
prime and vigor of his days and possessed of great
activity. You can make him your lieutenant; and
while you repose from your toils, he can carry on
the affairs of the colony with spirit and enterprise,
and all his achievements will redound to the ad-

vancement of your family, and splendor of your administration."

"But Balboa already has a wife," said the governor.

With a smile the bishop answered.

"He has an Indian mistress, but has never wed according to the forms of the church. I will dissolve the ties which bind him to her."

Both the governor and his wife were won by the bishop to his way of thinking, and soon after Balboa was notified that the governor had made him his lieutenant, and would entrust him with the exploration of the South Sea.

Almost ere he knew it, Balboa was in the high career of prosperity. His most implacable enemy was now his dearest friend, and was loading him with favors. The daughter whom the matchmaking bishop designed to become Balboa's bride was yet in Spain, but had been sent for. Meanwhile active preparations were made for exploring the South Sea. He went to Acla, where men and money were furnished him for constructing four brigantines to be launched in the Pacific or South Sea. Timber was felled on the Atlantic seaboard, and, with the anchors and rigging, transported across the lofty ridge of mountains to the opposite shores of the isthmus. For this duty several Spaniards, thirty negroes, and an army of Indians were employed.

6

Arduous and almost impossible as the task may seem, the vessels were built and launched. The town of Panama was laid out on the Pacific side, and thither came many Spaniards with their families, and thither came Fulvia. The explorer had just returned from a short cruise and was building larger vessels with the intention of exploring Peru, when his wife joined him. There was a mysterious change in Fulvia which Balboa could not understand. She was silent and sad. No more she greeted him with the fond affection of old, and one evening on entering the house he found her bathed in tears.

"What grieves you, Fulvia?" he asked.

"I know why the governor has changed toward you!" she answered. "He has sent to Spain for his daughter who is to become your wife, and then poor Fulvia is to be cast aside, or, perhaps, devoured by Leoncico."

Moved by her love and grief, Balboa clasped the beautiful princess in his arms and cried:

"Fulvia, you are my wife, and I swear I will have none other."

Startled by the declaration, Fulvia was silent for a moment; then a strange dread came over her.

"You will have to wed the governor's daughter; it will be death to refuse," she said.

"Fulvia, I can now defy the governor."

"Do not defy fate. Remember the prediction of Micer Codro, the astrologer, of which you have told me."

With an incredulous laugh he answered: "Behold the wisdom of those who believe in soothsayers, and, above all, in such an astrologer as Micer Codro! According to his prophecy, I should now be in imminent peril of my life; yet here I am, within reach of all my wishes, sound in health, with four brigantines and three hundred men at my command, and on the point of exploring this great southern sea. Above all I have for my wife a princess whom I would not exchange for the daughter of a king, much less a governor."

A footstep startled them, and, turning their eyes toward the door, they beheld the scowling face of Andres Garabito, Balboa's agent in exploring the South Sea. Being infatuated with the beautiful Fulvia, Garabito was madly jealous of Balboa. The rumor which spread over the colony that Balboa was to wed the governor's daughter gave Garabito a hope, but what he had just heard and seen dispelled it. Madly jealous, he seized the first opportunity to write the following to Pedrarias:

"PANAMA, *September* 4, 1517
"GOVERNOR PEDRARIAS :—
"In the name of our Gracious Majestie : I have to tell you of many things which it sorely grieves my heart to

relate. Vasco Nuñez de Balboa, whom you trust, is false to you, and is even now forming an insurrection against your authoritie. He has three hundred men and four brigantines and will defy you. Yielding most ungraciously to the influence of his Indian paramour, Fulvia, the daughter of Careta, he has no intention of solemnizing his marriage with your daughter. He has merely made use of the friendship of Pedrarias to further his own selfish views, and, as soon as his ships are ready, will throw off all allegiance to you, and put to sea as an independent commander, for so have I heard him declare this very day.

"Andres Garabito."

Not content with sending this mischievous missive, Garabito, who was entrusted with a message to the governor, managed at Darien to have himself arrested, and made a confession of his own guilt with Balboa in a conspiracy. The effect of all this on the hard and jealous governor can be better imagined than described. His wrath knew no bounds.

"Rejects my daughter for an Indian, does he? He shall die, I will strike off his head."

Meanwhile, Balboa, unaware of the pitfall yawning at his unwary feet, was pushing with all possible speed his preparations for a voyage on the South Sea. Every arrangement had been completed, and, with Fulvia, he came ashore to take the last leave of their recent happy home, before plunging into the great unknown.

"Let us set sail at once!" pleaded Fulvia. "There is no safety for us save in the unknown sea."

" We will sail in the morning," Balboa answered. "This is the last night we shall spend on the shore."

He sat in the door of his house, his wife on a low stool at his feet, when the tramp of hoofs reached their ears, and looking down the path, almost hidden by the dim gray twilight, they saw a horseman approaching.

"The governor's messenger!" exclaimed Fulvia.

"What have you?" asked Balboa, as the messenger drew in his reeking steed at the door.

"A letter from the governor," answered the messenger, handing him a sealed missive. While the messenger was gone to secure rest and refreshments, Balboa broke the seal. The letter was a hypocritical missive inviting Balboa to an interview at Acla, and so carefully had the deceitful governor worded it that it awakened no suspicion in his heart.

"Will you go to Acla?" Fulvia asked, when the letter was read.

"Certainly. The governor has summoned me for an interview, and I will obey."

"I dread your going."

"Wherefore should you?"

"I know not why; but I dread the governor. He talks with a forked tongue, and his paper has an inperceivable falsehood in it."

The conqueror laughed at his wife's fears, kissed her a good-night, and made preparations for the journey. At early dawn he was on the road, which had now become a considerable thoroughfare, accompanied by the messengers who had come for him. Won by his frank, open manner, they repented that they were leading him into a snare, and told him something of the governor's hostile intentions.

"I have not been guilty of treason," said Balboa. "Then I have friends at court who will protect me. I will face the governor and dispel his fears."

As they pressed on, he descried a band of horsemen in glittering armor coming up the road.

"It is Captain Pizarro and cavaliers," said one of the messengers. Pizarro being a friend, Balboa entertained no fears of him, and rode boldly toward the cavalcade. When the two parties met, Pizarro rode directly to the side of Balboa. "I must arrest you," he said.

"How is this, Francisco?" exclaimed Balboa. "Is this the way you have been accustomed to receive me?"

"I am only obeying the orders of the governor."

"Having never resisted or disobeyed a superior officer, I shall not do so now," returned Balboa.

Offering no resistance, he was taken in chains to Acla, where he was thrown into prison, and Bartolome Hurtado, once his favorite officer, was sent to take command of his squadron.

Bad news flies on the wings of the morning, and in an incredibly short time Fulvia heard of her lord's arrest. She hurried to Acla to console him with her presence, but was refused admission. The trial was a farce. On the testimony of Andres Garabito and a sentinel, who had also overheard what Balboa had said to Fulvia, he was convicted. Fulvia, being a heathen, was not permitted to testify in his behalf, and Balboa was convicted of treason and sentenced to death.

The governor, upbraiding the doomed man, said: "Hitherto, I have treated you as a son, because I thought you loyal to your king and to his representative, but, as you have meditated rebellion against the crown of Castile, I cast you off from my affections, and shall henceforth treat you as an enemy."

Balboa indignantly denied the charge, and referred to the confiding frankness of his conduct as a proof of his innocence.

"Had I been conscious of my guilt, what could have induced me to come here and put myself in your power?" he asked. "Had I meditated rebellion, what prevented me from carrying it into effect? I had four ships ready to weigh anchor, **three hundred brave men at my command, and an** open sea before me. What had I to do but spread sail and press forward? There was no doubt of finding a land, whether rich or poor, sufficient for me and mine, far beyond reach of your control. In the innocence of my heart I came here promptly at your request, and my reward is slander, indignity, chains, and death!"

Unable to answer an appeal so noble and generous, Pedrarias left the prison cell and went out upon the street. As he was going, some one touched his arm and a soft musical voice imploringly asked:

"Can I see him? Can I see him? Please, governor, let me see him!"

"It's Fulvia!" cried the governor. "Fulvia, the wild she-devil who has bewitched him. Away! or I will set the dogs on you."

The frightened Fulvia ran away, but hovered near, hoping to be able to get a glimpse of her husband. Again and again did Pedrarias drive her into the wood, threatening her with the dogs, until the populace, incensed at his cruelty, determined that she should talk with the doomed man. So urgently did they insist, that, on the night before the execution, the interview was granted. Fulvia rushed into the arms of Balboa, and burying her face on his shoulder, gave way to sobs.

"It is I who have brought you to death," she cried, when he sought to soothe her. "Denounce me, cast me from you, wed the governor's daughter, and live."

"No, Fulvia, I prefer death with your love to a kingdom without it," answered the hero, with a smile.

The dread morning of execution came. A scaffold had been built, and the grim executioner, with his black mask over his face, stood by the fatal block, leaning on his great shining axe. Three of Balboa's officers had been doomed to die with him, and from a secret place between the reeds of a wall, Pedrarias was a witness to the bloody scene. The scaffold was in the plaza or public square of Acla, and the prisoners, under a strong guard, were marched toward it.

From the hill a weeping woman watched them, and as they drew near the fatal scaffold, she ran to them crying: "Let it be me. I am guilty, not he."

"Away, she-devil!" shouted a soldier, striking her with the pole of his lance. "Away, lest I run you through."

"Slay me, if you will, but spare him!" she cried.

"Ask nothing of them," said Balboa. "Let not your tears rejoice their hearts."

The public crier who walked before Balboa, at this moment proclaimed: "This is the punishment inflicted by command of the king and his lieutenant.

Don Pedrarias Davila, on this man, as a traitor and an usurper of the territories of the crown."

"He lies!" Balboa indignantly answered. "Never did such a crime enter my mind. I have ever served my king with truth and loyalty, and sought to augment his dominions."

Fulvia's frantic grief began to move the multitude, and the officers having the execution in hand hurried Balboa forward. As he mounted the scaffold, the explorer gazed about over the scene. After wandering over the vast array of faces, his eyes finally fell on Fulvia, and as the executioners bound his feet together and tied his hands behind his back, his deep rich voice suddenly broke the stillness.

"Farewell, Fulvia, I die for loving you!" he exclaimed.

Then he was forced forward on his knees, his head held down on the block by his long hair; the executioner raised his terrible axe, it flashed like a gleam of vengeance in the sunlight, and fell with a sickening thud. There was a rush of dark blood over the scaffold, and the head of Balboa was severed from its body.

One prolonged shriek rent the air, and Fulvia fell in a swoon.

CHAPTER VI.

THE OPPORTUNITY.

FROM this dark spot on history's page we turn once more to Cuba, where affairs go better. Velasquez, though a fickle and jealous governor, did not possess the cruelty of Pedrarias. His reconciliation with Cortez seemed permanent. Cortez married the Señora Catalina and received a liberal share of lands and repartiamiento of Indians. He still lived in the neighborhood of St. Jago, and, being once more restored to good citizenship, renewed the acquaintance of Estevan.

"So the gay, dashing Cortez has settled down to mining and raising sugar-cane," said Christina, a few days after the marriage of Cortez to the fair Catalina.

"Yes, and promises to be a sober citizen," her husband answered.

"He is cruel," put in Christopher.

"Why?"

"He beat a slave to-day. I heard the poor Indian cry out in pain. Father Las Casas says it is very wrong."

Estevan and his wife were both amazed at the intelligence of their first-born.

"He will be a priest," remarked the father. "He has all the qualifications for a member of the Holy order."

Christopher heard the remark, and shook his head gravely.

"No, I will be a soldier and fight battles," he said.

"To fight battles you must be cruel."

"Not so cruel as to beat slaves; that is cowardly!"

A few days later, as Hernando Estevan and Christopher were going about the plantation, Cortez, mounted on a fiery horse, came riding along the road.

"Cortez, you have changed your course of life, I hear," cried Estevan.

"So I have. No more the roystering Cortez, but the sober, industrious miner and planter," he answered. "My soul has panted for conquest since first I came to the New World, but the opportunity has not presented itself yet; hence I am trying to become rich by mining, and growing sugar-cane."

"That opportunity may come, Cortez, for I hear strange stories of a far-off country which the great admiral failed to reach. Gold abounds there in such huge quantities that they use it for drinking cups. Is it the fair Cathay?"

"Perhaps; but where the devil is it? Ojeda is a beggar, and Nicuesa lost his life seeking it. News has just came that our friend Balboa has been beheaded."

"Executed by Pedrarias the governor of Darien?"

"The same."

"It was a wicked outrage, and was done because of Pedrarias's jealousy."

"Quite correct, Estevan. Though death seems to await all explorers from Spain, yet I long to take my place with them."

For several years the life of Cortez glided smoothly along in tranquil pursuits. He grew prosperous and, some thought, happy. Catalina, although beneath him in birth and station, made an excellent wife. Such was the state of things when Alvarado returned to Cuba with tidings of Grijalva's wonderful discoveries in Yucatan. Rumors of rich fields, of castles, towns, and temples of gold in far-away lands almost drove the people wild. The news spread throughout the island, and every one saw at once that these discoveries promised greater results than any which had hitherto been obtained.

"Estevan, have you heard the strange news?"

asked Cortez, meeting his friend on the great road leading from St. Jago.

"I have."

"Will the governor follow up these discoveries?"

"He will. He is even now casting about for some suitable person to command the expedition."

"Has he found one?"

"No. Several hidalgos have presented themselves, but from want of proper qualifications, or from fear of their assuming independence of their employer, one after another has been rejected."

"I am going to ask for the commission for myself," declared Cortez, after a moment's thought.

"Can you influence the governor?"

"I have powerful friends who can. There are two persons in St. Jago in whom Velasquez places great confidence. They are Amador de Lares the contador, and the governor's secretary, Andres de Ducro. I am in close intimacy with both these persons, and I shall urge them to recommend me as a suitable person."

"Cortez, if you command the expedition, I will be one of your followers."

"Give me your hand on that, for I will surely command it," cried Cortez.

As he seized the hand of Cortez, Estevan added:

"I mean it, Cortez, for my children are grown

out of infancy, and my affairs are in such shape that I can leave them."

"And you are enthusiastic for the enterprise?"

"I am."

"Come with me; we will go and see the contador and secretary at once."

They hastened down the street to the office of Andres de Duero. There are times in the affairs of men when luck, fortune, or fate, which ever it may be termed, seems to sweep one on to success. This was the golden opportunity for Cortez. He found Duero in his office and Amador de Lares with him. As soon as the two visitors were seated, Cortez broached the subject nearest his heart. Had they heard the report of Alvarado, and the determination of the governor to send an expedition to this unknown Eldorado?

They had, and were just discussing the matter.

"The governor seems at a loss for some one to command the expedition," remarked the contador.

"Why would not Hernando Cortez do?" Estevan asked.

"The man!" answered Duero.

"I had him in mind, but doubted if he would give up prosperous mines and plantations, with the ease and luxury of Cuba, for the dangers and vicissitudes of an explorer."

"You misjudged me, Lares," Cortez answered.

"There is untold wealth in those lands; help me to a commission to conquer them, and you shall share liberally in the rewards."

Cortez had touched the key to their hearts. The contador of the royal treasury and the secretary of state, both powers behind the throne, became his warm adherents. From this hour, the deportment of the future conqueror of Mexico underwent a change. His thoughts, instead of evaporating in empty levities or idle flashes of merriment, were wholly concentrated on the great object to which he was devoted. His elastic spirits were exercised in cheering and stimulating the companions of his toilsome duties, and he was roused to a generous enthusiasm, of which even those who knew him best had not believed him capable.

His friends were successful, and he received the appointment for which he had longed since his arrival in the New World. His commission, dated at Barcelona, November 13, 1518, arrived when preparations for the conquest of Mexico were well under way. Cortez applied all his money in fitting out the expedition, mortgaged his estates for more, and borrowed all that Estevan and his other friends could spare.

The expedition, fitting out in the harbor of St. Jago, kept the busy little city in a state of bustle and excitement. The most exaggerated stories of

that far-off land called Mexico reached the city,
and nearly drove the people wild with excitement.
From dawn till dark Cortez pursued his labors,
directing what should be
done, and sharing in the
toil with his own hands.

He was born to inspire,
to lead, and to conquer.

"Ho! Señor Cortez,"
cried Gerund, the gover-
nor's jester, a crack-
brained fellow, half wit
and half fool, who in
those days was essential
to every great man's es-
tablishment, "you have
grown quite sedate of late.
No more merry-making."

"I have serious matters
commanding my atten-
tion," answered Cortez.

"And are you happy?"

"Happy! What know

"DON'T YOU SEE HOW HAPPY
I AM?"

you of happiness? Cudgel your dull brain for
some poor joke to make your master laugh."

"I will! I will!" cried Gerund, with a comical
grin. "I will give him a jest that will crack his
sides. It makes me happy to think of it. Ha,

7

ha, ha, don't you see how happy I am?" and, holding his hands to his sides, Gerund roared with laughter.

As Cortez was turning away from the fool, he met Christopher Estevan, a lad now eight years of age. The boy's eyes followed the jester as he said:

"Even a fool, señor, can set the governor a-thinking."

"Watch him, Christopher, and if you learn that he is poisoning the governor's mind against me, let me know."

Christopher promised to do so. As he was a playmate of Antonio Velasquez, the governor's nephew, who was much of the time at the governor's house, he had an excellent opportunity to watch Gerund. Next day, as Cortez and the governor were walking from the mansion toward the port, they were startled by a voice calling from the garden. Turning about, both discovered Gerund the jester.

"Have a care, Master Velasquez," he cried, "or we shall have to go a-hunting, some day or other, after this same captain of ours. What think you of my joke, Señor Captain?"

"Do you hear what the rogue says?" asked the governor, as they passed on.

"Do not heed him," answered Cortez; "he is a saucy knave and deserves to be whipped."

Gerund overheard the remark· and sent a last shot after him:

"Fie, fie! Señor Captain, you would no doubt like to lay it on my back as you will on Master Velasquez."

They hastened out of hearing of the jester, but his words sank deep in the mind of Velasquez.

On returning to his house, the governor found a number of his relatives and personal friends await-ing him. Christopher Estevan and Antonio Velas-quez, who was three or four years his senior, were playing about the house, and young Estevan saw and heard all that was said and done. The gov-ernor's brother was there and seemed greatly vexed.

"Governor Velasquez," he said, "why do you send Cortez on an expedition which is sure to pro-duce both wealth and fame? Reliable information has reached our ears that Mexico contains more wealth than all the remainder of the world. Why neglect your own flesh and blood, and give all this to a stranger?"

"He has his commission, and his fleet is almost ready to sail," returned Velasquez, who began to entertain some fears.

"Recall the commission. Remember your ancient quarrel, for he is one who never forgives an affront, and will, ere long, supersede you."

"I have feared this. Bring Lares and Ducro here," said the governor. The secretary and the contador were summoned, and to them he said: "I have become distrustful of this fellow Cortez, and I want to detain the expedition a few days and then put it in other hands."

Lares and Ducro tried to dissuade the governor, but he was set in his way. Without seeming to take any note of the matter, Christopher Estevan had heard all. Excusing himself from his playmate, he hastened to his father's house, where Cortez chanced to be.

In as few words as possible, Christopher related what he had heard pertaining to Cortez, who, at the conclusion of the boy's narrative said:

"There is not a moment to lose, Estevan."

"No."

"We must sail to-night."

"But your fleet is not ready?"

"Nevertheless we must sail; delay is ruin."

"Lares and Ducro are your friends; why not consult them and learn if the boy's statement is true," suggested the father. "Christopher may have been misinformed."

"I was not, father."

"You may have misinterpreted their meaning, Christopher. Better see them, Cortez."

On going to the office of the contador Cortez

found both Lares and Duero, who confirmed the lad's story.

"And now, Cortez," concluded Duero, "I would advise you to expedite matters as much as possible, and if you would retain command of your fleet, get ready for sea at once."

"I will," he answered. "Although I have not my complement of men and my vessels are inadequately provided with supplies, I will sail this very night."

His officers were secretly informed of his design, and at midnight, when the town was hushed in sleep, there came on the air the muffled tread of troops, cautiously marching to the vessel. Supplies were silently hurried on board, and just before dawn of day the little fleet moved down the bay, where they cast anchor to wait for daylight to sail.

At early dawn Velasquez was awakened by his jester pounding at his door.

"Ho, master!" he cried, "awake, and see your good Cortez already under way without so much as bidding you adieu."

"What mean you, knave?"

"Behold the fleet ready to sail."

With a yell of rage, the governor leaped from his bed and ran to a window, from which he saw the fleet beyond the harbor.

"Bring a guard!   Bring me a horse!" he cried, hurriedly dressing.

Buckling on his sword, he donned his sombrero, and rushed out on the lawn where a retinue of cavaliers awaited him. He leaped on his horse, and, followed by his guard, galloped down to the beach, waving his hand at the fleet and crying:

"Ho, you knaves!   Come back, you villains!"

Cortez, discovering the approach of the governor and retinue, entered an armed boat and came within speaking distance of the shore.

"And is it thus you part from me?" exclaimed Velasquez; "a courteous way of taking leave, truly!"

"Pardon me," Cortez answered courteously; "time presses, and there are some things that should be done before they are even thought of. Has your excellency any commands?"

So exasperated was the governor at the cool impudence of the fellow that he turned to one of his attendants and cried:

"Garcia, you have a matchlock; dismount and put a bullet through the knave."

Garcia, dismounting, lighted the match in his gun, and, setting the rest, opened the pan. Cortez stood boldly in the stern of the boat, an excellent mark for a good shot, but when the guardsman pressed the trigger sending the match into the pan there was no explosion; the powder had been jolted out in the ride to the beach.

"Gonzalez, have you your crossbow," cried the governor.

"No, your excellency."

The governor's rage knew no bounds, as Cortez politely waved his hand and returned to his vessel. Turning to Christopher Estevan, who stood on the beach watching the fleet which now weighed anchor, the governor asked:

"Is your father aboard that fleet?"

"He is," the lad answered.

"Then, by St. Anthony, you will be an orphan, for I will hang every officer on the rebel fleet!"

With this threat Velasquez rode back to the house to digest his chagrin as best he might, satisfied that he had blundered both in appointing Cortez to the command, and in attempting to deprive him of it, after appointed.

Cortez sailed to Macaca, where he laid in such stores as he could obtain from the royal farms, which he declared to be "a loan from the king." Thence he proceeded to Trinidad, which had grown to be a considerable town on the south end of Cuba. He remained here some time, recruiting and taking in stores. About one hundred of Grijalva's men, just returned from a long and tedious voyage along the southern coast of Mexico, were persuaded to

join him. He also dispatched one of his officers,
Diego Ordaz, in quest of another ship, of which
he had heard, and ordered him to meet him off Cape
Antonio. From here he sailed to Havana, where
he spent his time boldly taking in supplies and recruiting his men.

According to historians, Cortez was, at this
time, thirty-four years of age. In stature he was
rather above middle size. His complexion was
pale, and his large, dark eyes gave an expression of
gravity to his countenance, not to be expected in
one of his cheerful temperament. Though his
figure was slender until later in life, his chest was
deep, his shoulders broad, his frame muscular, and
well proportioned. His body was a union of
strength, agility, and vigor, which qualified him to
excel in fencing, horsemanship, and other generous
exercises of chivalry. He was temperate in diet,
and drank little, while to toil and privation he was
perfectly indifferent. His dress was elegant, and
well adapted to set off his handsome person to advantage. Though becoming, rich and striking, it
was not gaudy, while his few jewels were of great
price. His manners were pleasing, frank, and
soldier-like, concealing a cool and calculating spirit
beneath them. With his gayest humor there
mingled a settled air of resolution, which made
those who approached him feel that they must obey,

and infused awe into the attachment of his most devoted followers.

In the month of February, 1519, the little squadron touched at Cape St. Antonio, where Cortez, mustering his forces, found they numbered one hundred and ten mariners, five hundred and fifty-three soldiers, including thirty-two crossbow-men and thirteen arquebusiers, besides two hundred Indians of the island, and a few Indian women for menial offices. He was provided with ten heavy guns, and sixteen horses; for Cortez rightly estimated the importance of cavalry, however small in number, both for their actual service in the field, and for striking terror into the hearts of the savages.

After making a short speech, in which he showed them the glories of the coming conquest, they sailed for the island of Cozumel. Here they found houses built of stone and lime, with magnificent temples towering several stories in the air. But the temples had been rifled of their treasures by Alvarado. While at Cozumel, a man dressed like a native came to Cortez one day, and saluted him in Indian fashion by touching his head to the earth.

"Call an interpreter," said Cortez.

"No need, captain, for I am a Spaniard like yourself," said the stranger. "I am Geronimo de Aguilar, a native of Ecija in old Spain, where I

was regularly educated for the church. I was established with the colony at Darien, and on a
voyage to Hispaniola eight years ago was wrecked
near the cost of Yucatan." Then he told a story,
so wild and weird as to make even the steel-clad
Cortez shudder.

"Are you the only survivor?" he asked at the
conclusion.

"No, I have one companion left from this
disaster," answered Aguilar; "but he has married
an Indian wife and adopted their manners and customs. He would not come with me, for he preferred
his wild life in the wilderness with his dusky wife
and children to his own people."

CHAPTER VII.

A YOUNG HUMANITARIAN.

A FEW days after the departure of the fleet of Cortez, the governor of Cuba, with his lieutenant, Narvaez, drew rein in front of Estevan's house and called to his wife, who was on the veranda. Christopher, who heard the governor, came from the arbor to learn what he wanted.

"Señora Estevan, is your husband with the fleet of Cortez?" asked the governor.

"He is," she answered.

"Then more is the pity for you."

"Why?" asked Christina, her heart giving great bounds, for she discovered that the governor was in a rage, and she had a dread of him.

"Because you will soon be a widow. I will hang every man aboard the fleet."

"They have done nothing worthy of death, governor."

"Desertion and treason are punishable with death?"

107

"They are surely guilty of neither charge. They sailed with your consent and the king's commission."

"My consent, indeed! Did I not recall them? But Cortez defied me; yes, defied me. I will hang every one of them."

"But, remember, the good Father Olmedo is with them!" put in the lad, who had early been taught that the priest was sacred.

"I will hang him, also. Señora, I warn you, if you do not keep that impudent son of yours quiet I will pull your house down about your ears," cried the governor. Dismounting from his horse, he went to the gate, where he stood shaking his fist at the señora, whose husband he hated. Christopher's blue eyes flashed with deadly fire, and, turning, he entered the house. There was an arbor at the side of the house with a door opening to it from within.

The señora, who was trembling for her own safety, was doing all she could to pacify the angry governor, when she was suddenly startled by the odor of burning wood. Leaving the governor to fume and rage alone, she hurried into the arbor from whence the odor came.

"Christopher, what are you doing!" shrieked the astounded mother. Her son was balancing an old arquebus on a cross-beam and aiming it through the trellised vines at the governor, while he held in his right hand a firebrand to touch it off.

"Keep quiet, mother, I will kill him."

Christina snatched the firebrand from his hand, and taking away the weapon put it in the house just as the governor, suspecting some mischief, entered the arbor.

"What are you about?" he demanded.

"Trying to shoot a tyrant, who would hang my father," boldly answered the lad, his eyes flashing fire.

Velasquez was not without his good qualities, and there was something so noble about the lad, that he could not but admire him. He turned to his lieutenant.

"What think you of such a youth, Narvaez?" he asked.

"He will make a dangerous rebel," was the reply.

"To tyrants I will be dangerous," cried the lad. "To men who beat Indian slaves until they fall dead, I am dangerous. Beware, Narvaez, for when I grow to be a man, your cruelty will end."

"By the mass, governor!" cried the impulsive lieutenant, "I do admire the lad's pluck."

"So do I, yet I would advise his mother to keep fire-arms out of his hands, until years may add discretion to his valor, or he may end his days on the scaffold."

"Many good men have," defiantly answered Christopher. "Balboa lost his life for refusing to wed the governor's daughter."

"Come, come, lad, make yourself a useful man, and for your sake I may spare your father; but Cortez shall hang."

"How will you get him?"

"I will send for him."

"Send your lieutenant, Narvaez, and he will return the worse for his mission."

"Hear you the young rogue, Narvaez?"

"I do, and trust I may some day prove he is no prophet."

"Come to my mansion, lad, and play with Antonio when you wish," said Velasquez, remounting his horse. "You are a brave lad, and will make a useful man, despite the fact that your father is a rebel." Velasquez and his lieutenant took their leave, and Christopher was alone with his mother.

She took occasion to reprove him, assuring him that he would increase his father's danger by open hostility to the governor.

"He won't dare harm my father," Christopher answered. "Father and Cortez are brave, and the governor fears them."

A child sometimes reads the heart more accurately than an adult. He is guided more by impressions and never-erring intuitions than false logic. He went straight at the truth and guessed the cause of the governor's antipathy. But childhood is forgetful and forgiving. In a few days Antonio and Christopher were again roaming the fields and forests about St. Jago with their small bows and arrows.

"The governor doesn't like your father," said Antonio.

"I know it. Look at that bird with a great red tail."

"Yes I see it. I believe I can hit it."

"Try. There, you missed and it flew away."

"Come, help me find my arrow!" As they wandered deeper into the wood, Antonio continued. "He don't like your father, because he was a friend of Christopher Columbus. You were named for Columbus?"

"I was."

"So much more the pity. I don't like you, either."

"Then why did you come for me to go birdnesting with you?"

"Because one doesn't want to go alone."

"There are other lads."

"But they don't like me. Here is my arrow sticking in a tree."

"See those great vultures soaring over the wood, Antonio?"

"I do."

"Why do they circle about one place?"

"There is something which attracts them."

"Let us go and see what it is."

With the curiosity of childhood, the boys hurried through the wood, which in places was a dense jungle. On the air made fragrant by tropical flowers, there was borne an offensive odor which increased as they approached the spot beneath the vultures. Suddenly Christopher seized the arm of his companion.

"Something is dead, Antonio," he said.

Filled with that unutterable awe produced by near approach to death, they cautiously advanced until they came upon a terrible sight. A dead Indian slave lay unburied in the woods to be devoured by the vultures. The slave had belonged to Narvaez, and, owing to his master's cruelty, had fled to the wood to be chased, torn, and slain by the dogs. The boys gazed for a moment in silence on the awful spectacle, then turned away.

"Is that the Narvaez plantation?" asked Christopher, pointing to some fields on a hill.

"Yes."

"See, he is already among his slaves."

"He beats them."

"How they scream! Antonio, he is very cruel."

"HOLD, LIEUTENANT; WOULD YOU KILL YOUR SLAVE?"

The boys now came to the Narvaez plantation, and saw him laying his whip about the naked shoulders of a young Indian woman.

"Hold, lieutenant! in God's name, would you kill your slave?" cried Christopher, rushing at the Spaniard.

Astounded at the fierce manner of the little fellow, Narvaez ceased to belabor the slave and stood for a moment gazing in astonishment at the lad.

"Are you not Christopher Estevan?"

"I am."

"You are too bold to interfere with my affairs. Are you not afraid I will lay my whip on your shoulders?"

"No! I would kill you if you did," cried the defiant little fellow, glaring at the slave-beater. "I saw one of your slaves dead in the wood. You can see the vultures soaring above the spot where he lies. If you continue to kill them you will soon have none, and then you must do the work yourself."

"There are plenty more in the forest," answered Narvaez, releasing the shrinking girl, who crept away to her labor in the sugar-cane. Narvaez, guilty tyrant as he was, was awed by his daring little accuser, and unconsciously recoiled from him.

"You say there are plenty in the forest," re-

8

sumed the boy, "but they are dying by hundreds. The woods are whitened with their bones. The Spaniard's cruelty reduces them so rapidly, that, ere many years, this great race of people will all be gone. God will surely avenge their wrongs. Narvaez, beware of God's vengeance," and the lad turned about and left the hidalgo overcome with amazement.

Antonio, alarmed at the boldness of his young friend, when he saw him charge defiantly on Narvaez, turned about and fled to St. Jago, about three miles distant.

Christopher was not alarmed at having to traverse the distance alone. His road led through a dense forest. It was a lonely road, and, as he trotted along the well-beaten path, he was suddenly surprised at hearing a voice call to him from the thicket. Halting, he gazed in the direction of the voice. There was a rustling and trembling of the branches, and then the oddest specimen of humanity he had ever seen stepped out in the path before him. It was an Indian woman, evidently of a great age, dressed in fantastic garb, half civilized and half barbaric. She wore a curious head-gear of feathers, and her feet and legs, to the knees, were naked.

"You are a good lad!" said the old hag, in excellent Spanish.

"Who are you?" he asked.

"Zuna."

"Where from?"

She pointed off to the south, and, with a sadness in her tone, added:

"It has been a long time since I left my people. I was young then, now I am old."

"Why did you come to this island?" he asked.

"I was brought here."

"As a slave?"

"Yes."

"By the white men?"

"No; by the cruel Caribs, who captured me years before the white men ever came to this land. I escaped from them and was captured by a cacique, but I cannot tell you my story now. If you would like to hear it, I will tell it to you some other time."

"I would."

"Do you know where the cavern below the town is?"

He had been to the cavern, and told her he knew where it was.

"I live there now, for I am hunted by a cruel master."

"Who is your master?" he asked.

"Narvaez," she answered. "He set his dogs on me, but I poisoned them and escaped. Since

then I have lived in the cavern. I am starving; I
must have food, for I have devoured all the lizards
and toads which creep about the cave. Bring me
food and I will tell you a wonderful story of a land
and people unknown to the Spaniards."

His boyish curiosity was roused, and he hastened
home for food for the starving slave. His mother
was absent; so, gathering up some loaves in a basket, he hastened to the cavern. The sun was low
in the west, but the prospect of hearing a wonderful story drove away all fears of darkness. Reaching the cavern, he paused a moment at the entrance
and heard voices whispering.

"He has come, he brings food," said one.

"Zuna!" he called.

"I am here."

"Alone?"

"No, an unfortunate slave, escaping from his
master, is here." (A few weeks later, and Zuna's
cavern became a famous resort for escaping slaves.)

"Here is food for you," said the lad, placing the
basket in her hands.

Zuna eagerly seized it, and she and a middle-aged
Indian, lame from the fangs of a bloodhound, began to devour the food.

"We have had no food for days," said Zuna,
who, despite her withered, hag-like appearance,
possessed a lofty bearing.

Far into the interior of the cavern, illuminated by a single torch, she conducted the lad. As soon as he could recover from wonder, he turned again to the woman.

"Zuna, you promised to tell me of your land and people," he said.

"I did," answered the old woman, finishing the food, "and I will. I am a child of the sun."

Gazing at her in wonder he said, "Of the sun?"

"Yes; the land of my birth is the land of the children of the sun. It is a strange, far-off land, across seas and mountains. There the skies are always bright and the people live in great houses of stone, roofed with gold.

"Many years ago our people were living in peace and splendor, when there suddenly appeared among us great birds which carried off many people.* Then there came two birds with faces like humans, and so large that, when they spread their wings, they darkened the sun as if a great cloud had come over it. They feasted on people, and devoured many. The largest bird, a female with the head and breasts of a woman, was the mother of the younger. Often they swooped down on great cities, snatched people up in the streets, and

---

*Zuna's story relates Indian legends current at the time of the Spanish conquests.

carried them away screaming, to be torn to pieces by their talons. At last all our warriors got bows and arrows and shot the old bird to death, when her son went shrieking away and was never seen again.

"When they were gone there came among us two strange people directly from the sun, Manco Copac, and his wife Mama. They were great and good people and gave us wholesome laws, which my people observe to this day."

"Where is this land?" the lad asked.

"Far away from here, beyond wood, seas, and mountains so tall that their tops seem to reach the sky. The people have ships almost as large as yours; they have swinging bridges, excellent roads, and carry burdens on animals."

"Horses?"

"No, not so large."

"Camels?"

"No."

"What?"

"Llamas!"

"What are llamas?"

"Animals with wool or hair on their backs, from which cloth is made." Then she continued to tell him of golden temples and cities of wondrous wealth, until Christopher thought it must be a land of enchantment.

"How did you come here?" the young humanitarian asked.

"Copac was at war with a tribe, and I was a child living on the frontier," she answered. "I was captured by our enemy and taken to the coast. I lived three years here, when a party of Caribs came over the sea in their boats and again I was captured and carried to their country. I escaped and wandered a long distance in the woods, when I was one day seized by white men and taken to Cuba, where I was sold to Narvaez, from whose cruelty I have but recently escaped."

The lad promised to bring her food regularly and keep her hiding-place a secret.

"When I am grown to be a man I will go to this wonderful country," he declared, on leaving the cavern.

It chanced a few days later, as he was playing with Antonio about the governor's mansion, that he related to him the strange story of Zuna. With childish enthusiasm he dwelt on the richness and mystery of a land in which cities were roofed in with gold. The governor, who chanced to be near, was an eager listener and when the story was ended he seized the lad's arm.

"Who told you this?" he demanded.

"An Indian woman."

"Where is she?"

"I will not tell."

"You shall," cried the excited governor. "I will have this story from her own lips."

With flashing eye, his whole manner expressing defiance, the brave lad replied:

"I will not tell, and you cannot make me."

The governor pushed him aside, and walked across the apartment impatiently.

"It is the same story that comes from Darien," he muttered half aloud, "and, by St. Anthony! the boy shall tell, or I will put him to the rack. Where in the devil's name has he gone?" demanded the governor suddenly, on discovering that young Estevan had disappeared. Even then Christopher was hastening to his mother.

CHAPTER VIII.

DOÑA MARINA.

THE Tobascans, a tribe of Indians at whose territory Cortez touched, showed a strong disposition to resist him. He gave battle and defeated the savages. They sued for peace, and among their propitiatory gifts were twenty female slaves, one of whom proved to be of infinite more consequence than was anticipated by either the Spaniards or Tobascans. Estevan and Cortez were standing side by side when the twenty female slaves were brought to the Spaniards. Never saw the Spaniards a queen more graceful or beautiful than one of those slaves.

"Mark you, Estevan, how she bears herself," said Cortez. "Such diamond eyes, ruby lips, and olive cheeks."

She was not attired in simple, barbaric costume, but wore a robe of rich cloth and beaded sandals on her feet, and her manner was modest and refined. Strangely moved, from the moment he set eyes on her, he felt he had met his destiny, and

121 ·

declared that she was the most beautiful being he had ever seen.

The mind of the Spanish commander, however, was not long in reverting to the chief object of the conquest. Among other presents, the cacique had brought him many gold ornaments. Through his two interpreters he asked from whence the precious metal came. The cacique pointed to the west.

"Mexico," he said.

Before taking his leave of the natives, Cortez caused the priests, Fathers Olmedo and Diaz, to enlighten their minds as far as possible in regard to the great truths of revelation, urging them to embrace the true faith in place of their own heathen abominations. The perceptions of the Tobascans had been materially quickened by the discipline they had undergone, and they made but faint resistance to this proposal. The next day was Palm Sunday, and their conversion was celebrated by one of those pompous ceremonies of the Church, which made a lasting impression on the minds of the Indians.

A procession of military and ecclesiastics was formed, each soldier carrying a palm-branch in his hand. The great concourse was swelled by thousands of Indians of both sexes, following in curious astonishment. The long lines moved through flowery savannas that bordered the settlement, to the principal temple, where an altar was raised, and the image of the presiding deity deposed to make room for the Virgin and the infant Saviour. Mass was celebrated by Father Olmedo, all the soldiers capable joining in the solemn chant. In silent wonder the natives listened, their hearts penetrated with reverential awe for the God of those terrible beings.

The religious ceremonies over, Cortez bade the converts adieu, well satisfied with the impression he had made. Going aboard their vessels the little fleet spread sails to receive the breeze and skimmed over the waves to the golden shores of Mexico. They held their course so near to land that the sailors could see the inhabitants along the shores of the gulf.

"We are approaching a grand country," said Cortez to Estevan.

"It is a noble land, general. Each hour unfolds new wonders."

When the fleet arrived off San Juan de Ulua, an island so named by Grijalva, and glided along under easy sail on the bosom of the waters, crowds of natives gathered on the shore of the main land and gazed at the strange phenomenon. Cortez gave orders to anchor under the lee of the island.

Scarce had the ships came to anchor, when Estevan from the forecastle called to Cortez:

"General, there comes a pirogue filled with natives from the main land."

"I see it, and they are heading directly for our vessel."

The Indians came on board with frank confidence, inspired by the accounts of the Spaniards spread by their countrymen who had traded with Grijalva. They brought presents of fruits and flowers, and little ornaments of gold, which they gladly exchanged for the usual trinkets. Cortez called Aguilar to interpret what they said, but he was unable to understand them.

"Can't you interpret their language?" Cortez asked.

"No, they speak Aztec, which I do not understand; but one of the twenty slaves whom you took from the Tobascans is an Aztec," answered Aguilar.

"Do you mean the beautiful maiden?"

"Yes."

"Send her to me."

When she came on deck, Cortez again surveyed her with a critic's eye. Her lofty bearing, gorgeous eyes, shapely bust, rising and falling beneath deep respirations, her olive-tinted cheek, clear enough to show the rich blood beneath the skin, and her ruby lips, were productive of a spell from which Cortez never recovered.

"By St. Anthony! such beauty never existed in my own race," he declared. He christened her *Doña Marina.* When Aguilar interpreted the remark of the general to the maiden, a glad glow came over her face. When she had interpreted what the Aztecs had to say, Cortez spoke to her.

"Henceforth you are to be my own, and I will teach you to speak Spanish," he said.

From that moment she was so attached to him that she was constantly at his side in time of danger or tranquillity. She rapidly learned the Spanish language, receiving her instructions at the feet of her liege.

Did he forget his marriage vows? Did he forget the wife, in his far-off Cuban home, who patiently waited and watched for him day by day? Yes.

Perhaps the truth too well told has robbed the hero of half his glory; but history is arbitrary, and even the novelist cannot mould it at will. The critical reader may say that Cortez never loved Catalina, and that his marriage with her was a matter of policy. But Cortez was a libertine, a gay, dashing fellow with flexible morals, and apt to fall in love with every pretty girl he met. He could no more resist the charms of Marina than winter's snow can withstand the April sun. Her artless simplicity was captivating. Uneducated in all the graces and accomplishments of civilization, and knowing nothing of the laws of society, save what she gleaned from the man she worshipped, she may be held excusable by the world.   So rapidly did she acquire Spanish that in a very short time she could converse with him quite freely.

One day, as she was sitting at the feet of her lord as was her custom, he said, " Marina, you have promised to give me a history of your life; do so now."

After a few moments' hesitation she began:

"I was born at Painalla, in the province of Coatzacualco, on the southeastern borders of the Mexican empire.   My father, a rich and powerful cacique, died when I was very young.   My mother married again, and, having a son by her second husband, determined to secure to him my rightful inheritance.   She gave it out that I was dead, and secretly gave me into the hands of some travelling traders of Xicallanco.   In order to make the deception more complete, she availed herself of the death of a child of one of her slaves to substitute the corpse for her own daughter, and celebrated the funeral with great solemnity.   My masters who purchased me were not very cruel, and soon after brought me to this part of the country, where they sold me to the chief of Tobasco, who delivered me to you." *

---

* The story of Doña Marina is given in Prescott's Conquest of Mexico, volume 1, chapter v., pages 292, 293.

"Your mother was cruel," said Cortez at conclusion of her story.

Marina was silent. Her natural affections and gentle disposition would not sanction her mother's censure, much as she deserved it.

"She was very cruel, and I will see to it that you are avenged," resumed Cortez.

"No, no," she answered, seizing his hand.

"Would you not have her brought to justice?"

"No, she is my mother."

Appreciating the value of Doña Marina's services, Cortez made her his interpreter, then his secretary, and, captivated by her remarkable charms, took her to be his mistress. She always remained loyal to the countrymen of her adoption, and her knowledge of the language and customs of the Mexicans, and frequently of their designs, enabled her often to extricate the Spaniards from the most embarrassing and perilous situations.

Cortez learned from the Indians that he was now on the shores of the great Mexican Empire. He was informed that the country was ruled by the great Montezuma, who dwelt on the mountain plains of the interior, nearly seventy leagues from the coast. The province at which Cortez first touched was governed by one of Montezuma's nobles named Teuhtlile.

"I have visited your country," explained Cortez to some embassadors, "to see your Aztec governor."

The invader loaded his visitors with presents and sent them away. Next morning, April 24, he landed with his entire retinue at the place where now stands the city of Vera Cruz. The country was a wide, level plain, save where the sand had drifted into hillocks by the perpetual blowing of the wind. On these sand dunes he mounted his little battery of artillery so as to command the surrounding country. The soldiers were employed in cutting down the small trees and bushes which grew near, to provide a shelter against the weather.

The landing of the Spaniards and their preparations for staying roused all the country round about, and Teuhtlile, the provincial governor, attended by a numerous train, arrived on the second day after their landing. He was taken to Cortez, who conducted him with much ceremony to his tent, where his principal officers were assembled. The Aztec chief was polite and courteous, though formal. Mass was said by Father Olmedo and a collation was served, at which the general entertained his guest with Spanish wines and confections.

"From what country did you come, and what is the object of your visit?" Teuhtlile asked.

"I am the subject of a powerful monarch beyond the seas," Cortez answered. "He rules over a

"FROM WHAT COUNTRY DO YOU COME?" INQUIRED THE AZTEC CHIEF.

powerful empire, and has kings and princes for his vassals. Having heard much of the greatness of the emperor of Mexico, my master wishes to enter into communication with him, and has sent me as his envoy to wait on Montezuma with a present, in token of his good-will, and a message which I must deliver in person. When can I be admitted to your sovereign's presence?"

"How is it that you have been here only two days and demand to see the emperor?" the Aztec noble haughtily demanded.

"I have a message for the emperor, and am in a hurry to deliver it," answered Cortez, not at all perturbed by the impatience and anger of his guest.

Teuhtlile was averse to the Spaniards going to Mexico. Montezuma, in his capital, desired to communicate with the invaders by embassadors, but he was not at home to Cortez in his own house.

"I am surprised to learn that there is another monarch as powerful as Montezuma," Teuhtlile said, after a brief silence. "But if there be one, my emperor will be happy to communicate with him. I will send my couriers with the royal gifts brought by you, and as soon as I have learned the wishes of Montezuma, I will communicate with you."

Estevan, who was present, wore a glittering steel helmet. This attracted the attention of Teuhtlile.

9

"Give me the glittering cap to send to Montezuma," he said, "that he may know the pale-faced
men, long prophesied by Quetzalcoatl, have come."

His strange request was made known to Cortez.

"Send your helmet to the emperor," he said to
Estevan; "you can get another one."

Estevan approached the governor to give him
the helmet. As he did so, he discovered an Indian
hastily making marks on a bit of canvas.

"Have you observed that fellow?" he asked
Cortez.

"No; what is he doing?"

"He is an artist. He has made a drawing of us,
the soldiers, the tents, and the arms."

Turning to Marina, who was always at his side,
Cortez asked her what the Indian was doing.

"He has been sent to make pictures of all he
sees, and take them to Montezuma," she answered.

In other words, the young Indian was a royal
reporter. The Aztecs had a system of hieroglyphics
by which thought was communicated. Estevan went to look at the canvas of the artist, and
discovered that it was not a bad sketch of Cortez,
himself, and the other Spaniards, with costumes,
arms, and, in short, every object of interest, in its
appropriate color, displaying no mean talent. Cortez caused the cavalry to be brought out on the
wet sands, and the wonderful war-horses, richly

caparisoned, inspired the Mexicans with dread; but when they heard the thunder of cannon, and saw the branches and bodies of trees shivered by iron balls, they were more than ever amazed, and retired, filled with awe of the invaders. When the governor left them, Cortez asked Doña Marina what the governor meant by the pale men of Quetzalcoatl.

" It is the popular tradition of Quetzalcoatl," she answered.

" Who was Quetzalcoatl?"

" *The fair god.*"

Filled with amazement, Cortez asked, " Who is the fair god?"

Doña Marina mustered up all the Spanish she knew, and answered:

" He was a god, who, many years ago, lived in Mexico. It was so long ago that the oldest people do not remember him. His face was fair like yours, and he had a long beard. He was good and noble, and after performing his mission of benevolence he left us. Under him, Mexico was more prosperous than ever before or since. He instructed our people in the use of metals, in agriculture, and in governing. The earth teemed with fruits and flowers without the pains of culture. An ear of maize was as much as a man could carry. The cotton, as it grew, took the richest colors, of its own accord, and the air was filled with intoxicating perfumes and sweetest songs of birds. Such days Mexico has never known since."

"Why did Quetzalcoatl leave?" Cortez asked.

"He incurred the wrath of one of the principal gods."

"For what cause?"

"Our people never knew."

"How did he go away?"

"He went from Mexico to Cholulu, where he halted, and his followers built a temple there and dedicated it to his worship. Then he went to the gulf, where he took leave of his followers, saying, 'I and my descendants will revisit you.' Then he entered his wizard boat, made of serpents' skins, and sailed for the land of Tlapallan. Teuhtlile believes you are either Quetzalcoatl or a descendant of his, for it is believed by all that his return is near at hand."

"Why do they think so?"

"I learned from them, that nine years ago the great lake of Tezcuco, without any occurrence of tempest, or earthquake, or any other visible cause, became violently agitated, overflowed its banks, and, pouring into the city of Mexico, swept off many of the buildings by the fury of the waters.*

---

*The above legends are given by Prescott and other historians.

One year later one of the turrets of the great temple took fire without any cause, and continued to burn in defiance of all attempts to extinguish it. One year later three comets were seen, and, not long before your arrival, a strange light broke forth in the east. It was broad at its base on the horizon, and, rising in a pyramidal form, tapered off as it approached the zenith, like a great sheet of fire thickly powdered with stars. At the same time, low voices were heard on the air, and doleful wailings, as if to announce some strange, mysterious calamity. Are you really the fair god returned?" Marina asked in conclusion.

"Tell them I am, and that I will destroy all who do not submit to me."

The shrewd Cortez was both politician and diplomat, and he determined to take advantage of the superstition of the Mexicans. Just as he seemed to reach smooth waters there arose a disaffection among his own followers. His people became divided. A part of them, loyal to Velasquez, wanted to return to Cuba, while another party, headed by Estevan, remained true to Cortez. The city of Vera Cruz (The True Cross) was laid out and duly incorporated in the name of the king of Spain. A mayor, alguacil, and officers were elected. Cortez shrewdly had his friends placed in office under the new municipality, and, resigning to them, asked that a leader be appointed. He was of course appointed governor general of Mexico, and thus claimed to have a commission from the crown, and a higher authority than Velasquez.

A number of persons, with the priest Juan Diaz at their head, ill-affected toward the administration of Cortez, laid a plan to seize a ship and make the best of their way back to Cuba and report to the governor. The plot was conducted with so much secrecy that supplies were placed on board without arousing suspicion, and had not one of the party relented at the last moment and betrayed the scheme, it would have been successful. The accused parties were arrested and found guilty. Two of the ringleaders were condemned to death, the pilot lost his feet, and all others, save the priest, who claimed benefit of clergy, were whipped.

One of the condemned men was Escudero, the alguacil who arrested Cortez before the sanctuary in Cuba. Although the governor, on signing the death warrant, regretted that he had ever learned to write, yet to Escudero he betrayed no such emotion.

"I promised to hang you, and you see I keep my word," he said.

At sun-rise next morning, the doomed men were hung.

"So perish all your enemies," said Doña Marina, who had been a witness to the execution, turning to Cortez.

"Doña Marina, will you always be faithful to me?" he asked.

Pointing to the swaying bodies, she answered: "When I am not, let my fate be the same!"

CHAPTER IX.

THE BLOODHOUND'S VICTIM.

Months and years went by and Christina awaited the return of her husband. Rumors of all sorts were rife, but authentic news was scarce. Velasquez came frequently to her house to try, by bribes and threats, to induce Christopher to reveal the hiding-place of Zuna, but in vain.

"Tell me where I can find the old slave, lad, who told you of the city of gold, and I will make it profitable to you. I will forgive your father his crime."

"I will not!"

"Will not, when I promise to forgive your father?"

"My father has done nothing to be forgiven—"

"By St. Anthony! he is too wise for his years. Come, good Christopher, tell me of the slave's hiding-place."

"You would drag her back and beat her. She would die on the rack before she would reveal the secret."

The governor occasionally lost his temper, and swore he would imprison the lad and torture the secret from him. But he dared not do this, arbitrary as his power was. One day, as Christopher was roaming through the forests near the town of St. Jago, he was startled by the crack of a matchlock. The report of a gun in the wood was too common to excite more than momentary attention, had he not immediately heard the shriek of a woman.

Christopher had grown to be a stout lad, and could wield a crossbow quite effectively. On this morning he had his weapon with him, and involuntarily seized a bolt on hearing the shriek of pain.

"It is another slave-hunter," he said. "Surely God will not let these crimes go unpunished."

Impelled by curiosity, the lad pressed on through the everglades and luxuriant shrubbery of the tropics, his heart beating wildly, and his hands clutching his crossbow. He came in sight of two Spaniards armed with arquebuses and swords. They did not see him, although he was so near that, crouching behind some palms, he could hear what they said:

"She has escaped, Bernardo," said one.

"But she bleeds, Pedro. Put the bloodhound on her trail and he will soon rend her to pieces, while we will go to Narvaez and report that she is slain."

Christopher now discovered that one of the men held a dog by a stout cord. The furious animal set up a howl that was calculated to freeze the blood in one's veins. The Spaniard released the bloodhound, and it bounded away on the trail of the fugitive slave while its masters went back to St. Jago.

"The beast shall not tear the slave," cried Christopher, his eyes filling with tears. "I will slay it."

Then he gave chase to shoot the dog with his crossbow. The occasional baying of the beast told him the course in which it was going. Two or three times he came in sight of the dog and raised his weapon to send a bolt to its heart, while it paused for a moment in doubt, sniffing the ground and wagging its tail, but each time it found the trail again, and bounded away with howls of rage.

"I will follow it from one end of the island to the other or save the victim."

The fugitive had been wounded by the shot from the matchlock; for Christopher saw an occasional drop of blood on the grass or leaves along the path. He had crossed a ravine, when just over the hill he heard a terrible shriek, and the howl of the beast indicated that the fugitive had been found. Christopher flew with all possible speed over the hill, through the mahogany trees. At last he came upon a sight calculated to melt a heart of stone. An Indian woman, who, despite years of suffering and deprivation, was still beautiful, held a child two or three years old in her wounded arm, and beat off a dog with a stick which she had snatched from the ground. She was unable long to resist the attacks of the furious beast, and, even as the boy knelt and aimed his crossbow, it leaped upon her, tearing her side with its awful fangs. With a shriek, she dropped the child.

"Fly, Christoval, for your life!" she cried in Spanish.

Too much horrified to move, the child stood rooted to the spot, and the dog continued to rend the woman. Christopher Estevan aimed his crossbow at the dog's side, and sent a bolt whizzing to the mark. Though mortally wounded, the furious animal continued to rend the woman, until Christopher rushed upon it and stabbed it to the heart with his dagger. For a moment the lad was at a loss what to do. The woman had swooned and the child stood sobbing with terror. He discovered that it was but a short distance to Zuna's cave, the place of refuge for fugitive slaves, and started to go there for assistance. Fortunately, he met one

gone to that God, and I shall follow. But for leaving our child, I would rejoice."

"Tell me your sad story, poor woman, for I have only heard part of your wrongs."

She gave Fulvia another drink of wine, while she sought to stop the flow of blood from the gaping wound in her side. Little Christoval gazed on the agonized features of her mother, and, though she realized that death would soon make her an orphan, she gave no outcry. She still clung to young Estevan as if she depended on him for protection.

The dying woman fixed her eyes on Christina.

"Would you hear my tale of woe and wrong?" she asked. "Listen, and learn what a devil jealous envy and hatred may make of a man, even a Spaniard. Balboa, was good, brave, and noble, and he loved me. I followed him through many of his terrible marches and still more terrible battles. My love was as potent in protecting him from poisoned darts, as was his quilted armor. The governor came and asked him to abandon me for his daughter——"

A paroxysm of pain seized her, and for several moments she was unable to speak. As soon as it had passed she resumed:

"But he would not give me up. He preferred death with me, to life and honors with the daughter of the governor. He said I was more to him than the queen on her throne. They knew this, and, seizing him, threw him into prison——"

Another spasm of pain, a few moments silence, and she continued:

"I saw him. Oh, how grand—how noble he looked, as he stood before his accusers! I begged them to slay me in his stead, but they would not. They drove me off. He turned to me as he took his last view of the world, and said, 'Farewell, Fulvia, I die for loving you.'

"Then they did the awful deed, and I swooned. I had seen blood shed until I thought I was accustomed to it; but never had I beheld such a sight. He lived like a lord, he died like a hero."

"Where have you been since Balboa's execution?" Christina asked.

"I have wandered part of the time with my own people, and part of the time with other tribes. Seven months after his death our child was born. I named her Christoval. The rage of the governor followed me wherever I went. He sought to make me and my child slaves; but I escaped from his dominion, and went to an island to live with people friendly to my father. About a year ago some Spaniards, coasting along the shore, saw me with my child on the beach.

"'Esclavos!' they cried, and landing, gave us chase. I fled, carrying my child in my arms.

"'Stop, or we will slay you,' cried one, discharging his crossbow and sending the bolt over my head. Encumbered as I was with my child, they outran me, and before I reached the savanna, where I hoped to conceal myself, I was seized and held in a grasp of steel.

"'The slave thought to escape with her brat,' cried one.

"'I am not a slave, I am the wife of Balboa,' I answered.

"At this they laughed, and one said:

"'By the mass! the child has white blood in its veins.'

"'But its Indian blood makes it a slave,' another answered. 'Narvaez will pay us well for the child, even if it is half white.'

"Vain were all my pleadings; they either believed me not, or, believing me, heeded not. I was put on board a ship with a number of other slaves, and brought to Cuba. At St. Jago I was turned over to Narvaez, in whose face I read cruelty at first glance. Falling on my knees, I implored him to spare me, and told my story. He smiled when I said I was the wife of Balboa, and answered that no Christian could wed a heathen. In vain I told him I had been baptized in the Spanish faith; he said I was nevertheless his slave. Then I appealed for our child in the name of my dead lord, but he said Balboa was an outlaw, and, having forfeited his life in rebellion against the crown, his child could gain nothing by his death."

She had exhausted her strength, and Christina gave her more wine and waited for her to resume. Though she grew weaker as she neared the dark portals of death, her suffering became less. After a few moments, she partially revived and resumed her story.

"For the last year my life has been one of toil, degradation, poor food, and the lash. Again and again I was ready to sink in despair, when my love for Balboa's child strengthened me. I could almost forgive my master as long as he permitted her to remain with me, for in her eyes I saw his. Her face and voice were those of my own Balboa again. Yesterday, however, my suspicions were roused, and playing the spy on my master, I learned that my child was to be sold and sent to San Domingo. Such intelligence was enough to madden a mother's brain. I spent the night in praying for strength to baffle them. I thought of taking Christoval and seeking freedom beneath the waters of the bay, preferring death to separation. But other slaves had escaped, and why not we? I watched my chance and when an opportunity came, I seized Christoval in my arms and fled through the tall cane to the woods. I was pursued by two or three

10

slave-hunters who fired and wounded me; then they put a bloodhound on my trail. I ran, I screamed, I fought, but the dog tore me, and now I must die and leave her behind. Who will care for Christoval?"

"I will," answered Christina.

"And keep her from slavery?"

"I will." It was a hazardous undertaking, but the brave little señora hesitated not.

"Take her, kind angel," gasped the dying woman, putting the child's hand in Christina's. "Guard her with your life, for she is the last of two noble families, one of the old and one of the new world."

"I will care for her as my own; but you may yet recover."

Fulvia shook her head, then closing her eyes she seemed to sleep. The señora brought a stool and sat by the woman, whose breathing grew more difficult every moment. Little Christoval, with her large, dark eyes open wide in wonder, gazed at her dying mother, while she clung to her young rescuer. The fugitive slaves moved about with noiseless tread. Some wax tapers had been brought and lighted, giving a ghastly light in the dark cave.

For two hours Fulvia slept, and then, awaking, she started up.

" Where is she?" she asked.

" Who?" asked the señora.

" His child."

" Here," anwered Christopher, leading the little girl to her dying mother.

Taking one little hand in her own, she seized Christopher with her other.

"She is his child, take her, keep her from harm," she said.

" I will," the lad answered.

"Swear it!"

" I do."

" Her father was a nobleman from Spain. He loved me, oh! he loved me more than the great governor's daughter. They slew him before my eyes because he would not give me up for a fairer bride; but he loved me, and I am going to him. Take our Christoval—go—fly with her—the slave-driver comes. No, no, it is Balboa—he calls me —my love!—I come. I come!"

She relaxed her hold, her eyes closed, and for a long time all thought she slept. Christina bent over, and gazed for a moment on the calm, sweet face.

" Lead the child away," she whispered to her son.

Then she covered up the mother's face, on which a smile rested. All was over. Balboa's bride had crossed the mystic stream to join him.

CHAPTER X.

THE GOLDEN CONQUEST.*

As the setting sun threw its last beam over the magical valley, Cortez gazed from afar on a most wonderful scene. It was an unknown city in an unknown world, peopled by a race evincing a high state of civilization. The little band of conquerors had fought their way inch by inch from the coast to the valley of Mexico. They were encamped on the hills above ready to descend into the valley early next morning.

Cortez slept but little the night before his triumphal march into the valley of Montezuma. His ambitious mind was busy with the future and the past. Like a terrible panorama, the events of the past few months swept before him as, wrapped in his cloak, he lay on the ground, his saddle for a pillow.

---

* In the description of the city and valley of Mexico given in this chapter, the author has taken Prescott for his guide.

145

Like a shrewd general and cunning politician, he had succeeded in dividing the enemy into factions, turning them against each other. While professing friendship to Montezuma, he incited his subjects to rebellion. His path from the coast to the valley of Mexico was a trail of blood. Ever at his side, encouraging him by word and act, was Doña Marina. In peace or war she was his counsellor and adviser. The darts never flew too thick to drive her from his side, until the Aztecs came to believe that she, as well as Cortez, was a supernatural being, not to be slain with mortal weapons. Next to Doña Marina was Cortez's friend Hernando Estevan. He who had been first to land with Columbus on the shores of the New World was in the van on that dangerous march to Mexico.

Long before dawn Estevan was awakened by voices, and, rising, he buckled on his armor.

"This day will witness the beginning of our triumph or our death," he thought. Estevan was now a battle-scarred veteran, who had come to regard death-struggles with indifference. He sat down to await the dawn, when again voices reached his ear. A female voice, low and soft as rippling waters was heard first.

"For shame! to fear now, when triumph is within your grasp. You know Cortez cannot be defeated."

It was Doña Marina, talking to some faltering soldiers.

" He is but a man," answered one of the soldiers, "and any man may fail. He destroyed our ships, led us into the heart of a hostile nation, and now proposes to take us into the capital where we may be butchered without mercy."

"Coward!" hissed Marina in disgust, "can you fear with such a leader? Montezuma will not dare resist Cortez, and if you murmur again, I will have you hanged."

The soldier slunk away, silenced for the time being by the threat.

Estevan rose to his feet, yawning and shivering with the damp and chill of early morning. Cortez came toward him at that moment.

"Estevan, is your company in readiness?" he asked.

" It is."

" Are the men in good spirits?"

" They seem to be, general."

" We will be in the valley before the sun sets. Bid your men be firm and watchful. Montezuma is a shrewd and treacherous knave. We must be watchful, for we shall soon be within his walls."

At early dawn the trumpet sounded the reveille, and the Spaniards formed for the march. The

troops, refreshed by a night's rest, succeeded soon
after sun-rise, in gaining the crest of the sierra of
Ahualco, which stretches like a curtain between
the two great mountains on the north and south.

A blast of trumpets gave the order to advance,
and the march began. It was a sublime sight.
The rising sun flashed on the glittering spears,
banners, and gayly caparisoned horses, prancing
in time to the martial music. They had not advanced far, when, turning an angle of the sierra,
they came suddenly on a view which fully com-
pensated them for the weeks of toil and hardship.
It was the valley of Mexico, or Tenochtlitan, as it
was called by the Aztecs. With its picturesque
groupings of water, woodland, and cultivated plains,
shining cities and shadowy hills, it lay spread out
like some gorgeous panorama before them. In the
highly rarefied atmosphere of these upper regions,
even remote objects have a brilliancy of coloring
and a distinctness of outline, which seem to annihilate distance. Stretching far away below them
were seen noble forests of oak, sycamore, and
cedar, and, beyond, yellow fields of maize, and the
towering maguey, intermingled with orchards and
blooming gardens. In the centre of the great
basin were lakes, then occupying a much larger
portion of its surface than at present. Their
borders were studded thickly with towns and

hamlets, and in the midst, like some Indian em-
press with her coronal of pearls, was the fair city of
Mexico, with white towers and pyramidal temples,
reposing, as it were, on the bosom of the waters—
the far-famed "Venice of the Aztecs." High
over all, rose the royal hill of Chapultepec, the
residence of the Mexican monarchs, crowned with
gigantic cypresses, which to this day fling their
shadows over the land. In the distance, beyond
the blue waters of the lake, and nearly screened by
intervening foliage, was seen a shining speck, the
rival capital of Tezcuco, and still further on, the
dark belt of parphyr, girdling the valley like a
rich setting which nature had devised for the fairest
of her jewels. Such was the beautiful vision
which greeted the eyes of the Spanish conquerors.

They gazed for the first time on a strange valley, a
strange people, and a wonderful city, in a land
which, forty years before, was unknown to the
civilized world. Overwhelming emotions stirred
the breast of Cortez, when, after working his toilsome way into the upper air, the cloudy veil parted
before his eyes, and he beheld these fair scenes in
all their pristine glory. The poetic feelings of
Cortez, roused by the grandeur of the scene, soon
gave way to more sordid thoughts, for he saw here
evidences of a civilization and power far superior to
anything he had yet encountered in the New World.

Estevan noticed that some of his own true and tried cavaliers began to shrink from the unequal contest before them and he galloped quickly to the side of Cortez.

"Some of the men shrink from the invasion, now that they see what a city we are to conquer," he whispered.

"We cannot turn back now," answered Cortez.

The scene had no such effect on the sanguine general. His avarice was sharpened by the display of dazzling spoil at his feet; and, if he felt a natural anxiety at the formidable odds, his confidence was renewed as he gazed on the lines of his weatherbeaten veterans, while his bold barbarian allies, with appetites whetted by the view of their enemies' country, seemed like eagles ready to swoop down upon their prey.

"Why have you cause to falter now?" Cortez asked his shrinking soldiers. "Have we not succeeded in overcoming every difficulty until the golden conquest is in our hands. We have reached the goal at last, and, now that the gates are open to receive us, should we turn back?"

He was ably seconded by Estevan in his efforts to restore the spirits of the faltering, until the faintest hearts caught some of their leader's fire, and the general had the satisfaction of seeing his hesitating columns, with buoyant step, once more on their march down the slope of the sierra.

Having desended to the valley, the army advanced by easy stages, somewhat retarded by the crowd of curious inhabitants gathered on the highways to see the wonderful strangers. Another embassy from the capital met them. It was composed of Aztec lords, bearing richer gifts of gold and robes, and more delicate furs and feathers, than they had hitherto seen. The object of the embassy was to bribe their return, Montezuma promising four loads of gold to Cortez, one to each of his captains, and a yearly tribute to their sovereign. The very offer increased the determination of Cortez to press on to the golden conquest, and he continued his advance to the city.

Meanwhile Montezuma was a prey to the most gloomy forebodings and apprehensions. When his last embassadors returned with the information that the mysterious strangers would not turn back, but continued to advance; that they had crossed the mountain chain and were on their march across the valley to the very threshold of his capital, his heart sank within him. From the first, he had believed himself in the web of inexorable fate, against which no precaution or foresight could avail. It was as if the strange beings, who had thus invaded his shores, had dropped from some distant planet, so different were they from all he had ever seen. Though a mere handful in numbers, they were so superior in strength and science, and all the fearful accompaniments of war, that all the banded nations of Anahuac could not prevail against them. They were now in the valley. The huge mountain screen, which nature had so kindly drawn around for its defence, had been overleaped by the pale-faced descendants of Quetzalcoatl. The golden vision of security in which Montezuma had so long indulged, the lordly sway descended from his ancestors, his broad imperial domain, were all to pass away. It seemed like some terrible dream, from which he was to awake to a still more terrible reality.

Halting at Ajotzinco, a town of considerable size, the army remained until morning, when, as they were preparing to leave the place, a courier came, requesting them to postpone their departure until the arrival of the king of Tezcuco, who was advancing to meet Cortez.

"Here is an opportunity to gain another ally!" said the wily conqueror to Estevan. Before long the king appeared on a palanquin which literally glittered with gold and precious stones, having pillars curiously wrought, supporting green plumes, a favorite color with Aztec princes. After an interchange of courtesies, and the most friendly and respectful assurances on the part of Cortez, the

Indian king withdrew, leaving the Spaniards
strongly impressed with the superiority of his state
and bearing over anything they had hitherto seen
in the country.

After his departure Cortez resumed his march,
keeping along the southern borders of Lake Chalco,
overshadowed, at that time, by noble woods, and
orchards glowing with autumnal fruits of unknown
names, but rich and tempting hues On every
side were cultivated fields, waving with yellow har-
vests, irrigated by canals introduced from the
neighboring lake, the whole showing careful cultivation, and looking to the invaders like a veritable
paradise.

Bewildered, the Spaniards advanced through the
wonderful country, half believing that they were
entering a new world. Leaving the main land,
they came to the great dike, or causeway, which
stretched some four or five miles in length, and
divided Lake Chalco from Xochialco on the west.
It was ten or twelve feet in breadth at the narrowest
place, and at others wide enough for eight horsemen
to ride abreast. It was a solid structure of stone
and lime, running directly through the lake, and
was the most marvellous piece of workmanship the
Spaniards had yet seen in this land of wonders.

As they passed along, they beheld the gay spectacle of multitudes of Indians darting up and down

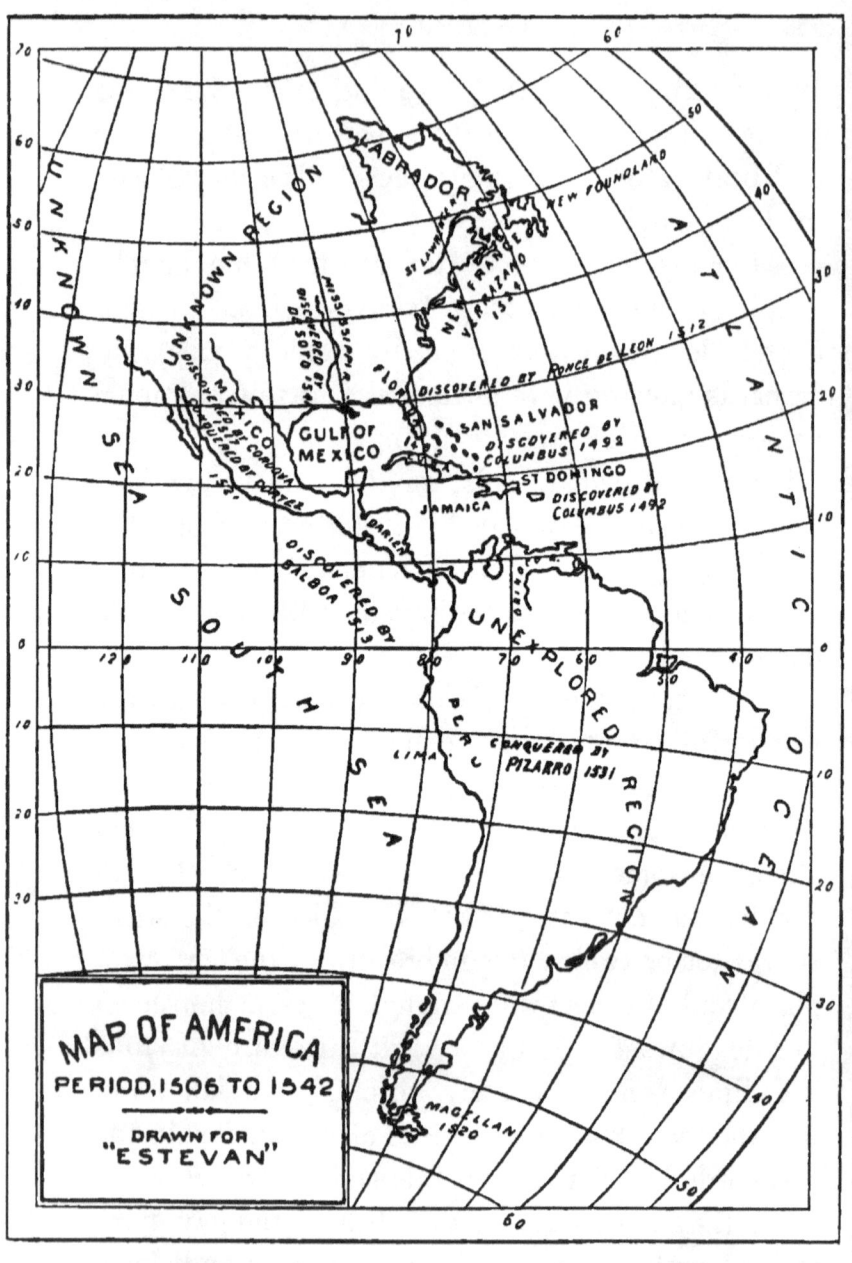

MAP OF AMERICA

PERIOD, 1506 TO 1542

DRAWN FOR
"ESTEVAN"

in their light pirogues, eager to catch a glimpse of
the strangers, or bearing the products of the country
to the neighboring cities. The *chinampas*, or floating gardens, those wandering islands of verdure,
teeming with flowers and burdening the air with
perfume, delighted and amazed the invaders. All
around the margin, and occasionally far into the
lake, they beheld little towns and villages, which,
half concealed by foliage, or gathered in white
clusters on the shores, resembled wild swans in
hiding. A scene so new and wonderful was like
an enchantment, and the Spaniards could compare
it with nothing save the magical picture in the
"Amadis de Gaula." No production of the most
fertile imagination could surpass the realities of
their own experience. The life of the adventurer
in the new world was romance put in action.

Half-way across the lake they halted at the beautiful town of Cuitlahuac for rest and refreshment,
and then resumed their march along the dike.
From the causeway, the army descended to that
narrow point of land which divided the waters of
the Lake Chalco from the Tezcucan lake, then over-
flowing many miles of earth now laid bare. Traversing the peninsula, they entered the royal
residence of Iztapalapan, a place containing twelve
or fifteen thousand houses, governed by the emperor's brother Cuitlahua. Cortez, Estevan, and all

the cavaliers, were here received with pomp and
ceremony in one of the great halls of the palace,
and presents of gold and delicate stuffs were made
to the invaders.   The excellence of the architecture
excited the admiration of the general, who declared
some of the stone buildings equal to the best in
Spain.   They were of great size, with spacious
apartments, and roofs of odorous cedar-wood, while
the walls were tapestried with fine cotton, stained
with brilliant colors.   Here the Spaniards took up
quarters for the night.

"Be on your guard," Cortez cautioned his
officers.   "We are not now among savages, but in
a land of civilization where points of strategy are
appreciated, and we are about to enter the capital
of a monarch who, we have abundant reason to
know, regards us with distrust and aversion.   Be
vigilant, and the golden prize I promised in the
beginning will be ours before another sun has set."

The capital, distinctly visible from their present
quarters, was but a few miles distant, and as its
long lines of glittering edifices, struck by the rays
of the evening sun, trembled on the dark blue
waters, it looked like a thing of fairy creation
rather than the work of mortal hands.

Next morning was the memorable eighth of
November, 1519, a day made conspicuous in
history by the Europeans setting foot for the first

time in the capital of the western world. With
the first faint streak of dawn, Cortez was astir,
mustering his followers. As the trumpet sent forth
its stirring sounds across water and woodland till
they died away in distant echoes among the mountains, the men gathered with beating hearts under
their respective banners. Through the gray twilight
of early morning could be seen the sacred flames
on the altars of numberless teocallis, indicating
the site of the capital. As it grew lighter, temple,
tower, and palace were revealed in the glorious
illumination of the sun.

The conqueror with his little body of horse
formed an advance guard to the army. Cortez,
mounted upon a snow-white horse, led the van,
while Estevan, mounted on a jet-black steed richly
caparisoned, led the second file of cavalry. Behind
the cavalry came the Spanish infantry with the
discipline and weather beaten aspect of veterans.
The baggage occupied the centre, and the rear was
closed by the undisciplined Tlascalan warriors, who
had first resisted and then joined the conquerors.
The entire army was less than seven thousand,
while the Spaniards did not number four hundred.

As they advanced, the Spaniards were more
than ever lost in admiration of the mechanical
science of the Aztecs, the geometrical precision
with which the work was executed, as well as the

solidity of its construction. Large towns, resting on piles, and reaching far out into the water, were to be seen on every side. Everywhere were evidences of a crowded and thriving population. The temples and principal buildings were covered with a hard white stucco, which glistened like enamel in the level beams of the morning sun. The waters were darkened by swarms of canoes, filled with Indians, who clambered up the sides of the causeway and gazed with curious astonishment at the strangers. Fairy islands of flowers, occasionally overshadowed by trees of considerable size, rose and fell with the gentle undulation of the waves.

About one mile and a half from the capital, they came upon the solid wall of stone, twelve feet high, which traversed the dike. It was strengthened at the extremities by towers, while in the centre was a ponderous gateway, opened for the passage of the troops. Several hundred chiefs were here to welcome the white strangers to Mexico and to announce the approach of Montezuma. The army experienced no further interruption until it reached the bridge near the gates of the city. It was built of wood and thrown across an opening of the dike. The structure was a drawbridge, and, as they crossed it, the Spaniards felt how thoroughly they were committing themselves to the mercy of Monte-zuma, who, by thus cutting off their communication with the outside world, might hold them prisoners in his capital. The drawbridge was crossed, and the army boldly advanced up the main street of this wonderful city, the fair Cathay of the unknown world.

"Close up the files, Estevan," said Cortez. "We are in the imperial city now, with a treacherous enemy on every side, and we must present a solid phalanx."

"Can the Tlascalans be depended on?" asked Estevan.

"They can. The national hatred they bear the Aztecs makes them our friends. Capture with them means death. Be watchful and keep a sharp lookout for treachery. Montezuma is a cunning warrior, and his boasted friendship may be an artful dodge to get us in his power. But be vigilant and brave and all this countless wealth will be ours."

In the midst of these unpleasant reflections they beheld the glittering retinue of the emperor emerging from the great street which led through the heart of the city. Amid a crowd of Indian nobles, preceded by three officers of state bearing golden wands, came the royal palanquin blazing with burnished gold. It was borne on the shoulders of nobles, and over it a canopy of gaudy feather-work, powdered with jewels and fringed with sil-

11

ver, was supported by four attendants of the same rank. They were barefooted and walked with slow, measured steps, their eyes on the ground. When the train came within a convenient distance, it halted, and Montezuma, descending from his palanquin, and leaning on the arms of his brother and nephew, advanced to meet the new-comers.

As the monarch walked under the canopy, attendants covered the ground with cotton tapestry, that his imperial feet might be uncontaminated with the soil. His subjects, high and low, bowed their heads as he passed, many of the humbler class prostrating themselves before him. The homage paid this Indian despot equalled the slavish forms of Oriental adulation of the period.

Estevan, who had heard much of the superior qualities of this emperor, was naturally very curious to see what he was like. He now beheld a tall, thin man of about forty years of age, with short black hair, a thin, dark beard, a complexion much paler than was usually found in the copper-colored race, and features serious without being melancholy. He wore the girdle and ample, square cloak, *tilmatli*, of his nation. It was made of the finest cotton, with embroidered ends gathered in a knot round his neck. He wore sandals with soles of gold on his feet, and the leathern thongs which bound them were embossed with the same metal. Both cloak and sandals were sprinkled with pearls, among which the emerald and the *chalchivitl*—a green stone of higher estimation than any other among the Aztecs—were conspicuous. On his head he wore no other ornament than a *panache* of plumes of royal green, which floated down his back, the badge of military rather than legal rank. He moved with dignity, and his whole demeanor was worthy of a great prince.

Dismounting, Cortez threw his rein to an attendant, and called on Estevan and Marina to accompany him.

"General, had you not better bring a few of the cavaliers to more fully impress the emperor with your power?" suggested Estevan.

"I will," Cortez answered, and he added a few of his principal cavaliers to the list.

As they advanced, Montezuma paused, his heart almost ceasing to beat, while his breath came hard, for he saw in this conqueror the strange being whose history was shadowed forth in one of his oracles, and whose achievements proclaimed him something more than human.

After a moment's pause, Montezuma advanced and received his guest with princely courtesy.

"I am very much gratified," he said, "to see so great a man as General Cortez in Mexico, and to welcome him to my capital."

"I have come to thank you, in the name of my king," answered Cortez, "for the many gifts you have bestowed upon his subjects, and to behold with my own eyes the greatness of Montezuma, as well as to give you substantial proof of the respect and love of my king for the emperor of this new world."

He hung a chain of colored crystals about the neck of the emperor, and was about to embrace him, when he was restrained by the two Aztec lords, who were shocked at the attempt to pollute the sacred person of their emperor by personal contact.

Montezuma seemed greatly pleased with the glittering ornament hanging about his neck, little dreaming that it was to become the clanking chain of a despotic conqueror. From that moment Montezuma was, in fact, a prisoner and his empire conquered. The pale strangers from an unknown land had planted themselves in the heart of his imperial city, and would not be ejected. He who had been a stern, daring soldier in other wars had, with this strange, new enemy, proved to be weak and unworthy the name he had won. But Montezuma was a fatalist, and, believing from the first that his empire was to be overthrown by the invaders, dared not resist them.

CHAPTER XI.

MATCHLOCKS IN THE AIR.

DAY by day, as reports of the success of Cortez reached Velasquez, he grew more and more desperate. He had declared the conqueror a rebel, and so reported him to the king.

"He shall hang to the highest mast on his ship!" exclaimed Velasquez, on learning of his triumphant march through the land of the Atecs.

"He has anticipated you, good master," said Gerund, who heard the governor's remark.

"What mean you, rogue?" demanded the governor.

"Surely you will not hang him to the tallest mast of his ship, since he has destroyed his fleet."

"Never mind, Gerund, we will hang him to some other ship then."

"There is catching, first, my lord."

"Who says we won't catch him?"

"Not I; yet the king may object."

"Why should the king object, since he is a rebel against the crown?"

Gerund made one of his comical grimaces.

"My lord, there is no knowing who is nearest the throne," he answered. "Put not your trust in princes. Cortez has sent embassadors to Spain."

"What if he has? Have not I done the same?"

"But, with his embassadors, Cortez sent great treasures of gold and precious stones, and I have been told that even the good king, like other Spaniards, is afflicted with a disease of the heart which naught save gold will cure."

"What the knave says has truth in it," said the governor. At this moment the very man above all others whom he wished to see, Panfilo de Narvaez, entered the room.

"I am glad you have come, Narvaez, for I wish to consult with you on a matter of great moment. Gerund, leave us."

"Don't make the stew so hot it will burn your lips," laughed the jester on quitting the room.

"The rascal has more wisdom than he gets credit for," said the governor. "But to business, Narvaez. You have heard of the rebel Cortez?"

"Have you heard from your embassadors?"

"No."

"Cortez, having conquered the richest nation in the world, has sent embassadors to Spain loaded with treasure to buy a good opinion of himself."

"I have feared as much," returned Velasquez.

"Report says that he has Montezuma a prisoner in his own city, and something must be done, governor, or all the glory and renown of this conquest will belong to Cortez."

"What can be done?"

"You have power to send and bring the rebel back."

"Whom shall I send?"

"Send me."

"Would you go?"

"That I would."

The governor rose and, grasping his hand, gazed a moment into his face to make sure he was in earnest.

"Narvaez, you are the very man I would have chosen," he declared, "and I only await authority from Spain to raise an army——"

"Why wait, governor, when you may take measures for redress in your own hand. The week Cortez sailed, a capitulation was signed by Charles V., conferring on you the title of Adelantado, with great augmentation of your original powers. Do not hesitate to send such a force to Mexico as will enable you to assert your new authority, and take vengeance on your rebellious officer."

Velasquez, deeply moved by the reports of treasure sent by Cortez to Spain, was in the mood for such advice. Rage, mortification, disappointment, and avarice distracted his mind. He could not forgive himself for trusting the conquest to such hands. The governor, who was a very corpulent man, rose and paced the floor for several moments, his florid face flushed with excitement and rage.

"I cannot go myself," he panted. "I am too fat to endure the hardships incident to such an expedition, and besides, my tenderness for my Indian subjects, who are wasting away with this epidemic, forbids that I should leave Cuba. You must relieve me at this trying hour and take the command."

Narvaez, who had longed for an opportunity to distinguish himself, did not hesitate. The compact was made at once, and, exercising his new authority, Velasquez commissioned Narvaez to command the expedition. The governor and his lieutenant were unwearied in their efforts to assemble an army. They visited every considerable town in the island, fitting out vessels, laying in stores and ammunition, and encouraging volunteers to enlist.

Of course Christina and her son learned of these efforts, and were alarmed at the formidable expedition which threatened the death of the husband and father. One day the lad was accosted by Narvaez himself in St. Jago.

"Do you know why all these preparations are being made?" the general asked.

"Yes, for a failure."

"No, we are going to hang the rebel Cortez, and your father to the same mast."

"Have a care, lieutenant, that you do not come back the worse for having met my father."

"Your father? Do you imagine that I fear him?"

"I know that you do not; but I am quite certain he has no fears of you, and would advise you to have a care, as you may not return as well in body and mind as you go."

Gerund, who was near enough to overhear the boy, put in:

> "'Tis an old saying I learned in my youth
> That fools and children speak the truth."

Narvaez was more annoyed than he would have admitted, though he continued his efforts to raise an army and fleet suitable for the expedition. The report of these proceedings soon spread through the islands, and drew the attention of the Royal Audience of San Domingo. This body was, at that time, intrusted not only with the highest judicial authority in the colonies, but with a civil jurisdiction, which, as "the admiral" complained, encroached on his own rights. The tribunal saw with alarm the proposed expedition of Velasquez, which, whatever might be its issue in regard to the parties, could not fail to compromise the interests of the crown. Accordingly, one of their number was chosen, a licentiate named Ayllon, a man noted for prudence and resolution, and dispatched to Cuba with instructions to interpose his authority and prevent, if possible, the sailing of the expedition. But Ayllon found that the flame had been fanned too long and the fire had gained too much headway for him to extinguish it. He accompanied the fleet of eighteen sail, but before he had gone far he was arrested and sent back in a ship to Cuba, though he prevailed on the captain to land him at San Domingo.

"I will hang the rebel Cortez," Narvaez declared; "all the licentiates in Hispaniola cannot prevent me."

On the 23d of April, 1520, the hostile fleet anchored off San Juan de Ulua, the spot where Cortez first landed on the sandy waste now covered by the city of Vera Cruz. From a Mexican, taken on board his ship, Narvaez gathered the particulars of all that had occurred since the departure of the envoys from Vera Cruz, including the march into the mountain, the bloody battles with the Tlascalans, the occupation of Mexico, the rich treasures found in it, and the seizure of Montezuma.

"Who rules the country?" asked Narvaez.

"Cortez rules the land like its own sovereign, so that a Spaniard may travel unarmed from one end of the country to the other without insult or injury."

Sandoval, a Spaniard left in charge of the post at La Villa Rica, had his suspicions aroused by the movements of Narvaez, and hurried messengers to the city of Mexico to warn Cortez. He then put his fort in the best possible state of defence. He even captured a priest, a notary, and four Spaniards sent to demand his capitulation, and, binding them, sent them hurriedly to Cortez at Mexico.

At the capital all was going well for Cortez. Montezuma had been induced to place himself under the protection of the Spaniards, practically their prisoner. The stern conqueror had checked every murmur of discontent on the part of the Mexicans. He was surrounded by every ease and luxury a monarch could desire, and, basking in the smiles of Marina, he forgot the wife at home.

Just when he seemed most secure, messengers from Sandoval at La Villa Rica arrived bringing information of the fleet of Narvaez. This alarming intelligence was at first confided to Marina and Estevan.

"What think you of the situation?" he asked.

"You should return to the coast without delay,

and strike a blow at the invaders," Estevan answered.

"You have excellent ideas of military movements, friend Estevan.   To hesitate is fatal, and
I shall take immediate action."

A soldier came and announced the arrival of a
party from La Villa Rica with the priest, notary
and four soldiers.

"Bring them to me," said Cortez, in no very
amiable mood.

The captives were brought to the conqueror, who
received them with marked courtesy, apologized
for the rude conduct of his companions, and loaded
them with presents, and by his most assiduous
attentions soothed the irritation of their minds.
When the priest Guevara was completely won over
to him, he proceeded to draw from him many important particulars.

"What are the designs of Narvaez?" he asked.

"To capture you and take you to Cuba for trial."

"On what charge?"

"Treason and rebellion."

"What are the feelings of the soldiers?"

"The soldiers in general, so far from desiring
a rupture with your army, would willingly co-ope-
rate with you, were it not for their commander.
They have no feelings of resentment to gratify.
Their object is gold."

"Is Narvaez very popular among his men?"

"His personal influence is not very great, and his arrogance and temper have already gone far to alienate him from the affections of his men."

When alone Cortez smiled shrewdly. He had gained the very information he wished. He dismissed the prisoners with a letter to Narvaez beseeching him not to proclaim their animosity to the world, as it would enkindle a spirit of insubordination among the natives, and prove fatal to both.

"I am ready to greet Narvaez as a brother in arms," he added, "to share the fruits of conquest with him, and if he will produce a royal commission, to submit to his authority."

The conqueror well knew that Narvaez had no such commission to produce. He dispatched an envoy in the person of Father Olmedo to confer with Narvaez.

Neither epistle nor envoy had any effect to retard Narvaez. He declared his intention to apprehend Cortez as a traitor, and release Montezuma. This unwise declaration made him no friends among the tribes of Mexicans hostile to Montezuma. Sandoval, who was still at La Villa Rica, kept Cortez posted of the movements of his enemies.

"The time for action has come," Cortez declared, on learning from Father Olmedo that his letter of conciliation was received in anger by Narvaez,

who gave way to the most opprobrious invectives
against his rival. "Are the soldiers as full of
wrath as their general, Father Olmedo?"

"The rank and file desire no collision," the
priest answered. "One blustering captain, Salvatierra, openly avowed his intention to cut off the
rebel's ears and broil them for his breakfast. His
soldiers are more ready to support Cortez than
Narvaez."

Cortez was active from the first. Shortly before
the appearance of Narvaez off the coast, he had
sent Velasquez de Leon, a trusted captain, with
one hundred and fifty men to plant a colony on one
of the great rivers emptying into the Mexican
Gulf. Though Velasquez was a kinsman of the
governor of Cuba, he was a true friend of Cortez.
The general dispatched a messenger to him to
acquaint him of the landing of Narvaez, that he
might arrest the advance of the invader. Velasquez had already been importuned by Narvaez to desert his general and enroll under the
banner of Cuba. This he declined to do and was
marching toward the city of Mexico when the
general's messenger met him with orders to wait at
Cholula. Cortez determined to head the army
against Narvaez himself. He left Pedro de Alvarado in command at Mexico with one hundred
and forty men, two-thirds of his whole force, all the

artillery, the greater part of the little body of horse, and most of the arquebusiers. With Estevan, and only seventy men, he began a rapid and unexpected march toward the gulf. Everthing depended on celerity of movement, and the Spaniards were as little encumbered as possible.

Cortez dispatched other envoys to Narvaez, more to throw him off his guard than with any hope of arriving at a better understanding. As he pressed on to the coast with all possible speed, he gathered up scattered forces here and there, augmenting his strength by Indian allies. The army marched hurriedly across the level plains of Tierra Caliente, on which nature has exhausted the wonders of creation. For most of the distance the march was through mud and rain, and the soldiers, illy prepared for this hardship, suffered not a little. On reaching the Rio de Canoas, or " River of Canoes," they found the inconsiderable stream swollen to a torrent. At one moment the rain poured in floods, and an hour later a tropical sun from a cloudless sky steamed their soaked clothing, only to be followed by another rain, thus alternating heat and moisture. After sunset the clouds became broken, and the sky appeared for a few moments in patches, studded with stars. The river was only a league from the camp of Narvaez, and, before seeking an available ford for crossing, Cortez allowed his men

to regain their exhausted strength by stretching
themselves on the wet ground. The shades of
evening gathered and the rising moon, wading
through dark masses of clouds, shone with doubtful
and interrupted light on the miserable little army.

A distant peal of thunder rolled along the sky.

"The storm will be on us again," said Cortez,
turning to Estevan, "and I do not regret it, for
we shall make the assault this very night. In the
darkness and uproar of the tempest our movements
will be effectually concealed."

Although he had given his trusted friend an idea
of his plan, he had not yet disclosed it to his men.
But as soon as it was quite dark, and he was well
assured that the retreating tempest had rallied to
renew the attack, he called his men about him and
began one of those stirring harrangues with which
he was wont to greet them before a desperate engagement.

"Faithful heroes of many hard-fought battles, it
is well to sound the depths of your hearts, and if
any falter, to reanimate your heroic spirits I left
Cuba duly commissioned for this conquest, and I
have since, by the municipal authority, which is
next to the crown, been elected general and governor
of the country. 'I came, I saw, I conquered,'
while my avaricious enemies at Cuba envied and
feared to do what we have done. We invaded the

enemies' country, braved dangers, surmounted difficulties, and gained victories against the most appalling odds ever known in the world's history. The treasure in gold, silver, and precious stones which has fallen to each man is fabulous. Of this they seek now to defraud us. Not holding legal authority from the crown, they are but a band of adventurers with no title other than force. We have established a claim on the gratitude of our country and our sovereign, This claim is now to be dishonored, our very services converted into crimes, and our names branded as traitors. But the time has come for vengeance. God will not desert the soldier of the Cross. Those whom He has carried victorious through greater dangers will not be abandoned in this last great trying ordeal Fail! Shall we, who never knew failure, fail now? And, if we should fail, better die like brave men on the battle-field, than, with fame and fortune in our grasp, be cast away, to perish ignominiously like slaves on the gibbet."

"If we fail it shall be no fault of ours!" cried Estevan and Velasquez.

"It is my purpose," Cortez resumed, "to attack the enemy this very night, while they are buried in slumber, and the friendly darkness throws a veil over our movements, charitably concealing the poverty of our numbers."

12

At this the troops, though jaded with tiresome marches, gave a joyful shout of approval.

"Lead us on to battle—lead us wherever you will!" they cried.

Meanwhile, Narvaez had remained at Cempoalla, passing his days in idle and frivolous amusement. But at last, alarmed by rumors and suggestions of friends, he put himself at the head of his troops, and on the very day Cortez arrived at the River of Canoes, Narvaez sallied forth to meet him. On reaching the river, Narvaez saw no sign of the enemy. The rain fell in torrents and the soldiers were soon drenched to the skin.

"Of what use is it to remain here fighting with the elements?" said the general's lieutenant. "There is no sign of Cortez, and little reason to fear his approach in such tempestuous weather. It will be wiser for us to return to Cempoalla; and in the morning we will be fresh for action, should Cortez make his appearance."

Acting on this unwise suggestion, Narvaez returned to the Indian town, where he occupied the principal teocalli. It consisted of a stone building on the usual pyramidal basis, and the ascent was by a flight of steep steps on one of the faces of the pyramid. In the edifice of the sanctuary above, Narvaez stationed himself, with a strong party of arquebusiers and crossbow-men. Two other teo-

callis in the same area were garrisoned by large
detachments of infantry. His artillery consisted of
eighteen small guns posted in the area below, and
protected by the remainder of the cavalry. Having thus distributed his forces, he returned to his
quarters and to repose.

In the mean while, Cortez, having crossed the
stream, arranged his forces to the best advantage,
and gave the last word of advice before the battle
began.

"Everything depends on obedience. Let no man,
from desire to distinguish himself, break ranks.
On silence, dispatch, and, above all, obedience to
your officers, the success of our enterprise depends."

Silently and swiftly they moved to the teocalli.
They came on two sentries, one of whom made his
escape. Cortez, not doubting that the sentinel's report would alarm the enemy's camp, quickened his
pace. As they approached, he discerned a light in
one of the lofty towers of the city.

"There are the quarters of Narvaez," he exclaimed to Sandoval, "and let the light be your
beacon!"

On entering the suburbs, they were surprised to
find no one stirring and no symptoms of alarm;
but, stealthily as they moved, they were soon heard
by sentries, who hastened to Narvaez with the
alarming cry:

" *Cortez!   Cortez!* "

Narvaez buckled on his armor and summoned his men to battle.   All this was the work of a few minutes, but in those few minutes the Spaniards had reached the avenue leading to the enemy's camp.

" Keep close to the walls of the building," commanded Cortez, that the cannon-shot might pass between the two files.   The artillery thundered forth its death-notes, but the guns were aimed too high, and only three men were struck down.

" Espiritu Santo!   Espiritu Santo!   Upon them!" cried Cortez, and in a moment Olid and his division rushed on the artillerymen, whom they knocked down or ran through with pikes, and got possession of the guns.   Another division engaged the cavalry and made a diversion in favor of Estevan and Sandoval, who, with their followers, sprang up the great stairway of the temple.   They were received by a shower of bullets and arrows.

The uproar of battle startled from their slumbers on the walls numerous *cocuyos*, a species of large beetle which emits an intense phosphoric light from its body, strong enough to enable one to read by it.   Seeing these wandering fires in the air and being unacquainted with their causes, the followers of Narvaez were overcome with terror.

" See the matchlocks in the air!" they cried.

"The matchlocks in the air! We are overwhelmed with a powerful army!"

"Santa Maria! I am slain!"

Narvaez heard the cry, but fought with un-daunted courage. Estevan and Sandoval gained the

platform and engaged the foes in a hand-to-hand
fight. The standard-bearer of Narvaez was run
through and fell dead at his feet. Narvaez received
several wounds, for his short sword was no match
against the long pikes of his assailants. At last
Estevan, aiming a thrust at his face, drove his
pike through the bars of his visor and into the left
eye of the unhappy cavalier, destroying the sight
of it forever.

"Santa Maria! I am slain!" cried Narvaez.

"Victory!" shouted the followers of Cortez, and
the battle was over.

Next morning, Narvaez, Salvatierra, and two or
three more of the leaders were brought before Cortez in chains. It was a moment of deep humiliation for the former commander, in which the anguish of body, keen as it was, was forgotten in that
of the spirit.

"You have great reason, Señor Cortez," said the
discomfited knight, "to thank fortune for having
given you the day so easily, and put me in your
power."

"I have much to be thankful for," the general
answered; "but as for my victory over you, I esteem it as one of the least of my achievements since
coming into this country." He then ordered the
wounds of the prisoners to be cared for, and sent
them under a strong guard to Vera Cruz.

CHAPTER XII.

OFF FOR SPAIN.

YOUNG Estevan and his mother still lived at St. Jago, though the father, having excited the hatred of the governor, dared not return. There were few opportunities for acquiring an education in the New World at this period. Learning was immured in the cloister, and convents were the schools. The priest, in the New World, was a missionary rather than a professor. Las Casas had undertaken to teach the lad some of the principles of grammar, reading and writing; but it was the great desire of his mother that he might be educated at Salamanca in Spain.

One other member of the household we must not forget; it is little Christoval, the child of Balboa. She grew more beautiful and winning every year, developing from childhood to maidenhood, fulfilling every promise of beauty and grace. Her large, dark eyes had about them a sad and drooping expression peculiar to tropical beauties. She was seldom known to smile, save when in Christopher's presence, and she was often known to heave bitter sighs when he was away.

Though he had grown to be a big, stout lad, and she was a coy little maiden, they still wandered about the beach as of yore, hand in hand. One day they had gone to their favorite stone and seated themselves to listen to the wash of waves upon the sands.

"Has it ever occurred to you, Christoval," he asked, "that we are almost grown?"

"No," she answered uneasily.

"I will soon be a man and you a woman. We can no longer wander in the woods in search of wild flowers and birds' nests, nor pick up shells on the sea-shore, nor play with toys and swings, for more serious thoughts must henceforth occupy our minds. There are great things in store for both of us."

"What are you going to do?" she asked, fixing her great, sad eyes on him.

"My plans in life are not fully laid. I want to go to Mexico, but mother has other views."

"What are they?"

"She wants to send me to Spain."

"Far, far away across the seas to the land from whence my father came?"

"Yes."

The girl's hands were clasped and there was a

slight convulsive twitching of the fingers, but by no other means did she evince the agony she suffered.

"Don't you want me to go?" he asked.

For a moment she was strangely silent; then, in the mellow tone of her mother's people, she answered.

"I don't know."

"You will be very lonely, Christoval?"

"Yes, but what is the Indian girl, that you should be mindful of her? Are not the hearts of all my race breaking?"

"You are also a Spanish girl."

"Nevertheless they would have made a slave of me, had you not rescued me from the bloodhounds. Perhaps, when you are gone away, they may even yet make a slave of me."

Laughing at her fears, Christopher assured her that there was no further danger. But the sad fate of her mother's race was enough to make Christoval sad, despite his assurances. Tens of thousands of her mother's unfortunate people had yielded to slavery's blighting effects and had gone to that mysterious land from whence there is no return. Could voices come back from that echoless shore, the wailing of wronged spirits would forever disturb the sleep of their Spanish butchers.

A gentle breeze blew over the sea, toying with

the dark, silken curls on Christoval's brow. Her bright eyes had grown moist, and she dared not trust her voice to speak. Her early life had been without sunlight. Having the blood of two proud families in her veins, her humble sphere in life was more galling than if she had been of more lowly birth. Her young rescuer had ever been her chief comforter. At times, when with him, the dark cloud seemed to lift, and she was gay and laughing, but it was only while in his presence.

"Then you will really go away across this ocean?" she said at last, gazing out over the water.

"Yes, I must go to Salamanca."

"With a sigh she answered, "Well, I suppose it is best."

The sun was sinking low in the western horizon. There was a beauty in the land and a splendor in the sea as they wandered hand in hand along the pebbly beach, her heart almost filled to bursting, yet she dared not speak. Occasionally, when he paused to gaze on some bird soaring over the water, or to pick up a bright shell, he found the large, dark eyes fixed on him with a look of wonderful tenderness.

"Christoval, do you want me to stay?" he asked.

"Yes," she answered.

"But our mother, who is older and wiser, says

I must go. If she thinks it best to give up her son, you surely can give up a brother."

"Yes."

The answer came after a few moments of silence, and with some hesitation. It was not a cheerful assent, though she never afterward expressed any regret that he was going.

Often, after that day, as they wandered among the orange and palm groves seeking the oriole or parrot's nest, or gathering bright shells on the sea shore, Christopher was inclined to speak of his departure, but the sad little face haunted him, and he decided not to do so.

One evening, on their return home, they found the señora reading a letter.

"Is it from father?" Christopher asked.

"It is."

"Where is he?"

"Still in Mexico. He dares not come home."

"Will he ever dare return to Cuba?"

"He hopes to do so soon. Cortez is going to Spain to lay their case before the king. He hopes matters may be so tempered that we may live here, despite the enmity of Velasquez."

"I wish the king would remove the governor and give us a better one."

The Estevans were soon to feel the governor's power more forcibly than before. A few days later, Christopher was standing on the dock, watching a large ship riding at anchor in the bay, when some one tapped his shoulder and, looking about, he saw Antonio Velasquez.

"You have discovered the ship in the harbor?" Antonio said.

"When did it arrive?"

"Last night. Can you guess who came in it?"

"Not my father?"

Antonio shrugged his shoulders, while his dark eyes flashed with fire, and a strange smile played over his face.

"No, not your father," he said. "My uncle would like to have your father and the rebel Cortez in his power now."

"How am I to know who came in yonder ship?"

"It was Panfilo de Narvaez."

"The blustering cavalier who went to bring back Cortez," said Christopher. "I'll warrant you he came back worse than he went."

"I saw him, and the poor gentleman is in a sad condition."

"He was wounded?"

"Wounded, yes. He was near to being slain in a combat with your father. The unfortunate gentleman lost an eye."

"I have heard as much."

"Your father attacked the governor's lieutenant,

driving the keen point of his pike through the bars of his visor and destroying his eye."

"Narvaez boasted that he would hang my father; can he be blamed for defending himself?"

"Yet it was a sorry day when he wounded the lieutenant. The governor now is more enraged against Estevan than Cortez."

"Why should he be? Was it not all done in fair and honorable combat?"

"Yet the sight of a trusted and valuable friend maimed for life drove him to fury. He has issued a special proclamation against Hernando Estevan, declaring him an outlaw and traitor, and ordering that all his estates and possessions be seized and confiscated."

Christopher, at first, could hardly believe his ears; but the fearful reality forced itself on him, when, an hour later, he heard the town-crier proclaiming the order. Hurrying home, he acquainted his mother with the governor's order, and, together, they set out to a monastery, where was a friendly and powerful priest, to whom they told what had been done.

"Go to your homes," said the priest, "and I will see what can be done."

Through the interposition of the priest that part of the order confiscating the property was rescinded; but Hernando Estevan was still an outlaw.

in thought. His reflections took an ill turn and he gesticulated angrily, striking his hand in the air, as if he were beating back an invisible foe. The cavalier, being blind in one eye, did not see Christopher, who passed on his blind side. The fist of the one-eyed knight shot out just as young Estevan was opposite him, and sent his guitar spinning into the street.

Nothing was more calculated to rouse this music-loving youth, and, before the cavalier could realize what he had done, Christopher knocked him down.

As soon as he could gain his feet, the cavalier drew his sword, and turned upon his assailant.

"Impudent upstart! what do you mean?" he cried.

"You struck my guitar from my hand."

"By my patron saint! I swear I have a mind to run you through!"

"It would be a deed befitting a gallant cavalier, as I am unarmed," was the ironical response. "Panfilo de Narvaez dares not fight an Estevan in fair combat."

"I recognize you now; you are the son of Hernando the traitor."

"You speak falsely, señor. My father is no traitor, and a braver man never lived."

Narvaez, though a man of violent passions, nevertheless possessed great pride.

"It shall not be said that Narvaez struck an unarmed man," he said, putting up his sword; "but
I will see that you are sent to join your rebellious
father."

Estevan laughed at the cavalier, and assured him
that, before many days, he would leave the island
of his own accord. Christopher's adventure tended
to hasten his departure. News of the assault on
the cavalier reached the governor's ears, and he
determined to banish Estevan. Friends managed
to get the order stayed for a few days. Meanwhile
every arrangement for the youth's departure for
Spain was completed.

The day came, one of those lovely tropical
mornings. The sunbeams danced upon the deep
like smiles on the face of a sleeping babe.

The little bay of St. Jago was a scene of bril-
liance and confusion. Early as it was, the town
was alive with people hurrying hither and thither.
A ship was about to sail for Spain, and there were
the usual sounds in the harbor and on the shore.
People about to depart were bidding adieu to
those on shore, and the joyful expectation of meeting loved ones in the Old World, was dampened by
regrets at leaving dear friends in the New.

A little group stood apart from the others.
Christopher Estevan, his mother, her other two
children, and Christoval Balboa constituted the

13

group. Young Estevan was on his way to Salamanca, the seat of European learning. His mother
was weeping, and, for the first time since Fulvia
was torn to death by the bloodhound, Christoval
evinced signs of grief. Another joined them; it
was Gerund the jester. The poor fellow had forgotten his jests, and wept with the others.

It was a sad morning for Estevan, who felt as if
he were really banished from his home by the edict
of a tyrannical governor, and his return forbidden.

"Don't weep, mother, it is for the best," sighed
Christopher.

"It is, in very truth, the best," put in Gerund,
"but, alas, we do not always like the best," and
he sobbed louder than before.

The boat was ready, and, bidding all a final
adieu, Estevan sprang into it and was rowed away
to the vessel. They watched him go aboard, saw
the anchor hoisted, heard the signal gun, and then
the great white sails, like clouds of snow, were
spread to the wind and the vessel sailed away.
Poor Christoval, unable to bear up longer, gave
way to her first and only violent fit of grief. As
Christina Estevan held the sobbing girl in her arms,
and gazed after her departing son, her mind went
back to the day in Palos, when she had seen his
father sail away with the white-haired explorer in
search of a new world.

CHAPTER XIII.

INEZ OVIEDO.

CHRISTOPHER ESTEVAN had been two years in Salamanca when, one day, he met Antonio Velasquez. He afterward learned that Antonio had come to Salamanca to take a scholarship in the famous convent, but, having been early expelled, was pursuing his studies under a private tutor. Under the circumstances, the meeting between the two could hardly be cordial. There was a sneer on the face of Antonio, and he was not backward in his expressions of dislike toward Christopher.

"You will not return to Cuba, I suppose?" he remarked.

"Why not?"

"The governor has banished you."

"Perchance, before I am ready to go home, the governor may be hanged."

"No, he has strong friends at court, and they will see that he suffers not, which is more than can be said of your father."

"Yet, under Cortez, he has given Mexico, with

195

all the treasures of the Aztecs, to the king, and kings know valuable friends too well to permit them long to live under a cloud. The failure of the Narvaez expedition proved that Cortez was no ordinary man."

Realizing that he was getting the worst of the debate, Antonio framed an excuse for going away. He hated Estevan so much that he wrote a letter to the governor of Cuba setting forth that Christopher was devoting his time and limited abilities to slandering the governor. The governor was so enraged, that he offered a reward for Estevan, dead or alive, on the ground that he was guilty of treasonable conduct. Meanwhile, Christopher, heedless of all danger, was busily engaged in his studies, or dreaming day dreams of the future. It was a romantic age, and the wildest rumors of golden conquests came from the western to the eastern continent. The student caught the spirit of the age and longed to leave the cloister for the battlefield. Exploration and conquest was the all-absorbing theme of the day.

Christopher was proficient in all the manly sports and accomplishments of the day. He could ride at a tourney or play the guitar with equal excellency. His fondness for travel and adventure fitted him to be an explorer and an able companion of Pizarro and De Soto.

At this time there stood, not a league from Salamanca, one of the most beautiful villages in all Spain, situated in a lovely valley, where all the charms of verdure so peculiar to the Peninsula seemed to have been scattered with lavish hand. Nothing remains of the village to-day save the tumble-down walls of a castle and the ruins of an ancient monastery; but at the time of Estevan it was a sight bewitching to all the senses. The citron and arbutus, growing wild, sheltered every cottage door, and the olive and laurel threw their shadows across the little stream which traversed the hamlet. The houses, observing no uniform arrangement, stood wherever the caprice or inclination of the builder dictated, surrounded by the neatest and cosiest of gardens. The undulating hills, soft blue skies, and transparent atmosphere imparted a picturesque feature to even the lowliest hut, while upon the craggy eminence, just south of this lovely village, there perched a dragon-like castle, looking silently down upon the peaceful hamlet with an air of protection.

This retired spot was one of the most quiet places in all the world. The birds sung all day long in the fulness of their joy, and all through the Spanish and Moorish wars not a rude alarm had come to disturb the repose of the village. Unmolested, the nightingale at evening poured

forth her song, and here peasantry and noble alike enjoyed a long season of uninterrupted peace.

The castle was owned by a hidalgo named Oviedo, noted for his kindness of heart and gallantry. He was a brother of the famous chronicler and historian who accompanied Ojeda to the New World, and whose faithful account of many of the conquests is authority to the present day. Don Oviedo was beloved by all the peasantry. Although only forty-five years of age, he had won distinction in the wars in which his country had been involved.

Don Oviedo was a widower, his wife having died in giving birth to a daughter, fifteen years before. Ever since, Oviedo had lived alone in his castle with his daughter Inez, who had grown to be one of the most lovely señoritas in all Spain. Genius and beauty combined to make Inez Oviedo one of those brilliant characters seen but once or twice in a life-time, and the most delicate modesty added a wonderful charm to the rich gifts of mind and body.

Naturally the fame of so lovely a being soon reached the ears of the student at Salamanca, and her praises aroused within Estevan a strong desire to meet her. He was informed one day by Antonio Velasquez, in the most insinuating way, that he was not only on familiar terms with Inez, but was her accepted suitor. Velasquez took pleasure in descanting on the matchless beauty and intelligence of the fair Inez.

"If what you say be true, then the Doña Inez is far from perfection in judgment," retorted Estevan, who could scarcely tolerate the fellow.

"What do you mean?" Antonio demanded.

"If she possessed such wonderful wisdom. Antonio never would have been her choice."

Antonio became enraged, shook his fist at the student, and gave vent to innumerable rash threats, to all of which Christopher listened with good humor, never rising from the couch on which he reclined. Having exhausted his rage in empty threats, Antonio rushed from the apartment.

"A good riddance," said Estevan, rising and tossing aside the book he had been reading. "I have said nothing to regret. If all he has said be true and she has chosen him, Inez Oviedo may be matchless in beauty and wisdom, but in her choice of a suitor she has displayed bad judgment."

One knows nothing of the bewitching spell of a pair of soft, dark eyes, until he has once come under their magical power. Estevan was soon to realize the power of a glance from the eyes of Inez. He was accustomed to take long walks about the convent, going half a league into the country and the surrounding hills almost every day. One day, as he was returning from a long stroll, he was startled at the sound of horses' feet, and, looking up, he saw a gentleman, richly attired, riding by the side of a young lady, mounted on a gayly caparisoned Andalusian pony. Her face was veiled, and he could not see her features, but he knew at a glance who the couple were. The gallant gentleman could be none other than Don Oviedo, who was a familiar personage at Salamanca. Christopher longed for a glimpse of the señorita's face. Just then, as if in answer to his wish, a breeze lifted the fleecy veil, and gave to his view that bright, nymph-like beauty, which for months had been the subject of his imagination.

For a moment only did he behold the delightful vision, yet that moment sealed his fate. The great, soft, dark eyes did the mischief.

The Spanish twilight fell like a noiseless curtain over the earth as the youth stood watching Doña Inez and her father, until their forms were no longer discernible. Then he started, as from a delightful dream.

"He has lied!" exclaimed Christopher.

This charge had no connection with the couple that had just passed. He was thinking of the boastful assertion of Antonio, and again he cried: "He has lied!"

For the next few days little attention was paid

to books. The schoolmasters noticed the strange conduct of their formerly bright pupil and marvelled of it.

When he tried to read philosophy, he saw only a pair of bright eyes on the page. When studying astronomy, the stars became the beaming orbs of Inez. Manfully he kept his secret. He wandered over the country more frequently than usual, going farther than he had ever gone before. The hamlet and castle became special objects of interest, and, from a far-off hill, he watched the sun set, casting its last fading ray on roof and tower. Then he would rise and begin his silent homeward march.

Again and again he wandered to the hill and the village, hoping to be repaid by another sight of Inez; but he was always disappointed. He grew madly jealous of Antonio. Reason told him that the boasting fellow had spoken falsely; but love is unreasonable, and takes to itself a thousand disagreeable forms and annoyances.

Would not the kind Heaven which sent the wandering breeze to lift her veil bring about some chance by which he might meet her? One evening Christopher had wandered as usual to the hill to gaze on the far-off castle which held the object dearest to his heart. In despair he turn to retrace his steps to Salamanca, vowing never again to come to the hill-top. He descended to the densely wooded valley and entered the Salamanca road, which was growing dim in the twilight.

As he paused here a moment, before retracing his steps, there came on the air from behind him a wild clatter of hoofs, and above the noise of thundering feet, a piercing shriek. Filled with wonder and alarm he involuntarily laid his hand on his sword. He was not long in suspense. A dark Arabian horse, with eyes emitting dangerous fire, came flying toward him, wild with rage and terror. On his back, sitting firmly in the saddle, holding the reins in both hands, was the vision of his dreams, Inez Oviedo.

"Saint Anthony be praised for this!"

Madly he leaped toward the frightened steed, hurling himself almost under its hoofs. It was a daring act; but he snatched the reins, and, with superhuman strength, hurled the animal back upon its haunches, holding him there with one hand, while with the other he assisted Inez to dismount.

"Thank you, señor!" the trembling maiden whispered in his ear.

King Ferdinand was not more proud at the fall of Granada, than was Estevan at this moment. The conquered horse stood trembling in the grasp of his master.

"This is a pleasure, I assure you," he stam-

"MADLY HE LEAPED TOWARD THE FRIGHTENED STEED."

mered, "to be of service to Doña Inez Oviedo. That is your name, I believe?"

"Yes, señor, and, if I mistake not, you are the student whom we passed the other evening."

"I am; Christopher Estevan is my name, and America my birthplace."

"A native of America! Are you one of those strange people of whom I have heard so much?"

"I am, like yourself, a Spaniard," he answered, smiling. "My parents were born in Spain, but emigrated to America soon after its discovery. My mother lives in Cuba, while my father is with Cortez in Mexico.

"Hernando Estevan?"

"That is his name."

"I have heard of him. My uncle, the chronicler, is also in the New World."

"How came your horse to run away with you?"

"He became frightened at some object at the roadside."

"It is dangerous for you to ride alone so late."

"Father was to accompany me. He was ready to mount, when something detained him a moment at the castle, and I thought I would ride a short distance and wait."

"He knows nothing of the runaway?"

"Nothing."

Before more could be said, there came from the

road toward the village a clattering of hoofs, and a moment later Don Oviedo came riding at full speed calling the name of his daughter. He was overjoyed to find her unharmed. She told her father of her rescue, and the don, who was every inch a gentleman, dismounted and, seizing Estevan's hand, thanked him warmly.

"You owe me no thanks, Don Oviedo," Christopher answered. "The happiness it gives me to be of service to Doña Inez doubly repays me."

The señorita heard this gallant response; her eyes met the student's and drooped beneath his gaze, while a soft flush stole over her face, perceptable even in the gathering twilight. Inez was the only child of the don, and the thanks welling up from his proud heart were poured forth without restraint. The don had known Estevan's father; while the story of his grandfather's (Roderigo Estevan's) long captivity among the Moors was a familiar tale in Spain.

"You came of good stock," declared the old cavalier. "The house of Estevan is one of the oldest and proudest in Spain. Your ancestors were men who feared neither Christian nor Moor, and always chose the side of right. So the Estevans have been transplanted to the New World; well, I trust they may flourish there as long as they have in Spain. America must be a wonderful country.

I have a brother there, and, God willing, I may some day visit it myself."

Estevan was invited to the castle, and most gladly accepted the invitation, thinking himself the happiest of mortals. He could now meet his rival on equal footing. The bitter feud between his family and that of Velasquez was destined to become more bitter still, as he and Antonio now had a subject worthy of a quarrel. Christopher had many advantages over his rival. He was taller, handsomer, and had a more gallant bearing. He was skilled in all the accomplishments of the period, and well calculated to win the heart of a fair lady. No more daring horseman ever rode a joust or tourney. He was one of the best swords-men in Spain, and, at the same time, was a skilful performer on the guitar, and the possessor of a rich, musical voice.

From this day he became a favorite at the cas-tle. Antonio soon learned of these visits, and his hatred of Estevan increased a thousand-fold, for bitter jealousy was added to the ancient family feud. Antonio was shrewd and cunning. There was nothing bold, open, or noble about him; he was trained in the school of deception, and could wear an affable and smiling exterior, while, beneath, he was a raging devil. What Christopher was calcu-lated to win by boldness, he sought to gain by

intrigue, and, though he avoided any open rupture, he set on foot schemes to ruin the young
student.

Meanwhile, Estevan lived a new life, for there
had dawned for him a joy he had never known
before. At times he was silent and melancholy,
then boisterous and happy. The birth of this new
emotion had changed his entire being. He loved
to wander alone among the hills about the old
castle, or gaze on it from afar, and ask himself at
which window sat the fair conqueror who held
his heart captive. At deepest night, when all the
world was hushed in sleep, and the high moon
alone beheld his devotions, he would steal to the
castle, the temple of his heart, and woo his beloved
after the beautiful fashion of Spain, common to
this day. In the wing of the castle where the fair
Inez slept was a room with a balcony. Beneath
this window he would come and charm the long
summer night with the sound of his melodious guitar, and such verses as the inspiration of the moment sufficed to weave.

One night, after the last trembling note of his
guitar had died, he waited, hoping and fearing, for
what, he dared not say. Would the serenade be
favorably received, or was his music wasted on the
dark walls of the old castle? A moment of suspense; then the lattice-work parted, and something

white fluttered from the balcony above. He cast
his eyes upward, catching just a glimpse of a
small white hand in the moonlight, when a delicate
object, burdening the air with its rich perfume,
dropped at his feet. With heart wildly beating
with hope and joy, he picked it up. It was a
beautiful nosegay of rare lilies surrounding a blood-
red rose. He knew the emblem, and, seizing the
precious flowers, he pressed them to his lips, and,
too happy to longer contain himself, fled from the
scene. The joy of his soul overleaped itself, and,
wandering over the hills, he blessed every object
of nature. It seemed as if he could not quit the
hills and woods, while the castle became an en-
chanted spot. It was late before he recovered
sufficiently to return, and, as he was entering Salamanca, a dark form suddenly arose before him, and
Estevan recognized his angry rival.

"For a student your conduct seems unbecoming," he said, in a voice which trembled despite
his efforts to be cool. "Where have you been?"

"Why should I render account to you?" was
the indignant response.

"Do you hesitate to tell?"

"Are you my confessor? God forbid I should
ever have such an one!"

"God forbid that I should ever have to give
absolution to an outlaw and the son of a rebel!"

Stung to the quick, Estevan started back to draw his sword, when the nosegay, which he had until this moment kept concealed, fell at his feet. The circle of snow-white lilies with the blood-red rose in the centre caught the jealous eye of his rival, and the hot blood mounted to his cheek.

"It came from the castle!" he cried.

"It concerns not you whence it came!" returned Estevan, drawing his sword. "Stand aside, or I will run you through."

"Is that a challenge?" and Antonio, who was no coward, drew his own blade. "This is a quarrel of your own seeking; I shall not be responsible for the consequences."

Both were excellent swordsmen, and as they clutched their slender Toledo blades, there was blood in their eyes. Velasquez was cunning, and he tried to get Estevan off his guard by alluding again to the nosegay.

"She gave it to you; you would rob me of her —die!"

He aimed a well-directed thrust at Estevan, which he parried with the skill of a fencing-master, and, recovering his position, delivered a thrust in return. The combat began in earnest. Like flashes of lightning the glittering blades played together, now darting side by side, now whirling like meteors, with the swiftness of thought, then clinking alongside again with the wary darts of serpents' tongues. As they became thoroughly warmed up to the work, and realized that their lives hung on the points of their swords, they grew more cautious and at the same time more deadly. The blood trickled from the cheek of Velasquez, and Christopher's sword arm had been slightly punctured between the elbow and the wrist. The blood, flowing down to the handle of his weapon, made it slippery, and his hold became uncertain. The conflict had just reached its height, when Father Philip, a priest friendly with Estevan, returning after a late visit to a dying sinner, was attracted to the spot by the clashing of the swords, and the heavy breathing of the combatants. Boldly rushing between them, he hurled them aside:

"Put up your swords!" he commanded.

Instinctively they obeyed, and each went his way.

14

CHAPTER XIV.

LOVE AND HATE.

WHILE young Estevan was making love in Spain, great events were transpiring in the New World, concerning most of which his mother's letters kept him posted. Years had rolled by since he left Cuba. He was still an outlaw, and as the hatred of the Cuban governor seemed to increase with time, he dared not return. His father still lingered in Mexico; but Cortez was soon to set out for Spain to lay their cause before the king, and Christina Estevan hoped he would win the good opinion of the sovereign, so that the banished husband might return.

One of her letters contained the following:

"One of your enemies is no more. I allude to Panfilo de Narvaez, who lost his eye in Mexico. Narvaez was ambitious to conquer a country and reap such rewards as have fallen to Cortez. From Charles V., he obtained a commission to explore the country which Ponce de Leon discovered sixteen years ago and named Florida. It seems, from what can be learned, that the expedition, which set out from here in June, 1527, reached Florida, where they found the natives quite hostile. They either made efforts to repulse the Spaniards, or kept aloof from them. The explorers landed and wandered through a strange, wild country, where the trees grow so tall that their tops seem to brush the sky, and through the densest of foliage the awful roar of the lion frequently smote their ears. Strange birds and beasts, such as the white men of Europe never looked on before, were found in abundance in this wonderful land, but no rich mines nor cities, such as in Mexico, were discovered. To delude them, the natives spoke of a hill of pure gold, and they wandered for a great distance, crossing rivers on rafts and scaling mountains. Many perished of hunger, or sunk in the swamps, and the Indians killed many more, so Narvaez discovered that they must all soon perish. They wandered back to the coast, but a handful of those who had landed in Florida. There some of them, under Caleza, we:e discovered and rescued; but it is quite certain that Narvaez perished, his frail bark foundering at sea.

"A man who is your father's friend is engaged in a most remarkable conquest. His name is Francisco Pizarro and he is the one who was with Vasco Nuñez de Balboa, our Christoval's father, when Don Pedrarias, Governor of Darien, had him beheaded. Pizarro says there is a vast country beyond the South Sea, greater in magnitude and wealth than Mexico. He also says there is a wonderful city of gold in this far-off land called Peru. Pizarro was promised help from Darien and from Spain to discover this country, but all failed him. For a long time he was left with a few followers at a strange island in an almost starving condition. At last a ship was sent to bring them off, and Pizarro refused to return. Drawing his sword, he traced a line with it on the sand from east to west. Turning toward the south he said:

"'Friends and comrades! On that side are toil, hunger, nakedness, the drenching storm, desertion, and death; on this side ease and pleasure. There lies Peru with its riches ; here, Panama and its poverty. Choose, each man, what best becomes a brave Castilian. For my part, I go to the south,' and he stepped across the line, followed by his brave pilot Ruiz; next by a Greek named Pedro de Candia, and eleven others. With these thirteen followers, he commenced the conquest of Peru. Many months have elapsed and the wonderful land has not been reached. I have just learned that Pizarro contemplates going to Spain to enlist the king in his enterprise. Should he succeed, he will be the richest conqueror the world has ever known.

"Before I close this letter, I must tell you of Christoval. She is now a beautiful woman, but as strange and mysterious as ever, and my own daughter does not love me more. She never sleeps, I think, without breathing your name in her prayers. She is meek, patient, and lovable, but I can't understand her. Every day she goes to the beach where you wandered so often, and gazes out across the ocean, as if looking to see you come back. Once I found her there bathed in tears. I asked her why she wept, but evading me, she ran to the house. I think she was weeping because her brother was away. I hope affairs may soon change so that you and your father may both be able to come home ; but I fear, yet dare not tell Christoval so, that we are destined to spend our lives in different lands. For the present adieu.

"Your mother,
"CHRISTINA ESTEVAN."

Carefully folding his mother's letter, Estevan placed it between the leaves of his book. Strange thoughts had been aroused by the perusal of the epistle. His father, whom he had not seen since childhood, his mother, brother, sister, and Christoval, all seemed to claim anew their place in his affections. But that part which aroused the latent ambition in his breast was the reference to Francisco Pizarro.

"He is coming to Spain to fit out for the conquest of Peru, the wonderful land of which old Zuna the fugitive slave told me. There are the cities whose houses are roofed with gold. I will go with him," declared Estevan. "When he comes, I will join him."

His love for Inez Oviedo had not abated his ambition to become an explorer. There were more worlds to conquer and he resolved to conquer them; but for a while longer he dallied at the feet of the beautiful being of his adoration, reading to her the poetry and romances of the day, or amusing her with his guitar. He kept from her ears the story of his encounter with Antonio. He and his rival frequently met, but they never spoke.

The student was more often at the castle than at the convent, and was always warmly welcomed. He often went riding with Doña Inez, and on one of these occasions met Velasquez in the road. He greeted them with silent amazement and hatred. His look bode the successful lover no good; but what cared Estevan for danger, while basking in the sunlight of the señorita's love? He found Inez such a fountain of wisdom and purity that he could

forget sorrows and dangers in her presence. Day
by day his affection grew stronger, until he loved
her madly. As her mind, richly stored with useful accomplishments, each day unfolded some new
beauty, that love become almost worship. It
seemed as if she was born to inspire all who knew
her with noble thoughts. Those who could not
understand her soul were made spiritual, as it were,
by the magic of her beauty. Those who had no
heart for poetry had ears for the music of her
voice.

The lovers were much together, riding, walking,
or rowing in the Spanish gondola. They could not
have told on what subjects they conversed. Their
talk was not of love, but every word and glance was
love itself. Estevan told her of his home in the
New World, of his parents and their persecution,
and Inez listened, absorbed and mute. Dearer were
those simple stories than all the extravagant praises
of her numberless admirers. Their love was sudden
but it was strong. Heart, brain, sense, imagination,
all were its ministers. When the betrothal vows
were spoken, they could scarce remember, so
naturally did the wonderful event come about.
Young, beautiful, and gifted—of noble birth and
lofty souls—there was harmony in their union, on
which the heavens smiled; but dark clouds were
rising in the horizon, and beneath the altar of their

happiness a hissing serpent had coiled, ready to strike them with its deadly fangs.

Antonio had not surrendered his claim to the fair Doña Inez. He was only biding his time and perfecting schemes which would bring disaster and ruin upon his hated rival.

"Fool! does he think an Estevan superior in wit to a Velasquez? I shall first ensnare him in a web of disgrace and ruin, and then try my chance with the rich and beautiful señorita."

With Estevan all was going well. He told the old Don of his love for Inez, and their betrothal received the blessing of the proud old hidalgo. The youth kept it a secret from his parents and friends, designing a happy surprise for them. Alas! what misery that precious secret brought to one he loved, the world will never know.

One night he stood beneath the casement of Inez' room to sing a love serenade. The castle was dark from frowning battlement to drawbridge, but on her window-pane a coquettish moonbeam played. He held his lute a moment in his hand, gazing on the crimson roses which, stirred by the gentle zephyrs, tapped against the pane.

"She awaits my voice to come forth and join me on the balcony," he thought.

As he was about to touch the strings, he heard a noise, and, turning suddenly, saw a flash issuing from a clump of bushes beyond the drawbridge. Dropping his lute he snatched his sword from its sheath and flew to the spot whence came the flash. He found no one, though hastily retreating footsteps told him that a foe had lurked near. He was about to pursue him, when he stumbled over a matchlock. The match was still burning, but the powder in the pan was gone out in the flash he had seen, failing to ignite the powder in the barrel.

"I have an enemy cowardly enough to resort to assassination," he thought.

Nevertheless, he returned, sang his song, and received his reward from the balcony above.

School was forgotten and the student lived only in the presence of Inez. Walking together, galloping on fiery Arabian steeds over the rugged country, they were almost inseparable. But, most of all, they loved to glide down the narrow stream side by side in the beautiful gondola.

Such happiness was not destined to last, and the rude awakening came all too soon.

One morning Father Philip, who had always been his friend, entered the apartment of Estevan, his face deathly pale, his frame trembling, and tears in his eyes. Estevan started to his feet, and seized his friend's hand.

"What is the matter, father; what has happened to distress you?" he asked.

"Alas! I have sorrowful news for you, my son."

"Have you come to tell me of the death of my parents?"

The good priest shook his head.

SIDE BY SIDE, THEY FLOATED DOWN THE NARROW STREAM.

"Then what can be the trouble?"

"It is something which causes more grief than death, my son—disgrace!"

"Disgrace!" gasped Estevan, his cheek deathly pale. "Who is disgraced?"

"Don't blame me, my son. I did all I could to spare you, but I was overruled."

"Holy father, in God's name, what do you mean?" he asked, starting up in alarm and gazing in amazement at the priest.

"Serious charges were brought before the faculty against you—and—you were expelled from the convent."

Estevan started to his feet, and gazed at the priest like one stunned by a blow.

"Expelled!" he repeated.

"Would to heaven it were otherwise! but it is too true," sobbed the priest.

"Of what offence am I charged?" he asked as soon as he could speak.

"The charges are numerous; three of them are insubordination, heresy, and treason to the crown."

Covering his face with his hands, Estevan tried to collect his scattered faculties, and think wherein he had been guilty of such serious offences. After a moment's silence, he sat up and fixed his great blue eyes on the priest.

"Holy father, I know not how I have given offence as indicated."

"Nor I, but, though I have tried to convince the

Bishop of Burgos, for some cause he is immovable from his purpose."

"The Bishop of Burgos is Juan Rodriguez de Fonseca, is he not?"

"He is."

"I begin to understand it now. He was an enemy of Christopher Columbus, and my father, being a personal friend of the admiral, drew down on him the hatred of the bishop. Governor Velasquez and his nephew Antonio are likewise enemies of my father and myself, and have helped to poison the mind of the bishop against me."

The priest groaned.

"The bishop is all-powerful and we are forced to obey him," he said. "Recalcitration will be impossible; the order has been issued, and you must bow in mute submission."

"I dare not return home."

"Why?"

"I am outlawed. Governor Velasquez proclaimed me an outlaw."

"For what reason?"

The student told the priest of the old feud and the bitter rivalry between himself and Antonio over Doña Inez Oviedo.

"If I had known all this sooner I might have averted this blow," sighed the priest.

"Is it too late?"

"It is. You are even now in danger of arrest and chains."

"I will carry my cause to the throne," he cried.

Again the priest shook his head.

"It will not avail you, my son; it's too late— too late. Do nothing, say nothing for the present. King Charles is determined to uphold the governors in the New World."

Estevan went out from the principal seat of learning of the world in disgrace. His proud spirit felt most keenly the deep humiliation of this expulsion.

"Antonio has gained the ear of the bishop," he thought, "and most cruelly maligned me."

The gentle twilight of an autumnal evening was falling, as the student, sad and dejected, wended his way along the well-beaten path to the castle on the hill.

How would she receive him? Was she already aware of his disgrace, or would she first hear it from his own lips? The castle, grim and silent, loomed up before him. The sun had set, and the moon was shedding a silvery light upon the scene. Estevan was walking hurriedly toward the frowning castle, when a tall, dark form suddenly came from the shadows of some wide-spreading oaks and advanced to meet him.

"Stop, Señor Estevan!" said a deep, solemn

voice. It was Don Oviedo himself, and, trembling with dread, the youth came to a halt. "I must forbid you my castle, señor. You may not sing and play beneath my daughter's balcony. I have learned of your disgrace, and my daughter cannot wed an outlaw and heretic."

For a moment Estevan strove to speak; but he was unable to utter a word. Don Oviedo saw the effort.

"I know what you would say," he added, "but it's no use, señor, I have it all from the bishop."

"The bishop is an enemy to my family," Estevan gasped.

Don Oviedo was a religious zealot, and to utter a word against a priest was an offence not to be condoned. He raised his hand to enjoin silence.

"Do not say aught against the bishop. He is above petty jealousies or envy. He is too great to be questioned; but as this has come to my ears from the best authority, which cannot be doubted, you must consider your engagement to my daughter broken off."

"Don Oviedo, will you not consult your daughter's happiness?"

"I am doing so."

"Give me time to establish my innocence. Give me a few months, a few weeks to prove that the good bishop has been deceived."

The Don considered the matter a moment.

"I will give you a week," he said; "but, meanwhile, you must not come to the castle."

"A week, a whole week," said the student hopefully, as he turned and walked away. "A stay of opinion has been granted for a week. Heaven grant that I may be able to establish my innocence."

The intrigues of Antonio and the bishop went on. The day after the scene we have witnessed, Antonio met Inez, but, knowing that she had learned of Estevan's disgrace, he was too shrewd to add more. He saw her frequently, and each time he strove with consummate skill to prepare her for the impressions he designed to have her receive. Inez read him like an open book, and knew that, while he never recurred to the disgrace of Estevan, he was secretly exulting over his downfall. She took great care to conceal her anguish; but she had a cunning man to deal with, and, if she read Antonio, he was no less slow in discovering her inmost thoughts. One day, by a seeming accident, Estevan's disgrace was referred to, and Antonio treated the subject as unworthy of consideration.

"I warned you against the adventurer and outlaw," he said. "Could more be expected than that he should be expelled from the convent?"

"He is not the only one who has been expelled,

señor," was the spirited answer. "I have heard that even you study under a private tutor."

He stammered, blushed, and after many efforts made a partial explanation and took his leave. On reaching Salamanca, he discovered his rival leaving the town on a mule.

" Why have not the officers done their duty?" he asked himself. "Diego and Miguel should even now have him in chains on shipboard. Once get him to Cuba, and he will be put out of my way."

Antonio lost no time in hunting up the officers who had the warrant for Estevan's arrest, and told them that their man had just made his escape, and was on his way from town by the old Seville road, riding a mule. By Antonio's aid the officers procured a pair of swift horses and started in hot pursuit.

"Slay him if he resists—and he will resist," was Antonio's parting instruction to Diego and Miguel.

CHAPTER XV.

PIZARRO AND CORTEZ.

GLOOMY and despondent, Estevan jogged along
the road, and Salamanca was soon lost to view
among the hills. The day was well advanced, and
he had a long and dangerous journey before him,
and a relentless and subtle foe in his rear; but his
thoughts were not of himself. Misfortune, disgrace,
and death were forgotten in the fear that he had
lost the only being who would make his life worth
living.

A clatter of hoofs startled him from his painful
revery, and, turning his eyes to where a road from
the hamlet intersected the path he was travelling,
he saw a man riding a horse and leading another.
He waved his hand for Estevan to stop.

"Wait, señor; I have a better steed for you!"
he called after him.

"Who are you?" asked the amazed youth as the
strange horseman approached him.

"I am your friend Sancho, sent to bring you a

horse, and accompany you on your journey, for you have enemies in hot pursuit."

"Have I met you before? Are you a retainer at the castle?"

"Lose no time in conjecture. I am your friend come to guide you to safety; trust in me and all is well. Your enemies ride hard behind you."

Turning his mule loose, he mounted one of the horses and set off with his mysterious guide at full speed for Seville. Although Estevan's pursuers followed him for several leagues, he managed to shake them off, and then the faithful Sancho, bidding him God-speed, left him as mysteriously as he had approached him.

Reaching Seville in safety, Estevan remained quietly among friends until danger was thought to be over. One morning he was strolling in disguise toward the bay, when he discovered a large vessel which had just come into port. He at once conjectured that it had come from the New World. At this moment he heard loud, angry voices, and discovered a commotion at the quay, toward which great crowds of people were hurrying.

"It is a scurvy trick for Bachelor Encisco to arrest him just now," one man declared.

"Who is arrested?" the youth asked.

At this moment some officers came up the hill with a tall, sunburned, battle-scarred man, whose

15

long beard and abundant hair bore evidences of a
wild life. This man, Estevan learned, was Francisco
Pizarro, who had just returned from America.

Pizarro, with his officers, had reached Seville that
morning (early in summer of 1528). There happened to be in Seville at that time a person known
in the history of Spanish adventure as Bachelor
Encisco. He had taken an active part in the
colonization of terra-firma, and had a pecuniary
claim against the early colonists of Darien, of whom
Pizarro was one. Immediately on his landing,
Pizarro was, by Encisco's orders, seized for the
debt. Pizarro, who fled from his native land as a
forlorn and homeless adventurer, after an absence
of more than twenty years, most of which time was
passed in unprecedented toil and suffering, now
found himself, on his return, the inmate of a
prison. Such was the commencement of those
brilliant fortunes which, as he had trusted, awaited
him at home.

While Estevan stood watching them take the
man away to a debtor's prison, he heard more than
one expression of indignation from the bystanders.
Here was a man who had been the friend of his
father suffering the most intolerable persecution.
Estevan determined to see the prisoner and try to
aid him. Soon after his incarceration, he demanded admission to Pizarro's cell, and after some

difficulty was admitted. The bronzed, battle-hardened conqueror fixed his eyes on the youth in amazement.

"Who are you?" he asked.

"Christopher Estevan."

"The son of Hernando?"

"Yes, señor."

"He was my friend."

"And so am I, señor. I come to offer my services to you, poor as they may be."

"Why are you in Seville?" asked Pizarro, regarding the young man with interest.

Estevan told his story, concealing nothing save his love and betrothal to Inez.

"You have been as illy treated as I," said the great conqueror, when he had concluded. "I came to lay before the king my plans for the conquest of the richest country in the world. I have brought samples of gold and treasure from Peru, such as the king has never seen. The moment I touched my foot on my native shore I was arrested for a debt for which I am no more responsible than Governor Pedrarias. It was Balboa who dispossessed Bachelor Encisco and not I."

After a long consultation over the matter, Estevan became so interested in the conquest of Peru that he determined to accompany Pizarro's officers to Toledo, where they proposed to lay the matter

before that monarch, although there was danger of
his own arrest.

As yet the king had received too little returns
from his transatlantic possessions to give them the
attention they deserved.   But as the recent acquisition of Mexico, and the brilliant anticipations
respecting the southern continent, were pressed upon
his notice, he felt their importance as likely to
afford the means for prosecuting his most ambitious
and expensive enterprises, and he was therefore
willing to listen to Pizarro.   He ordered his release
at once and commanded that he should be sent to
him.   Much to the disgust of Enciso, the debtor
was released.

Estevan accompanied Pizarro to Toledo.   Entering the city, Estevan and Pizarro were walking
along one of the chief thoroughfares, discussing
the proposed conquest, when they suddenly came
upon a cavalier as bronzed, swarthy, and battle-
hardened as the hero of Panama.   Though it had
been years since Estevan had seen that face, a
glance at it recalled the early morning at St. Jago
when the angry governor, mounted on his fiery
horse, thundered down to the water's edge and
demanded the return of the man whom he had
commissioned to the conquest of Mexico.   Estevan
was but a child then, yet he recognized him, and,
bounding forward, he seized his hand.

"Cortez!" he cried.

The cavalier glanced at him in astonishment.

"Who in the devil's name are you?"

"Estevan, son of the man who sailed with you from Cuba to conquer Mexico ten years ago."

"I know you now," said Cortez, embracing him.

"Have you forgotten me, and the night nearly a score of years ago, when, at the house of this lad's father in San Domingo, we talked of Ojeda's expedition?"

"Pizarro—cousin!" interrupted Cortez, grasping the hand of the hero of the Isthmus. Cortez always acknowledged Pizarro as his cousin, and, in fact, the conqueror of Peru was a soldier with whom no one need be ashamed to claim relationship.

Estevan was anxious to learn of his father, and as soon as greetings between the conquerors were over, he began to ply Cortez with questions about his parent, and to ask if he could return to Cuba.

"I have come to lay an empire at the feet of my sovereign," answered Cortez, "and to demand in return redress for our wrongs and recompense for our services. Your father shall not be forgotten, and will be the first for whom relief is asked."

"What are the chances of success?"

"Good; I am sure that every boon I crave will be granted."

"Can you assist me?" asked Pizarro. "You are at the close of a brilliant career, and I am at the beginning of mine."

"All that I can do to further your cause, Pizarro, shall be done."

Thus those two men, so wonderfully alike in some particulars and so dissimilar in others, were united in a common interest. The conqueror of the north and the conqueror of the south; the two men appointed by Providence to overturn the most powerful of Indian dynasties, and open the golden gates through which the treasures of the New World were to pass into the coffers of Spain, were to assail the throne in the interest of Pizarro. While preparations for laying Pizarro's case before the king were being made, the three were almost inseparable. It was arranged that Estevan, the outlawed youth, should become one of the recruits for the Peruvian expedition, concerning the success of which neither Cortez or Pizarro entertained a doubt.

When granted an audience with Charles V., Pizarro stated that he had come to satisfy his royal eyes by visible proofs of the truth of the golden rumors of Peru, which had time and again been borne to Castile. Despite his illiteracy and humble birth, Pizarro, unembarrassed in the presence of his king, maintained his self-possession, and showed that decorum and even dignity in his address which belong to Castilians. He spoke in a simple and respectful manner, but with the earnestness and natural eloquence of one who had been an actor in the scenes he described, and who was conscious that the impression he made on his audience was to decide his future destiny. The king and the court listened with eagerness to the account of Pizarro's strange adventures by sea and land, his wanderings in the forests, or in the dismal and pestilential swamps on the sea-coast, without food, almost without raiment, with feet torn and bleeding at almost every step, his few companions daily becoming fewer by disease and death, and yet pressing on with unconquerable spirit to extend the empire of Castile, and the name and power of his sovereign. When he described his lonely condition on the desolate island, abandoned by the government at home, deserted by all but a handful of devoted followers, his royal auditor, though seldom affected, was moved to tears.

The king examined the various objects brought from Peru with great care and attention. He was particularly interested in the llama, remarkable as the only beast of burden yet known in the new world. The fine fabrics made from its shaggy coat gave it a much higher value in the eyes of the sagacious monarch, than any they could possibly possess as domestic animals. But the gold and silver ornaments, and the wonderful tale which Pizarro had to tell of the abundance of precious metals, satisfied even the cravings of royal cupidity. On his departure from Toledo, Charles V. commended the affairs of his vassal in the most favorable terms to the consideration of the Council of the Indies.

Meanwhile Estevan seemed partially forgotten by his enemies. He sent a letter to Inez and received an answer in which she stated she did not believe the charges against him, and assured him of her love. He determined to see her before leaving Spain.

The business of Pizarro went forward at a tardy pace, and he found his limited means melting away under the expenses incurred by his present situation. At the last moment the queen, who had charge of the business in her husband's absence, in order to expedite affairs, on the twenty-sixth of July, 1529, executed the memorable capitulation, which defined the powers and privileges of Pizarro.

According to the stipulation therein, Pizarro was to receive the rank of governor and captain general of the province, together with those of adelantada and alguacil mayor for life, and an allowance necessary to retain suitable military officers. Throughout the long, tedious negotiations, Estevan was with Pizarro, acting as his private secretary and amanuensis. Estevan was full of buoyant hope and eager for a wild life of adventure. When all was completed, Pizarro and Estevan set out for the former's birthplace, Truxillo in Estremadura, where he would be most likely to meet with adherents for his new enterprise.

No doubt Pizarro made this visit to gratify his vanity by displaying himself at the home of humble childhood in the promising state of his present circumstances. If vanity was ever pardonable, it certainly was so in this man, who, born in an obscure station in life, without family interest or friends to back him, had carved out his own fortune in the world. Pizarro had four brothers, all of whom were poor, but proud and fond of adventure, and they were easily persuaded to enlist in his enterprise.

While at Truxillo, the enemies of Estevan discovered his whereabouts and he was arrested and thrown into prison. The authorities deeming all engaged in this expedition free from arrest, he was soon released. As soon as he regained his liberty, Estevan determined to pay the promised visit to Inez. He travelled in disguise, heavily armed, for he knew that his subtle foes would not hesitate to assassinate him. When the vicinity of

Salamanca was reached, he did not allow himself to be seen by daylight, but went secretly to Father Philip and secured his assistance. The priest managed to convey to Inez the information that Estevan wished to meet her on the following night beneath a large tree below the hill.

When the appointed hour for the rendezvous came, Estevan with trembling limbs and palpitating heart wended his way to the place. The night was very still. Even the nightingale's song was hushed, or so far away that it could not disturb the lovers. He threw himself on the ground and waited impatiently. Would she come? Hark! what was that? Surely he heard footsteps. Starting up, he saw an armed man approaching. Filled with alarm, Estevan laid his hand on his sword, but the new-comer spoke, and he recognized in him faithful Sancho, the guide who brought him a horse and led him in his flight from Salamanca.

"I came to see if you were here," he said.

"Who sent you?"

"Doña Inez."

"Go to her, Sancho, and tell her I am waiting."

Sancho went back toward the castle, and Estevan again threw himself on the ground and clasped his hands over his heart to stop its wild beating. Again the sound of footsteps fell upon his ear; this time the tread was lighter than before.

"Is she coming?"

She was coming, he knew it, and, starting to his feet, he saw a beautiful being clad in white, moving toward him.

"WITH A GLAD CRY, SHE WAS IN HIS ARMS."

"Inez!"

"Christopher!" and, with a glad cry, she was in his arms. For a moment neither spoke a word. After a while he regained his voice.

"Inez, you have heard all?"

"I have, and I believe you blameless."

"If you could but know the persecutions to which my family has been subjected, you would understand why I was outlawed. I am going away to the New World with Pizarro to Peru, and I hope to win honors and gold to buy the friendship of the king."

"We go also to the New World," said Inez.

"What! Inez, speak again; did I understand you?"

"We are going to Panama. My uncle is already there, and through him father has purchased large tracts of land. He has consented to take me with him."

"Heaven be praised! We both shall be on the same continent. When will you sail?"

"In one month."

"Then you will come on the fleet that follows ours," said Estevan.

"We will."

CHAPTER XVI.

THE cannon from the port at St. Jago boomed forth the arrival of a ship from the Old World. In a moment the town was wild with excitement. What vessel was it? what tidings did it bring from the Old World? whose friends were in the ship? were the questions asked by nearly every one.

The boats which pulled out to the vessel learned that it was on the way to Darien with supplies and recruits for Pizarro's expedition.

Among the first to disembark was a handsome young fellow about twenty or twenty-one years of age. He gazed about, from right to left, as if trying to recognize some familiar landmark, and then passed quickly up into the town. He glanced curiously at the faces he met as though in search of a friend. Here and there an old resident would give the young stranger a more than passing glance, which he returned with a nod or smile, and passed on boldly up the street like one who had known the place all his life.

237

"Now may I never make another pun, and may I forever lose my wits if I haven't seen that face before," declared Gerund the jester, gazing in the young man's face.

"It would be impossible for you to lose your wits, my friend," answered the stranger with a smile.

"Why would it, my merry fellow?"

"Because you have none."

"Well, I will admit that, for once, Gerund has been worsted. But, pray thee, tell me who you are?"

The stranger was not ready to reveal his identity, and, with a laugh, hurried through the town into the suburbs, where stood a stately mansion.

"Here, as elsewhere, all has changed," he said. "The forest, so grand in my childhood, has shrunk farther and farther away; the little cottage has grown to a stately mansion; faces once so familiar are grown out of recognition, and I have changed also, for no one knows me. Will *they* recognize me?"

As he approached the mansion, he saw a white-haired man, with a cane, walking in the garden. He had all the bearing of a veteran soldier. Years had rolled by since he sailed with Cortez to conquer Mexico. The tall, handsome young fellow was a child then. The white-haired man was astounded when the young stranger came toward him, and, with extended arms, cried:

"Father!"

The soldier's eyes opened wide, and he gazed at the face before him.

"My son! my son! can this be my little Christopher?" he exclaimed.

"It is, father, but little no longer," answered Christopher, embracing him. "I am now grown to be a man."

"I have been so long accustomed to think of you as the little boy I left here long ago, that I can hardly realize that you are a man. Why did you leave Spain?"

"I am on my way to Peru, father!"

"And have you given up your studies?"

"For good cause, as I will explain in time. Francisco Pizarro came to Spain beating up recruits for Peru, and I am going with him. Our ship touched here and will remain a few days to take in wood and water, and I availed myself of the opportunity to pay you a visit."

The mother, who was not far away, heard voices in the garden and went to see who was there. Her eyes were quick to recognize in that tall, manly stranger her first-born, and she hurried to embrace him and welcome him as only a fond mother can. The other members of the family followed

her to rejoice over the arrival. From behind one of the massive columns supporting the roof of the long piazza, he caught a glimpse of a slender girl. The loose, straight gown of the period, gathered at the waist with cord of gold, clung to her, giving a quaint, nymph-like contour of beauty. A casual observer would at once be attracted by her delicate profile and her large, dark eyes. Christopher Estevan recognized in this slender, graceful, olive-cheeked girl his adopted sister, Christoval Balboa. One glance, and Christopher sprang to her side and seized her hand before she could escape.

"Christoval, Christoval, don't you know me? Don't you know your brother?"

She trembled like a captive bird, and Christopher's brotherly kiss seemed to set her cheek aflame; her breath came in gasps, and she looked as if she would faint.

"It is your brother returned; fear not, Christoval."

She gazed at him with her great, dark eyes, as if she feared it might all be a dream from which she would awake. Before long she was sufficiently recovered to sit at his side on the rustic seat and hold his hand in her own, as if she feared he would escape.

Before many days she grew reconciled to the change in her brother, and again they wandered among old familiar scenes, or sat on the beach to hear the ocean's roar. He told her much of the Old World which she was destined never to see; of his expulsion from Salamanca and the attempt to

"YOU ARE GOING AWAY TO PERU?"

arrest him; but he told no one of Inez. That was a secret which he kept safely locked up in his heart.

"You are going away to Peru?" she asked, as they sat on the great stone on the beach.

16

"I am," he answered.

For a long time both were silent. The surf dashed mournfully upon the sands and the pebbles glistened in the sun; while in the distance porpoises could be seen sporting in the water. Sea-fowls soared in the air above, and from afar came the subdued sounds of life in the town. Christoval heaved a sigh, and a look of sadness came over her face.

"Don't you want me to go?" he asked.

"No."

Another mournful silence of shorter duration followed, which was broken by Christoval saying: "What matters it to me? I am only an Indian."

"Christoval—sister, don't use that term in self-reproach, for the best blood of Spain flows in your veins. Your father made a name which will last through all time. Has any one reproached you on account of your Indian blood?"

"No."

"Have we not always been kind to you?"

"Forgive me; I am very ungrateful. It is perhaps my proud Indian blood which makes me so; but I see my mother's race conquered, humiliated, and enslaved, and feelings of bitterness will arise in my heart."

"You have done nothing to be forgiven," he answered. Then she grew more cheerful, and they discussed the coming conquest and Estevan's prospects for bettering his fortune.

"There are great dangers in the path of the man who would conquer Peru," said Christoval.

"I realize them all," he answered.

"Do you remember the stories told by Zuna, the old woman of the cave, of rivers infested with dragons, of huge birds with human faces, which feed on people? Did she not speak of mountains of flame, and gulfs that would swallow up armies?"

"Yes, and she told of cities of gold, of splendor such as kings might envy, of such fabulous wealth as the world has never known. Who deserves the wealth of the heathen more than those who came to spread the Gospel among them?"

The Spanish conqueror was a religious robber. Mingled with the idea of conquest and gold was the one thought of extending the dominion of the Cross. The Spaniard was ever a Crusader. He was, in the sixteenth century, what Cœur de Lion and his brave followers were in the twelfth, with this difference: the cavalier of the earlier period fought for the Cross and glory; while gold and the Cross became the watchwords of the Spaniards. The spirit of chivalry somewhat waned before the spirit of gain; but the fire of religious enthusiasm burned as brightly under the quilted mail of the American

almost gave way. Her heart beat wildly and her face glowed as it never had before. When alone in her room that night, the señorita fell on her knees and thanked the Holy Virgin that she had lived to enjoy this hour.

"He loves me, he told me so, and his lips would not lie," the poor, deluded girl sobbed in her joy. "Cortez loved Marina, and he loves me. He loves me as Balboa loved Fulvia. Oh, this hour of bliss repays for ages of torment!" She was in a state of excitement, her hands were firmly clasped and she rocked her body from side to side.

"He is going away!" and she started again to her feet. "Thousands have gone to those far-off lands and never returned. He may sink down in battle, or perish by disease, but he loves me. Yes, even in death, he will be mine."

While Estevan slept the sweet sleep of peace and dreamed of Inez in far-off Spain, Christoval Balboa stole with noiseless feet to his bedside, and, bending over him, pressed her cold lips so gently to his forehead that the sleeper imagined it a passing zephyr.

Estevan was destined not to remain long at home. His ship was still detained at St. Jago taking supplies and beating up recruits, when another came from Spain, bringing Antonio Velasquez. He landed in great pomp and was greeted by relatives and friends congratulating him on his return. He was not long in St. Jago when he learned that Estevan and his father were both on the island. By some fatal oversight the pardon for Hernando Estevan did not include his son Christopher. Antonio was not long in inducing the governor to issue a new warrant for the arrest of his rival.

Christoval was wandering alone in the grove on the hill, when she discovered Gerund the jester coming toward her at a run. His usually jolly face wore an expression of alarm and anxiety.

"I have bad news, Christoval," he said excitedly. "By the mass! it would be more glorious if it were my funeral." Then the fellow told her of Antonio's arrival and the issuing of the warrant for the arrest of Christopher Estevan, which a party of soldiers were to execute that very night. His movements were to be closely watched and he would be slain if he made an effort to escape.

The Indian girl listened with the stoicism of her mother's race. She resolved at once upon a plan to save the man whom she loved more than life. She ran to a hut on the coast two miles above, where dwelt some humble fishermen, under obligation to her for past kindness, and persuaded them to seize a small caravel, and at midnight await off a point of rocks for the fugitive. This done, she hastened home, reaching the house at dusk, and found Estevan in the garden.

"You must go, fly with me at once," she whispered, seizing his arm.

"Why?" Estevan asked, fearing she had lost her reason.

"Your life is in danger, they are coming to kill you. Antonio has landed and procured a warrant for you, and is coming with soldiers to arrest or slay you."

"My father and I were pardoned by the king's proclamation."

"Only your father was pardoned."

Estevan realized his danger. By this time it had grown quite dark, and the clank of arms could be heard down the street. A deed too heinous for light of day was to be done under cover of darkness. There was not a moment to lose. He dared not wait to secure arms or bid parents adieu.

"You must go at once," whispered the Indian señorita, "a moment lost and distruction is certain. Come, I will lead you to safety, and, returning, explain all."

She took his hand and led him through the arbor, down an avenue of trees, and entered a dense forest. From this they discended into a ravine and followed it until the roar of beating surf fell on their cars. Almost before he was aware of it they had gained the point of rocks, and a boat awaiting him bore him away to the caravel. Christoval Balboa, with tear-dimmed eyes, stood on the great rock watching the caravel bound over the waves bearing him she loved to Panama and adventures and dangers greater than she imagined.

CHAPTER XVII.

A MYSTERIOUS FRIEND.

THE first arrival of white men on the South American shore was nearly ten years before the death of a powerful Inca named Huayna Capac, when Balboa crossed the Gulf of St. Michael and obtained the first clear report of the empire of the Incas. Hitherto this powerful nation, the farthest advanced in civilization of any tribe on the western continent, had lived in its secure retreat unknown to the European. Rumors of pale men, charged with thunder and lightning, breathing death and destruction, and riding terrible life-destroying beasts, reached their ears and filled the breast of the Inca and his nobles with alarm. Huayna Capac was disturbed not only by this news, but by the many supernatural appearances which filled the whole nation with dismay. Comets were seen flaming athwart the heavens; earthquakes shook the land; the moon was girdled with rings of fire of many colors; a thunderbolt fell on one of the royal palaces and consumed it to ashes, and an eagle, chased by several hawks, was seen one day screaming in the air above the great square of Cuzco. When pierced by the talons of his tormentors, the king of birds fell lifeless in the presence of the Inca's nobles, who interpreted it as an augury of their own destruction. Believing his end to be drawing near, the Inca called his chief officers about him, and prophesied the downfall of his empire by a race of white and bearded strangers, as the consummation predicted by the oracles after the reign of the twelfth Inca. Thereupon he warned his vassals not to resist the decrees of heaven.

On a former visit to Tumbez, Pizarro brought back with him two or three Peruvians to be instructed in Spanish and to act as guides and interpreters. Among them was a youth whom the Spaniards named Felipillo, or "Little Philip." Not having time, and, in fact, not being competent to instruct the Peruvians himself, Pizarro entrusted that duty to others, and Felipillo proved to be an apt scholar. By the time Pizarro returned to Panama to push matters for the final invasion, Felipillo had almost mastered the tongue of his conquerors.

"I know enough Spanish now to talk with you, and I want to tell my story," he said, one day, to Pizarro.

Knowing that he might have some valuable information to impart, Pizarro bade him proceed, as
he would gladly hear anything he had to say.

"I have heard that you are going to Peru to de-
throne the Inca Atahualpa, now at war with his
brother Huascar, whose power he usurped. If
such is the case, great captain, I will gladly join
you in slaying the bold, bad man."

"Do you hate him, Felipillo?"

"I have cause to hate him."

"Why?"

"Lend an ear to me, great captain, and I will
tell you my story. I once lived happily in Peru
in my mountain home on the great road not far
from Caxamalca. I loved a Peruvian maiden; she
loved me and was to become my wife, but one day
the evil eye of the Inca Atahualpa fell on her and
from that moment we were doomed. He determined to make her another victim of his infernal
harem, where so much of the beauty of Peru lan-
guishes. I protested, but was declared an outlaw,
and driven to the forests, where for days I lived
like a wild beast, hunted day and night by the
Inca's spies. I made my way to Tumbez, and, after
a hundred hair-breadth escapes, was leaving the
country in a balsa, when you found me. Meanwhile my beautiful Pruilla was seized and carried
away to the harem of the hated Inca. When I

met you, I thought, 'Here are the pale men charged
with thunder and lightning, who breathe destruction, and bestride those life-destroying beasts. If I
can but enlist them in my cause, I can invade the
country of the cruel Atahualpa, slay him in his
palace, and recover my beautiful Pruilla, for the
Inca dare not resist the pale men from the unknown
world.''

Pizarro, shrewd old warrior that he was, realized
that here was an opportunity to secure a faithful
ally. There was a flash in the Peruvian's eye and
an earnestness in his voice which proved that his
story was no idle romance. Felipillo was more
anxious for the overthrow of the Peruvian empire
than any steel-clad warrior from Spain. The
general assured him that Pruilla should be restored
to him, and the face of the Peruvian glowed with
delight.

During preparations for the expedition to Peru,
Estevan reached Panama, about the latter part of
December, 1530. He had escaped his foes in
Cuba, and, being with Pizarro, he was now perfectly safe from their machinations. A few days
later supplies and recruits from the ship which had
touched at Cuba arrived. Many Cubans, some
Spaniards, and some Indians had joined the expedition. Among the recruits was an olive-com-
plexioned boy, a very quiet young fellow, named

Nicosia. Although he spoke Spanish quite fluent-
ly, there was evidently a dash of Moorish or Indian
blood in his veins. Estevan asked the captain of
the ship from whence the young fellow came.

"Cuba," was the answer. "On the morning
we sailed from St. Jago, a boat, manned by some
fishermen, came alongside our ship. They hailed
us and put this boy on board. I asked him where
he was going, and he said, 'To join Francisco
Pizarro.' I brought him, though I believe the
general will reject him on account of his extreme
youth."

When the forces of Pizarro were mustered for
the last grand review, the veteran warrior went
from man to man, giving each a critical examination. He alone knew what was to be borne by
that devoted band, and he realized that it required
nerves and sinews of steel to endure the dangers
and hardships in store for them. When he came
to the dark youth, he paused, and gazed fixedly
into his eyes.

"Who are you, child?" he asked.

"Nicosia, from Cuba."

"Why are you here?"

"I am going to conquer Caxamalca."

"By the holy war! I like your spirit," returned
the battle-scarred Pizarro, and then to the surprise
of every one, who expected to see Nicosia rejected,

he passed him by. There was something daring in the young fellow's manner, which pleased Pizarro.

Nicosia was quiet and retired, mingling little with those in camp. He kept aloof from the carousals and brawls in which the Spaniards indulged. He lacked skill in the use of arms at first; but so diligently did he apply himself in acquiring the art, that before many weeks he was an adept with the slender sword and crossbow. He had not been long in the army, when he formed the acquaintance of Estevan, who became his tutor in the use of arms.

"I want to be with you," said Nicosia one day at the conclusion of a fencing match. "I want to be your comrade in arms, and march at your side through the dangers we are to encounter."

"I am willing," Estevan answered. "Though I have known you but a few weeks, I like you."

The ship which was to bear Inez to the Isthmus had not yet arrived. Day by day Estevan expected Don Oviedo and his daughter at Panama, but was disappointed. Preparations for the departure of the little army upon their terrible expedition were pushed forward with all possible speed, and Estevan feared they would not arrive before his departure. Early in January, 1531, Pizarro was ready to sail on his third and last expedition for the conquest of Peru, and nothing had yet been heard from the ship which was to bring Don Oviedo and his daughter to Darien. Estevan had to give it up and depart without a last interview with Inez.

Pizarro's army for this stupendous enterprise consisted of one hundred and eighty men, with twenty-seven horses for cavalry. His fleet was composed of three vessels, two of them of good size. Like his cousin Cortez, Pizarro was a shrewd politician, and, knowing that there were dissensions and civil wars among the Peruvians, he determined to take advantage of their division. A united Peru could have defeated a much larger force than he brought with him; but with one half arrayed against the other and ready to join the invader to crush their brothers, the scheme of conquest was practical.

As the vessels sailed away from Panama, Estevan stood leaning against the bulwark, gazing off at the fast receding shore.

"Will I ever return? will I ever see her again?" he murmured, half aloud.

"The blessed Virgin grant you may!" a voice at his side answered, and, turning, he beheld his mysterious friend Nicosia. Before Estevan could utter a word, the young fellow, overwhelmed with confusion, turned and went away.

"He is a strange fellow," thought the youthful adventurer. It was many hours before his friend rejoined him.

The fleet was headed for Tumbez, which promised such magnificent treasure; but, as usual, head winds and currents baffled the purpose of Pizarro, and after a run of thirteen days, much shorter than the period formerly required for the same distance, the little squadron came to anchor in the bay of St. Mathew, about one degree north. After a consultation with his officers, Pizarro resolved to disembark his forces at this place and advance along the coast, while the vessels held their course at a convenient distance from land. Estevan was among the first to land and begin the march, which was painful in the extreme. The road was intersected by streams, which, swollen by the winter rains, widened at their mouths into spacious estuaries. Pizarro, having some previous knowledge of the country, acted both as commander and guide. Reaching the first hamlet without being seen, the Spaniards charged into it, uttering their battle-cry. So sudden was their appearance, and so rapid the flight of the natives, that they failed to carry away with them their gold and jewels, which were found in great abundance in the cabins. The gold and silver ornaments were gathered from the buildings, and piled in a heap. After setting apart one-fifth

17

for the crown, according to the stipulation with Columbus and all subsequent explorers, the remainder was divided among the soldiers.

Having refreshed his men, Pizarro continued his march along the coast, but no longer accompanied by his vessels, which returned to Panama for recruits. As they advanced, the road was broken with strips of sandy waste, and the sand, drifted about by the winds, almost blinded the soldiers, and afforded a treacherous footing for man and beast. The glare was intense, and the rays of a vertical sun beat so fiercely on the iron mail and thickly quilted doublets of the soldiers that they were almost suffocated. To add greatly to their distress, a strange epidemic broke out in the little army. It took the form of hideous warts of enormous size, which covered the body, and when lanced, as was the case with some, such a quantity of blood escaped that the sufferer died. Pizarro lost several of his men by this frightful disorder. It was so sudden in its attack, and attended with such prostration, that those who lay down at night were frequently unable to lift a hand the next morning.

Estevan was among those who were stricken. Nicosia, his comrade, remained at his side and ministered to his wants. After two days he was able to follow the army, but was so weak that he fell behind, and at nightfall the army was out of sight. Nicosia spoke words of cheer and refused to leave him, even to save his own life. In the dead of night they were roused by a terrible roar, and an animal which they thought to be a tiger,

"NICOSIA ADVANCED TOWARD THE BEAST."

but which was probably a jaguar, suddenly burst through the underbrush and crouched near them for a spring. Estevan, too feeble to raise a weapon, sank powerless to the earth. Nicosia flung some faggots on the smouldering fire to make it burn up brilliantly, raised his shield so as to protect his breast, drew his keen sword and advanced toward the beast.

Either the fire-light, the secret power in the eyes of the youth, or the gleaming blade made the beast cower before him, and retire with growls into the woods.

Next day Estevan was better and they rejoined the army. He was mounted on a horse and thus enabled to keep up with the others. The little army had suffered frightfully and all were growing discouraged, when they were suddenly gladdened by sight of a vessel from Panama with supplies and reinforcements. From these Estevan hoped to receive some news of Inez; but although one of the recruits had seen Don Oviedo, who had arrived at Panama two days after the departure of Pizarro, he knew nothing of his daughter, and was quite sure she had not accompanied him. Recruits from Spain were also sure she was not there; then where was she?

"Would to heaven I could have seen her before leaving Panama," Estevan thought, and he sighed in his perplexity.

But the ambitious, restless Pizarro gave him little time for sighs and regrets. They pressed on over a country which became less sandy and more fertile. Some of the Spaniards wanted to halt and establish a colony, but Pizarro was more intent on conquest, and pushed on toward Tumbez. He made his first halt at the island of Puna in the Gulf of Guayaquil at no great distance from the Bay of Tumbez, where he rallied his forces, and prepared to make his descent on the Indian city.

They had not long been here before a deputation of natives with their caciques at their head crossed over in their balsas from the mainland to welcome the Spaniards. Felipillo put the general on his guard and warned him against treachery, and Pizarro arrested some of the caciques. This so enraged the people of Puna that they sprang to arms and assailed the Spanish camp. Though the odds were greatly against the Spaniards, they made up in arms and discipline what they lacked in numbers.

Estevan was a little apart from the others, and in a moment was surrounded by howling and screeching foes. He drew his sword and fought as best he could; but would have been soon overpowered, had not a horseman, with lance in rest, bore down on the group, scattering them like chaff before a whirlwind. Pizarro, at the head of the cavalry, put the Indians to rout, and then gave his attention to landing his forces at Tumbez. This port was but a few leagues distant, and he crossed over with his main force in the ships, leaving a few men to transport the baggage and military stores in balsas.

The first balsa that landed, some distance ahead
of the others, was surrounded by the natives, and
the three persons on it taken into the woods and
brained with war-clubs. The second balsa was in
command of Estevan, with seven men guarding
Pizarro's wardrobe. It was also assailed the moment it touched the shore.

Pizarro, with a dozen mounted men, among
whom was Nicosia, had landed a little lower down
the beach. Estevan's party had four guns among
them, and, as the savages advanced, they lighted
their matches and fired a volley at them, bringing
down two or three. The rest they attacked with
pikes and battle-axes.

"Look! they are in danger, general!" cried
Nicosia, as the report of matchlocks reached his
ears.

"Santiago!" cried Pizarro, and away went the
cavalry, Nicosia and Pizarro riding neck and neck.
A broad tract of miry ground, overflowed at
high tide, lay between the cavalry and the party
threatened. The tide was out and the bottom
soft and dangerous. With little regard for peril,
however, the bold cavaliers spurred their horses into
the slimy depths, and, with mud up to their saddle
girths, plunged forward into the midst of the
natives, who, terrified at the strange apparition,
fled precipitately to the forest.

On reaching Tumbez the town was found deserted, the houses demolished, and almost wholly stripped of interior decorations of gold and ornaments. The soldiers were quite cast down over the disappointment. Instead of the fabulous wealth of Tumbez, so graphically described to them by the natives, they found only barren walls and ruins.

While wandering about the city, Estevan suddenly met an old Indian who had a scroll of paper in his hand. He gave it to the young cavalier without a word and disappeared. Hastily unrolling the paper so mysteriously handed him, Estevan read as follows:

"Know, whoever you may be that may set foot in this country, that it contains more gold than there is iron in Biscay."

He took the paper to Pizarro, who caused it to be read to the soldiers. The document was evidently written by one of the Spaniards who had been left at the town on a former visit. The soldiers, however, treated it as a cunning device by the general to arouse their hopes.

"What do you think of the mysterious scroll, Nicosia?" Estevan asked his mysterious friend.

"I believe every word it contains to be true." he answered.

There came with Pizarro to Peru, a Spanish cavalier destined to make a name that will live as long as the history of the United States of America shall be read. His name was Hernando de Soto. He was a young, daring fellow, with a mind combining many noble qualities. He was ambitious, brave as a lion, and possessed excellent judgment. Without him it is doubtful if Pizarro would have succeeded in his conquest. He early formed a strong attachment for Estevan and next to Nicosia seemed his best friend.

Pizarro wanted a small party of horse to explore the wooded skirts of the vast sierra on the east and south, and De Soto and Estevan were selected to lead the expedition. Nicosia asked to become one of the party, but Pizarro refused his request. De Soto watched the expression on his face as he turned away, and, as the party rode toward the Andes, he asked Estevan:

"How long have you known Nicosia?"

"I met him first at Panama."

"There is some deep mystery about him."

"There is."

"Can you guess what it is?"

"No."

They did not discuss the subject further, for there seemed no key to the solution of the problem. In all their journey toward the foot-hills of the

Andes the matter was not mentioned again. They were destined to be the first white men to gaze on the wonders of Peruvian scenery, and for days they wandered through forests, beneath giant branches, through which the mountain winds swept in a weird and solemn symphony. A few savages were seen; but they fled into deeper forests at sight of the strangers. De Soto returned and made a report to Pizarro of what he had seen. After spending some time in reconnoitering the country, Pizarro came to the conclusion that the most suitable place for a settlement was in the rich valley of Tangarala, thirty leagues south of Tumbez, and traversed by streams which communicated with the ocean.

To this spot the army repaired, and with great ceremony began building the first town of the Europeans in Peru. Pizarro named the town San Miguel. Here he rested for some time with his troops, preparatory to his great achievement.

Estevan still lived in the hope that some ship from Panama would bring him tidings of Inez; but he was still doomed to disappointment. His mysterious friend Nicosia noted his drooping spirits and became serious on his account. He knew not the cause of Estevan's despondency, for, lover-like, the young cavalier kept his secret safely locked in his breast.

CHAPTER XVIII.

A CITY OF GOLD.

THE time had come for the Spaniards to cross the Andes and march to the interior. Caxamalca and Cuzco, the dream of the conqueror's life, lay beyond those snow-capped mountains. Their march had, hitherto, been along roads where they could occasionally catch a glimpse of the broad and lovely sea. It was with a sigh of deep regret that Estevan heard of the intended march across those wonderful mountains; not that he dreaded the journey, for he loved to explore great, unknown wilds, and there were no heights he would not dare climb, and no depths he would not descend, in search of the wonders and wealth of the earth; but not a word had he received from Inez since leaving Spain, and he began to entertain fears that he was forgotten. Perhaps, after all, Antonio might have won her from him. But for fear of being branded a coward he would have left Pizarro and returned to Panama.

One evening, late in September, De Soto came

to the tent in which Estevan and Nicosia were sitting.

"To-morrow we leave San Miguel for Caxa-malca," he said.

Estevan made no response. Although every step across those mountains took him further from Panama and Inez, yet he was tired of inactivity, and as she had not answered his letter, he felt the more willing to place the great natural barrier between them.

"The sooner we go the better; anything is more bearable than this inactivity," he declared, with a sigh.

Nicosia raised his soft, dark eyes to his face.

"Can I go with you?" he asked.

"I suppose every one who wishes can go."

"But I mean at your side—your comrade."

"I know not what disposition Pizarro may make of his men, and we must obey his orders."

Without another word Nicosia rose and left the tent.

"I know where he has gone," remarked De Soto.

"So do I."

"All will depend upon the humor in which he finds Pizarro."

"I hope, for the boy's sake, his mood may be amiable."

"Have you solved the mystery about him?"

"No."

"Won't he tell you anything of his life, who he is, where he has lived, and the cause of his strange attachment for you?" asked De Soto.

"He will reveal nothing. All I know of him is that he is well acquainted with the world. He has travelled or read much. He seems acquainted with every part of this mysterious country."

After a few moments Nicosia returned as quietly as he had left, a happy gleam in his eyes indicating that he had found Pizarro in one of his agreeable moods.

Five months after landing at Tumbez, on the 24th of September, 1532, Pizarro marched at the head of his hardy adventurers out from the gates of San Miguel, leaving a party there to colonize the valley and await the recruits under Almagro. Putting himself at the head of his troops, the chief struck boldly into the heart of the country in the direction where, he was informed, lay the camp of the Inca. This was perhaps the most daring enterprise yet engaged in by any Spaniard in the New World. With a handful of followers, and, as yet, few Indian allies, he determined to penetrate the very heart of a powerful empire, and present himself face to face before the Indian monarch in his own camp, encompassed by the flower of his victorious army.

On the morning of the march, Nicosia placed himself at Estevan's side and remained with him through the toil and danger of the expedition.

Having crossed the Piura, the little army continued to advance over a level district intersected by streams descending from the neighboring Cordilleras. The country was in places covered with a shaggy forest, occasionally traversed by barren ridges, which seemed to be off-shoots from the adjacent Andes, breaking up the surface of the region into sequestered valleys of singular loveliness. The soil, though rarely watered by rains, was rich, and, whenever refreshed by natural irrigation, as along the margins of the streams, it was covered with the brightest verdure. The industry of the inhabitants had turned the streams to the best account, and canals and aqueducts crossed the low lands in all directions like a vast network, spreading fertility and beauty around them. The air was fragrant with the perfume of flowers, and everywhere the eye was refreshed by the sight of orchards laden with unknown fruits and fields waving with yellow grain, or rich in vegetables of every description.

Estevan was filled with wonder at the high degree of civilization of these people. The Peruvians had developed the science of agriculture to greater perfection than any people yet found on the American continent; and as the Spaniards journeyed

through this paradise of plenty, they could not but
contrast it with the dreary wastes and wilderness
of mangroves through which they had passed so
recently.   They were everywhere received by the
trusting natives with confiding hospitality.   In
every town of considerable size was found some
fortress or royal caravansary, which furnished
abundant accommodations for the little army of
white men.   Thus they were provided with quarters along their route, at the expense of the very
government which they were preparing to overturn.

The further they advanced, the more Estevan
realized the magnitude of their enterprise, and he
was not surprised to hear whisperings of discontent
among the men.   After five days' march from San
Miguel, Pizarro called a halt in one of the beautiful
valleys, to allow his troops a little rest and make a
more complete inspection of men and arms.   The
men numbered one hundred and sixty-seven, of
which sixty-seven were cavalry.   He mustered
only three arquebusiers and twenty crossbow-men
in his entire army.   The arquebuse was regarded
as too heavy and cumbersome for a long, toilsome
march over the mountains.

The watchful eye of the commander had noted
such evidences of discontent among some of his
men that he grew uneasy.   If this spirit grew

contagious, it would ruin the enterprise, and he determined to remove it at once, if possible. Consequently he called the troops about him, and, mounting a stone so as to see and be seen by every one, he addressed them:

"Fellow soldiers and Castilians, a crisis has now arrived in our affairs to meet which demands all our courage. No man should think of going forward in this expedition who cannot do so with his whole heart, or who has the least misgivings as to success. If any of you repent having taken a share in it, it is not too late to turn back. San Miguel is but poorly garrisoned, and I would be glad to see it strengthened. All who choose may now return, and they shall be entitled to the same proportion of lands and Indian vassals as the present residents: have no fears on that score. With the remainder," he concluded, "be they few or be they many, I will pursue this adventure to the end."

This remarkable and unexpected proposal filled Estevan with wonder and alarm.

"What does he mean?" he exclaimed to De Soto, who stood near him. "Surely he will drive two-thirds of the army back to San Miguel; the expedition will be a failure."

De Soto shook his head.

"No; what he is doing is best. Pizarro knows that a single malcontent is more to be feared than

a thousand enemies. We are better off without
them. Very few, however, will return.

De Soto was correct; for, notwithstanding the
fair opening thus afforded, there were but nine who
availed themselves of the general's permission—five
cavalry and four infantry. The others declared
their resolve to go forward with their brave leader,
and, if there were some faint voices amid the
general acclamation, they at least relinquished the
right to complain in the future, having voluntarily
rejected the permission to return.

"Why didn't you go back?" asked Nicosia, his
great, sad eyes fixed on Estevan.

"Why should I?" Estevan asked.

"There is greater danger in store for you than
you imagine."

"Why did not you accept the offer?"

Nicosia shrugged his shoulders.

"I will go if you do," he replied.

Having winnowed out the few grains of discontent, which might have become dangerous if left to
grow in secret, Pizarro resumed the march, and, on
the second day, reached a place called Zaran, situated in a fruitful valley among the mountains.
Some of the people of this town had been drawn
away to swell the army of Atahualpa. The conquerors as yet saw no signs of their approach
toward the royal encampment, though more time had

already elapsed than was originally calculated on to reach it.

Being informed that a Peruvian garrison was established in a place called Caxas, among the hills not far from Zaran, Pizarro dispatched Hernando De Soto with Estevan and ten men to reconnoitre and bring back an account of the actual state of things. As days passed and no tidings were received of the reconnoitering party, Nicosia became greatly distressed, and even Pizarro grew uneasy. On the eighth morning De Soto appeared, bringing with him an envoy from the Inca, who brought with his message a present to the Spanish commander. The envoy had met De Soto at Caxas. The wily Spaniard understood the object of this diplomatic visit to be less a courtesy to the invader, than to secure information of the strength and condition of the Spaniards. He took great care that the envoy should be treated with all due regard to his rank and station. On his departure, Pizarro presented him with a cap of crimson cloth and some showy ornaments of glass, charging him to tell his master that the Spaniards came from a powerful prince beyond the waters; that they had heard much of the fame of Atahualpa's victories, and were coming to pay their respects to him, and offer their services against his enemies, and that they would not halt on the road longer than was

18

necessary before presenting themselves before him.

When the envoy was gone, De Soto informed his general that on entering, Caxas, he found the inhabitants ready to give battle; but, on assuring them of their peaceful intentions, they received the Spaniards with courtesy.

After sending a messenger to San Miguel with some treasures already collected from the Peruvians, Pizarro acquainted himself with the most direct route to Caxamalca.* The first halt was at the town of Motupa, pleasantly situated in a fruitful valley, among the hills which cluster around the base of the Cordilleras. Here the general halted four days, hoping to be joined by reinforcements from San Miguel.

"Why don't he press on?" asked Nicosia anxiously. "The Inca all this time can be augmenting his forces." He seemed so wise, to know so much about Peru and the Inca, that Estevan, gazing at him, asked:

"Have you not been here before?"

The mysterious youth became confused and answered, "No."

De Soto heard the answer and noted the confusion.

---

* The name has since been changed to Caxamarca.

"I don't believe him," he said. "He has a knowledge of Peru and Peruvians which can only be acquired by personal contact."

As no reinforcements appeared, they continued their march, advancing across a country in which sandy hills were relieved by broad expanses of verdant meadow, watered by natural streams. They were compelled to halt at one stream wider than the others, and Pizarro sent his brother Hernando across with a small detachment. Then they cut down trees from the woods, and made a floating bridge on which the army crossed next morning.

Taking every possible precaution, Pizarro pushed on, and at the end of three days reached the base of the mountain behind which lay the ancient town of Caxamalca. Before them rose the stupendous Andes, rock piled upon rock, their skirts below dark with evergreen forests, varied here and there by terraced patches of cultivated garden, with the peasant's cottage clinging to their shaggy sides, and their crests of snow glittering high in the heavens, presenting altogether such a wild chaos of magnificence and beauty as no other mountain scenery in the world can show. Across this tremendous rampart, through a labyrinth of passes, easily capable of defence by a handful of men against a large army, the troops were now to march. To the right, bordered by friendly shades, ran a road broad enough for two carriages to go abreast—one of the famous routes to Cuzco. Some of the officers were of the opinion that the army should choose this road, but Pizarro determined to hold to his original course.

"We have everywhere proclaimed it our intention to visit the Inca in his camp," declared Pizarro in a brief address to his followers. "This purpose has been communicated to the Inca himself, and now to take an opposite direction would draw upon us the charge of cowardice, and would incur Atahualpa's contempt. No alternative remains but to march straight across the Sierra to his quarters. Let every one take heart and go forward like a good soldier, nothing daunted by the poverty of our numbers. In the greatest extremity, God ever favors his own; so doubt not, he will humble the pride of the heathen, and bring him to the knowledge of the true faith, the great end and object of this conquest."

Every campaign-hardened warrior was roused to enthusiasm by this speech.

"Lead on!" they cried. "Lead wherever you think best; we will follow, and you shall see that we can do our duty in the cause of God and the king."

Estevan and Hernando Pizarro were sent in advance with a small party. They followed a road which was conducted in the most skilful manner round the rugged and precipitous sides of the mountains so as to best avoid the natural impediments of the ground. In places the cavalry were compelled to dismount and lead their horses, which could scarcely climb the rugged steeps. In many places they were crowded by an overhanging crag to the very verge of the precipice, where a single misstep would precipitate horse and rider into the dreadful abyss below. The wild passes of the Sierra, practicable for the half-naked Indian, or the sure-footed mule, became formidable to the Spaniards and their horses, encumbered with armor and supplies.

In one of these impregnable passes the army came suddenly upon a frowning fortress built of solid masonry, the lower part excavated from the solid rock. The fort was empty; not a Peruvian was in sight, and Pizarro took up his quarters there for the night.

Next morning the army proceeded still deeper into the intricate mountain gorges. From intense heat the climate changed to intense cold. Even vegetation changed, the gorgeous foliage of the tropics giving place to the Alpine plants and herbs of the north, while the dreary wilderness was nearly abandoned by the animal creation. The light-footed vicuña, roaming in its native wilds, might sometimes be seen looking down from some airy cliff, where the foot of the boldest hunter dared not venture. Instead of the feathered tribes, whose gay plumage sparkled in the deep gloom of the tropical forests, the invaders beheld only that great bird of the Andes, the loathsome condor, which, sailing high above the clouds, followed with doleful cries in the track of the army, as if guided by instinct in the path of blood and carnage.

The crest of the Cordillera was at last reached, and Estevan, with the shivering Nicosia at his side, stood gazing at the mountains spread out in a bold and bleak expanse with scarce a vestige of vegetation, except dried grass. Below were rocks rich in gems, and mountains big with mines, for they were approaching the famous mines of Caxamalca. Nicosia was almost frozen. His warm blood was untempered to the rigors of the frigid zone.

The Spaniards pressed persistently on, surmounting every obstacle, and overcoming every difficulty. Envoys were met who tried to detain or turn aside the invaders; yet they pressed on down the eastern descent, until they arrived in the valley of Caxamalca, which, clothed with all the beauties of cultivation, lay like a rich and variegated carpet of verdure, in strong contrast with the dark forms of the Andes which rose on every side. Below, with its white houses glittering in the sun, lay the city of Caxamalca. Columns of vapor, a league further away, marked the place of the famous hot baths, so much frequented by the Peruvian princes. Along the slope south of the hills white pavilions covered the ground as thickly as snowflakes for the space of many miles. The city was comparatively deserted, for the Inca and his people were in their camp. It was the 15th day of November, 1532, during a storm of rain and hail, that Pizarro's little army entered the city in battle array.

Hernando Pizarro, Estevan, De Soto, Felipillo and a few others were sent as envoys to the Inca, who was encamped just outside the city with a vast army of men. When informed of the visit of Pizarro he said:

"Tell your captain I am observing a fast which will end to-morrow morning. I will then visit him with my chieftains. In the mean time let him occupy the public buildings on the square, and no others until I come, when I shall direct what is to be done."

Observing the wonder with which the Inca watched the fiery steeds, De Soto determined to exhibit his horsemanship before him. Giving his war-horse the rein, he struck his iron heel into its flank and dashed wildly over the plain; then, wheeling him round and round, displaying all the beautiful movements of his charger, he suddenly checked him in full career, bringing the animal to its haunches so near to the person of the Inca that some of the foam which flecked the sides of the charger was flung on the royal garments. But Atahualpa was unmoved.

Estevan, who had trembled with dread and apprehension at the feat of De Soto, was disappointed at the Inca's unconcern.

On reaching the city, Estevan was placed on guard duty. It had grown dusk, and Estevan was pacing to and fro, when he descried a slender form stealing toward him. He was about to challenge him, when he recognized Nicosia.

"Estevan," he whispered, "I have come to talk with you." Then, drawing nearer, he asked, "Have you learned the general's desperate plan?"

"No; what is it?"

"He has determined to seize Atahualpa to-morrow."

"How can he do that?"

"When the Inca enters the square, at a given signal we are all to rush upon him."

"It will be a desperate undertaking, for they are a thousand to one of us."

"I realize it. Let me remain by you, and if we must fall, let us die side by side."

He consented, and then, regarding the grave occasion as a fitting one for the unravelling of mysteries, he asked Nicosia to tell who he was. But he shook his head and heaved a bitter sigh.

"I cannot now—I cannot now!"

The awful night of November 15, 1532, closed on a scene of hushed excitement. Only the careful tread of the sentry, or some soldier breathing a prayer in whispers, broke the stillness.

CHAPTER XIX.

LATE in the night Estevan was relieved, and retired to his quarters; but he did not sleep. There
was something portentous in the whispering among
the officers of the army. Occasionally the rattling
of a sword, the tread of a sentry, or the murmur of
a sleepy soldier reached his ears; all seemed to fill
the coming morrow with dread. Estevan sat in his
quarters with Nicosia at his side, and, not feeling
inclined to sleep, prepared to pass the night in
watching.

"Can you not sleep, Nicosia?" he asked.

"No."

"Do you dread the morrow?"

"I fear some dread calamity will befall us, señor.
If it comes not to-morrow, it will not long delay."

"Is life so sweet that you dare not take the desperate chances of winning the jewels a king might
envy?"

"It is not that life is sweet, but that death is
awful," replied Nicosia. "I have little to hold

282

me to this world; but I dread that leap into dark futurity."

Estevan made no reply. He was strangely impressed by Nicosia's remark. His own life had been a checkered one; for the few bright patches of happiness there had followed broad stretches of misery. His mind naturally recurred to Inez. Had she arrived at Panama without sending him any message? Her long silence was sufficient to fill him with forebodings, and in his conjectures he concluded that her ardent love had consumed itself in its own warmth, and he was forgotten.

"This farce called life will soon be over," he thought. "To-morrow may see the end of it all." The night was well-nigh spent when he slept.

On awaking, he found the dark clouds of night passing away and the east growing rosy with light. At his side sat Nicosia, still awake and grasping his spear. Rising, Estevan gazed off to the east to witness perhaps the last dawn of day upon earth. It was Saturday, the 16th of November, 1532, a memorable day in the history of Peru. With the first streak of dawn, a blast of trumpets called the Spaniards to arms, and Estevan, rubbing the sleep from his eyes, saw the grim general Pizarro hurrying along the lines, posting the men, and briefly acquainting the officers with the plan of assault.

The public square, or plaza, in which the Span-

ish army was formed, and which it was understood
the Peruvian Inca would enter to meet the white
strangers, was defended on three sides by low ranges
of buildings, consisting of spacious halls, with wide
doors or dormitories opening into the square. In
these halls Pizarro stationed his cavalry in two
divisions, one under his brother Hernando, and the
other under De Soto. The infantry he placed in
another of the buildings, reserving twenty chosen
men to act with himself as occasion might require.
Pedro de Comedia, with a few soldiers and the artillery—two small pieces called falconets—he established in the fortress. All received orders to
wait at their posts until the arrival of the Inca.

Estevan was at the side of De Soto, mounted
on a powerful black Arabian steed, and on his left
was Nicosia on a white one. All waited with trembling anxiety and eagerness. Felipillo, with eyes
gleaming, hurried hither and thither, muttering
sometimes in Spanish and sometimes in his native
tongue,

"The hour of vengeance is come."

All had heard of the seizure of his bride by the
Inca and knew to what he referred. From his
post Estevan had a good view of the plaza.

"Do they come?" asked an impatient soldier in
his rear.

"No."

All waited in trembling silence. Hour after hour passed, until the sun reached the meridian and began its descent, and still the Inca came not. The soldiers became uneasy and restless, and began to murmur, but were not allowed to break ranks. Some began to fear that Atahualpa had discovered the design of Pizarro and had determined to not place himself in his power. Even the captain-general grew anxious. The middle of the afternoon had passed, when suddenly there came a whisper from the lookout on the watch-tower:

"*They come! They come!*"

As the news passed from soldier to soldier, every man became erect and the lines were dressed. The cavalrymen straightened up in their saddles, seized their lances and lowered their visors in a most determined manner. Some craned their necks to get a glimpse of the coming procession.

"I see them!" whispered Nicosia, who was well to the front.

"Are there many?" asked De Soto with evident concern.

"There seems no end to the procession."

"Do you see the Inca?"

"Yes, he is coming, borne high above his vassals on a throne of gold, in a palanquin lined with richly colored plumes."

With glittering splendor and nodding plumes

the vast procession filed into the plaza, opening to the right and left for the royal retinue to pass. Everything was conducted with admirable order, and while the monarch traversed the plaza he saw not a single hostile demonstration. Some five or six thousand of his people entered the place, and Atahualpa halted and gazed about him.

"Where are the strangers?"

Fray Vicente de Valverde, a Dominican friar, and chaplain to Pizarro, came forward, his Bible in one hand and a crucifix in the other, with Felipillo as his interpreter.

"I come by order of my commander," he said, "to expound to you, Inca of Peru, the doctrines of the true faith, for which the Spaniards have come a great distance to your country."

He then proceeded to discuss the doctrines of the Trinity, beginning with the creation of man and ending with the crucifixion and the ascension of Jesus Christ, when the Saviour left the apostle Peter as his vicegerent upon earth, which power had been regularly transmitted to the successors of the apostles, good and wise men, who, under the title of Popes, held authority over the powers and potentates on earth. He concluded as follows:

"The Pope now reigning has commissioned the Spanish emperor, the greatest monarch in the world, to conquer and convert the natives in this

Western Hemisphere; and his great general, Francisco Pizarro, has come to execute this important mission. I beseech you to receive him kindly, to abjure the errors of your own faith, and embrace that of the holy Catholic Church now proffered to you, the only one by which you can hope for salvation. Furthermore, I beseech you to acknowledge yourself a tributary to the emperor Charles V., who in that event will aid and protect you as his loyal vassal."

The eyes of the Indian monarch flashed fire, and his dark brow grew dark with indignation.

"I will be no man's tributary," he replied. "I am greater than any prince on earth. Your emperor may be a great prince; I do not doubt it when I see that he has sent his subjects so far across the waters; and I am willing to regard him as a brother. As for the Pope of whom you speak, he must be drunk or crazy to talk of giving away countries which do not belong to him. I will not change my faith. Your own God, as you say, was put to death by the very men whom he created. But mine," he concluded, pointing to the sun sinking behind the mountains for the last time on the glory of Peruvian power, "my God still lives in the heavens and looks down on his children. By what authority do you say these strange things?"

"By this book," and he handed the Bible to the

Inca.   Atahualpa, taking it, turned over the pages
for a moment; then, as the insult he had received
flashed more forcibly across his mind, he hurled the
sacred volume from him.

"Tell your comrades they shall give me an account of their doings in my land," he exclaimed.
"I will not go from here until they have given me
full satisfaction for all the wrongs they have com-
mitted."

Hastily picking up the book, the indignant monk
returned to Pizarro, and informed him of what had
been done.

"Do you not see," he added, excitedly, "that
while we stand here wasting our breath in talking
with this dog, full of pride as he is, the fields are
filling with Indians?   Set upon them at once; I
absolve you."

Every Spaniard was waiting with wildly palpitating heart the terrible onset.   Nicosia grasped his
sword nervously.

"The hour has come," he whispered to Estevan.
"See there!   Pizarro waves his white scarf in the
air—the signal!"

Estevan gathered up the reins and couched his
lance.

"Boom!" went the fatal gun from the fortress.

"St. Jago, and at them!" cried Pizarro, leaping
into the plaza.   Like one tremendous thunderbolt

the Spanish horse and foot burst into the square, and with the fury of a whirlwind threw themselves upon the astounded Indians. Stunned by the thunder of artillery and matchlocks, the echoes of which reverberated from the surrounding buildings, and, blinded by the smoke which rolled in sulphurous volumes along the square, they were seized with a terrible panic, and knew not where to fly. Indiscriminately trampled down by the fierce war-horses, cut right and left by flashing swords, and beholding horse and rider in all their terror, it is no wonder that they were helpless with dread. The avenues of escape were soon choked up with the dead bodies of men in their vain endeavors to fly. A breach was made in the wall and many escaped through it, while hundreds perished in their efforts to reach this only avenue of escape. Every sword grew redder with each successive stroke, and the great square was drenched with blood.

"Pruilla, we shall be avenged!" cried Felipillo, leaping at the Inca with upraised dagger.

"Let no one who values his life harm the Inca!" cried Pizarro, stretching forth his brawny arm to save the monarch's life. The dagger fell on his own arm, and Pizarro's was the only Spanish blood which flowed that day.

The struggle around the royal litter momentarily

19

became more fierce. It swayed and reeled like a
ship in a storm as the nobles supporting it fell beneath the swords and lances. Suddenly it was
overturned, and the Indian prince would have fallen
to the ground had not Pizarro and Estevan caught
him in their arms. A soldier named Estete
snatched from his temples the imperial *borla*, and
the unhappy monarch, strongly secured, was removed to a neighboring building, where he was
carefully guarded. A king had been seized by a
mere handful of adventurers, in the midst of his
army.

The Peruvians were too much overcome by the
attack to make much further resistance. Nearly
ten thousand had been slain, and the remainder
were humbled.

It was three days before Estevan recovered from
the terrible shock produced by the indiscriminate
slaughter. He and Nicosia were selected as guards
over the imprisoned king, and they did all in their
power to alleviate his sufferings. Pizarro, too, was
kind to him, and allowed his family to visit him.
But for the watchful care of the guards, Felipillo
would have satisfied his hatred by slaying the royal
prisoner. He forced his way into the harem where
he found his adored Pruilla, whom the Inca had
torn from his side. The joy of this meeting is
beyond description. Clasping the lovely Peruvian

in his arms, Felipillo exclaimed: "Peru has lost king, liberty, and glory, but I have gained more than all these—she who is the sunlight of my life."

One day Pizarro, fearing that his royal prisoner would attempt to escape, went to him and said: "Any effort on your part to escape, or on the part of your friends to rescue you, will force me to put you to death."

The wily captain knew that this would be communicated to the Peruvians all over the country. Bereft of crown and kingdom, the unhappy monarch felt that a terrible fate was settling about him. But amid all his woe, he evinced no little curiosity and interest in the strangers. One day he asked his guard how the Spaniards communicated by writing. Explaining as best he could, Estevan wrote the word "God" on the Inca's thumb-nail.

"That is the word God," he explained, "and any of our men can tell you the same by looking at it." A few moments later De Soto entered, the test was tried and he answered correctly. Nicosia came next and several others, and all gave a correct answer. Unfortunately for Atahualpa, Pizarro entered his prison-chamber, and he tried him with the test, but only a blank, expressionless stare was the answer. *Pizarro could not read.*

"Is it possible that the great captain has not the knowledge of a common soldier?" said the royal prisoner in a tone of contempt. Pizarro was sensitive on the subject of illiteracy or humble birth, and from that moment became a personal enemy of the Inca. Atahualpa was not long in realizing that he was hated by the captain, and began to fear for his personal safety. Knowing that Pizarro loved gold, he offered him a heavy ransom for his liberty.

"How much will you give?" asked Pizarro. "Will you cover the floor of this room?"

"I will not only cover the floor but fill the room with gold as high as I can reach," he answered, standing on tiptoe and reaching up as high as he could.

The apartment was about seventeen feet broad by twenty-two feet long, and the line indicating how high it was to be filled was nine feet from the floor, making five thousand three hundred and forty-six cubic feet of gold which Pizarro was to receive as ransom for the Inca. The gold, however, was to retain the original form of the articles in which it was manufactured, that Atahualpa might have the benefit of the space which they occupied. He further agreed to fill an adjoining room of equal size twice over with silver, for which he was to have his liberty.

Pizarro had no faith in his being able to accumulate such a fabulous amount of treasure; but the Inca sent orders to his vassals throughout the land,

and temples, public houses, and private dwellings of the rich were despoiled and the rich treasure came pouring in. Estevan, who received the gold and placed it in the apartment, was amazed at the exquisite workmanship of many of the ornaments.

Rumor reached the ears of the captive Inca that Huascar, his brother and rival, whom he feared and hated, was seeking to take advantage of Atahualpa's imprisonment and seize the Peruvian throne. Atahualpa became greatly alarmed and determined to do away with his brother. Accordingly Huascar was assassinated before Pizarro could interfere. The conqueror was very indignant at the assassination of Huascar, and boldly accused Atahualpa of instigating the crime. This the captive denied. All the while the treasure flowed in, and Estevan reported that the room would soon be filled with gold to the required height.

It was reported, about this time, that there was an uprising of Peruvian forces who were concentrating in the neighborhood of the city of Huamachuco. When accused of this supposed treachery, and also informed that the required amount of gold was still incomplete, the Inca was astounded.

"No one of my subjects would dare appear in arms or raise a finger without my orders," he declared. "You have me in your power. Is not

my life at your disposal, and what better security
can you have for my fidelity?"

A small party of horse, about twenty in number,
was sent to Huamachuco to ascertain if the rumor
of the uprising was true. Meanwhile, gold and
silver continued to pour in. Never, perhaps, was
there such an accumulation of precious metal. The
amount of gold still lacked three and a half inches
of reaching the nine-foot line, when again rumors of
an uprising in the interior reached the general's ears.
De Soto was ordered to take a party of cavalry and
to go and learn if there were any truth in the rumor.

"Send some one else!" plead the captive Inca,
on learning that De Soto, who had always been his
best friend since his captivity, was to be sent away;
but Pizarro heeded not his request and ordered De
Soto to prepare for the expedition.

The horses' shoes being worn out by the journey
across the Andes, and there being a dearth of steel
and iron, De Soto shod his horses with silver, which
was far more plentiful.

"Is he gone?" Atahualpa asked Estevan the day
after the departure of De Soto.

"He is," the guard answered.

"Then I am doomed," groaned the unhappy
Inca. "The only friend able to protect me has
been sent away, and the cruel Pizarro will now put
me to death."

In vain Estevan strove to rouse his drooping spirits. Believing himself the victim of the malicious Felipillo and his terrible master Pizarro, as well as an unrelenting fate, the Inca refused to be consoled. When Estevan was relieved, Nicosia, who had overheard his remark, came to Estevan.

"What the Inca says is true, señor. Pizarro will, on some pretext, put him to death."

After the departure of De Soto to Huamachuco to reconnoitre the country and ascertain what grounds there were for the rumored insurrection, the agitation among the soldiers increased to such a degree that Pizarro consented to bring Atahualpa to immediate trial. A court was organized over which the two captains, Pizarro and Almagro, presided as judges. The charges preferred against the Inca were drawn up in the form of interrogations, twelve in number. It was charged that he had usurped the crown and assassinated his brother Huascar; that he had squandered the public revenues since the conquest of the country by the Spaniards, and lavished them on his kindred and minions; that he was guilty of idolatry and bigamy and had attempted an insurrection among the Spaniards.

"The charges are unjust, and no fair trial can be obtained from them," declared Estevan.

"Why are they unjust?" Pizarro asked.

"Most of them are against the usages and customs of the people over which we have no jurisdiction."

"The judges must settle those questions," answered Pizarro.

"Defer, I pray you, the trial until De Soto returns."

"Wherefore should we?"

"That the Inca may have one powerful friend who will see to it that he has justice."

"De Soto is not in command," cried Pizarro so fiercely that Nicosia, becoming alarmed, led Estevan aside and implored him not to cross the general in his purpose, as he might incur his displeasure, and the hatred of Pizarro was something to be dreaded. The examination proceeded, and the trial was so manifestly unjust that Estevan again raised his voice in defence of the prisoner, and was surprised to find himself with considerable following. Atahualpa was found guilty and sentenced to be burned alive in the public square of Caxamalca. Father Valverde signed the death warrant.

Estevan was so open in his denunciation of the sentence that he very nearly came to blows with some of the opposing party. He tried to prevail on them to wait until De Soto's return, but was over-ruled.

When the sentence was read to the Inca he was greatly overcome by it. He asked to see Pizarro, and when the captain entered the presence of the royal prisoner, the Inca burst into tears.

"What have I or my children done, that I should meet such a fate?" he exclaimed. "And from your hands, too—you, who have met with friendship and kindness from my people, with whom I have shared my treasures, who have received nothing but benefits from my hands! Spare my life!" he piteously cried, "and I will give you any guarantee of safety that may be required for every Spaniard in your army. I have filled this room with gold, and I will fill it again; but oh! do not doom me to that horrible death!"

Pizarro was visibly affected, but he was not to be moved from his purpose. He had determined on the conquest of Peru, and that could not be accomplished while Atahualpa lived.

Estevan had roused the hatred of the conqueror and his followers, and nine-tenths of the army were against him. Discovering that he could do the unfortunate Inca no good, he bade him a tearful farewell, and, with Nicosia, went to another part of the city that he might not be a witness to the horrible sight. On the 29th of August, 1533, Atahualpa was led out in chains and fastened to the stake. In order to avoid the painful death of burning, the Inca professed to embrace Christianity, and his sentence was commuted to the milder form of the garrote, a mode of punishment by strangulation used for criminals in Spain.

A day or two after the tragedy, Hernando De Soto returned from his expedition, and was greatly astonished and indignant on learning what had been done in his absence. Estevan and Nicosia met the cavalier some distance from the town and told him of the death of the Inca.

"Will God forgive such a barbarous deed?" groaned De Soto, reeling in his saddle as if he had received a blow. He sought out Pizarro and found him with a great felt hat, by way of mourning, slouched over his eyes, and his dress and demeanor exhibiting all the show of sorrow.

"You have acted rashly," said blunt but honest De Soto. "Atahualpa was slandered. There were no enemies at Huamachuco; no rising among the natives. I have met nothing on the road but expressions of good will, and all is quiet. If it was necessary to bring the Inca to trial, he should have been taken to Castile and judged by the emperor. I would have pledged myself to see him safe on board the vessel."

"It was hasty," admitted Pizarro, "but I was deceived by Riquelme, the royal treasurer, and Valverde and others."

These charges soon reached the ears of the treasurer and the Dominican, who, in their turn, exculpated themselves and upbraided Pizarro to his face, charging him with the entire responsibility for the deed. The dispute ran high, and they were soon heard giving one another the lie. This vulgar squabble among the leaders, so soon after the event, is sufficient proof of the iniquity of their proceedings.

CHAPTER XX.

A BANQUET OF DEATH.

THROUGHOUT all the stirring events we have described there was ever uppermost in the mind of Christopher Estevan the memory of one sweet face in far-off Spain. What can banish the faces of loved ones? Perchance not even death can do it. By day and by night, through sunlight and gloom, he saw the sweet, thoughtful face of Inez. Her name he never breathed aloud, and those who were his constant companions little dreamed that her face was the guiding star and beacon light which cheered his footsteps across the rugged Andes.

Others had taken up the quarrel with Pizarro, and he did not again refer to the murder of the Inca, though it became painfully evident that Pizarro's dislike for Estevan was increasing every day.

"He hates you," Nicosia said one day. "He would kill you if he could."

"He dares not do that, Nicosia."

"He dares do anything to gain his selfish ends," Nicosia answered.

Estevan consulted De Soto on the growing antipathy of Pizarro toward themselves.

"He dares not harm us," De Soto asserted; "but
he will grow so reckless and bloodthirsty with
power that we will either have to forsake him or
our honor."

"Whither goes the army now?"

"To Cuzco."

"Who will be the next ruling Inca?"

"Toparca is the choice of Pizarro, and his choice
will fix the matter," answered De Soto. "Pizarro
is a shrewd knave, and knows that he who crowns
the king owns him; consequently Toparca is
selected."

"Do you know anything of this fellow Toparca?"
Estevan asked.

"Nothing whatever, though probably he has re-
signed himself without reluctance to a destiny
which, however humiliating in some points of view,
is more exalted than he could have hoped to obtain
in the regular course of events."

"When is the coronation to take place?"

"At once."

Within the very week of the above conversation,
Toparca was crowned according to the Peruvian cus-
tom, the imperial *borla* being placed on his head by
Pizarro.

De Soto was correct in his surmises; for the new

Inca was no sooner crowned than the Spanish invaders and their allies turned their attention toward
Cuzco. The soldiers were all in good spirits at the
prospect of doubling their riches. Almagro had
joined them with reinforcements, and they entertained little doubt as to success. Their numbers
had grown to be formidable, and by the disheartened
natives they were thought to be invincible. The
young Inca and the old chief Challcuchima accompanied the march in their litters, attended by a
numerous retinue of vassals, and moving in as
much state and ceremony as if they were the pos-
sessors of real power instead of puppets in the
hands of their conquerors.

They journeyed along the great road of the Incas, the like of which has never been known in the
world. They beheld the wonderful swinging
bridges, and all the beautiful ingenuity of a race
which had begun to fade from the earth. They
passed temples erected to gods unknown to them,
and which, in wonder, magnificence, and richness
of jewels, have never been surpassed. These the
ruthless invaders hesitated not to despoil of their
treasures. The road is to this day a thing of wonder. Sometimes it crosses a smooth valley, at
others it follows the course of a mountain stream,
flowing round the base of some beetling cliff, leaving small space for foothold.

It was a formidable passage for cavalry. The mountain was hewn into steps, and the rocky ledges cut the hoofs of the horses; and, although the troopers dismounted and led them by the bridle, they suffered severely in their efforts to keep their footing.

"Señor Estevan, have a care," cried Nicosia, as the young cavalier's horse nearly stumbled over into the awful depths below. "Dismount, I pray you, dismount as others have done, and lead your horse."

Estevan was forced to do so. They had not proceeded far before they came to where a deep torrent rushed down in fury from the Andes. This was crossed by one of those hanging bridges of osier, whose frail materials were after a time broken up by the heavy tread of the cavalry, and the holes made in them added materially to the dangers of the passage. Then the Spaniards were forced to make their way across on rafts, swimming their horses by the bridle.

"Do you suffer much from the cold?" Nicosia asked Estevan as they wended their way up the mountain.

"Not much, Nicosia; how is it with you?"

"My teeth are chattering again," he answered, as he drew his cloak closer about his shoulders.

"If these bleak winds penetrate our harness, how much more must the Peruvians suffer!"

"They do," he answered.

De Soto, who had been riding in the van, came back to the young cavalier as they neared Xauxa.

"We will meet opposition soon," he said. "You can see great bodies of Indians like clouds in the valley below. They are concentrating somewhere."

He was correct. They concentrated at Xauxa, where the invaders found the bridge destroyed, and were compelled to ford the stream. The enemy, in vast numbers, were drawn up on the other side to receive them. De Soto and Estevan led the cavalry at a charge, and, plunging into the water, with their terrible battle-cry, waded and swam across the stream, so disconcerting the Indians that they fled.

Pizarro halted a few days at Xauxa, and sent De Soto with a detachment of sixty horse, including Estevan and Nicosia, to reconnoitre the country. Drawing near the Sierra of Vilcacauga, they were informed by their scouts that a large body of Indians lay in wait at a dangerous pass in the mountains.

"What shall we do?" De Soto asked his officers, "wait for the infantry, or press on to Cuzco?"

"Press on to Cuzco," answered the impetuous Estevan, and every one agreed with him. They pushed on with their weary horses, and when they were fairly entangled in the rocky defiles, a multitude of armed warriors, with terrific yells, seemed to start from every nook and corner of the mountains.

"Holy Virgin preserve us!" cried Nicosia in an undertone, yet loud enough to be heard by Estevan.

"Santiago, and at them!" roared the steel-clad warriors of Castile. Like a mountain torrent the Indians rushed down upon the invaders, overturning men and horses in the fury of their assault, so that the foremost files rolled back on those below, spreading ruin and consternation in their ranks. De Soto in vain endeavored to restore order and charge the assailants. The horses were blinded and maddened by the missiles, while the desperate natives, clinging to their necks, heads, legs, and tails, tried to prevent their progress. Estevan cut down two who clung to his horse's head. Nicosia's steed stumbled and fell, and had not Estevan hurled himself between the fallen youth and his enemies, the former would have been run through with Indian spears.

De Soto saw that unless he gained the level ground which opened at some distance before him all would be lost. Cheering on his men with the old battle-cry, which always went to the heart of a Spaniard, De Soto struck his spurs deep into the sides of his maddened charger and shouted:

20

"Follow all who can!"

Like a thunderbolt he dashed upward, gallantly supported by his troops, and broke through the dark array of Peruvians, shaking them off to the right and left as a spaniel does the water from his sides, and finally succeeded in gaining the plateau. Here, as if by mutual consent, both parties paused.

"It has been a hard struggle," Estevan remarked.

De Soto wiped away the blood which flowed from a trifling wound in his face and turned to his men.

"Here is a stream of water; let your horses drink," he said.

"The Peruvians are all about us," panted one of the almost exhausted officers.

"They will fight no more to-night," returned De Soto. "Darkness is almost on us, and they will wait until light of day to renew the conflict."

Both parties withdrew from the field, taking positions within bow-shot of each other.

"Have we lost many?" asked Estevan, who had been so busily engaged in rescuing Nicosia that he had forgotten to note how the battle was going.

"Several cavaliers were slain, as well as some horses," answered De Soto. "One poor fellow was struck down at my side with a Peruvian battle-axe which clove his skull to the chin."

"Who directed this assault which came so near to being successful? It was no ordinary leader,

"FOLLOW, ALL WHO CAN!"

but evidently some one of considerable military experience."

"Doubtless it was the old Peruvian general, Quiz-quiz, and right well did he plan the fight; but we have nothing to fear. If we were able to beat off the enemy while our horses were jaded and our strength nearly exhausted, how much easier it will be to come off victorious when all are restored to strength by a night's rest. Trust in the Almighty God, who never deserts his faithful followers in their extremity."

Notwithstanding the faith and assurance of De Soto, his little band of brave followers, lying on their arms, within hearing of a powerful enemy, were by no means comfortable. Estevan was lying on the ground listening to the shouts of exultation of the enemy, who threatened to annihilate them on the morrow, when a small hand was gently laid on his arm, and a soft voice whispered:

"Do you fear to die?"

"No, Nicosia, though I would rather live, for I have much to live for."

"Should you fall in the coming fight, señor, and I survive, have you no message to send back to loved ones at home?"

"I have a father and mother in Cuba," he answered. "Tell them I did my duty as a soldier for my king and my God."

"And no other?"

"Yes, I have sisters and a brother in that far-off island; you can tell them the same, and that I never forgot them."

"Is that all? Is there none other in all this wide world to whom you would send a last parting message?" the youth asked, with a half-suppressed sob.

"Yes!" he gasped.

There was one—one who amid toil and danger was ever uppermost in his mind, and he was about to breathe aloud, for the first time, the name of Inez, when cliffs, crags, and peaks, echoed with the blare of bugles. The sleeping Spaniards were up in a moment, and, seizing their own trumpets, gave forth a blast in return. Pizarro and Almagro were hurrying on through the night to reinforce De Soto, whom they had learned was hard pressed.

The Peruvians, dismayed by the reinforcements, fled at early dawn without striking a blow. The victory was celebrated by mass with prayer and thanksgiving, and all went to Xauxa.

While at this town, the young Inca Toparca, the creature of Pizarro, suddenly and mysteriously died. Suspicion fell on the old general Challcu-chima, who was also accused of instigating the Peruvians to revolt, in order to secure his own freedom. In the vale of Xaquixaguana, a valley noted for its picturesque beauty and delightful climate, the army halted to bring Challcuchima to trial.

"Another act of cruelty will be perpetrated," said Estevan to De Soto. "Pizarro is more devil than man."

"Don't say more," interposed Nicosia. "It will only bring the hatred of Pizarro in full force on you."

Estevan promised his mysterious young friend to say no more, but he proved correct in his surmise; for the Peruvian general was condemned to death and burned at the stake.

Soon after this barbarous event Pizarro was visited by the Peruvian noble, Manco Capac, a brother of the unfortunate Huascar. He announced his pretensions to the throne and claimed protection of the strangers. In this new scion of the royal stock Pizarro saw a more effective instrument for his purposes than he could have found in Toparca, of the family of Quito, with whom the Peruvians had but little sympathy. Pizarro received the young man, therefore, with great cordiality, and assured him that he had been sent into the country by the king of Spain, in order to vindicate the claims of Huascar to the crown and to punish the usurpation of his rival.

With the young noble and his train they set out

at once for Cuzco, and, after another sharp skirmish
with the natives in the Sierras, pressed on until
late one afternoon the conquerors came in sight of
the object of their toils and hopes. The sun was
streaming in broad rays full on the imperial city,
where many an altar was dedicated to its worship.
The low ranges of buildings appeared like so many
lines of silver light, filling up the bosom of the
valley and the lower slopes of the mountains, whose
shadowy forms hung darkly over the fair city as if
to shield it from the menaced profanation.

The army camped near the city, the soldiers
sleeping on their arms, and on the following day,
the 15th of November, 1533, Pizarro, forming his
little army into three divisions, entered Cuzco. A
countless multitude of natives had flocked from the
city and surrounding country to witness the showy
and, to them, startling pageant. From their dazzling arms and fair complexions they believed them
to be real children of the sun. As Estevan and
Nicosia rode side by side down the narrow street,
they were amazed at what they beheld. The
splendor and wealth that abounded in the utmost
profusion bewildered them. They were lost in
wonder and admiration at the magnificent Temple
of the Sun, with its gardens and broad parterres
gleaming with gold. The exterior ornaments were
quickly removed by the soldiers, but the frieze

of gold, which, imbedded in the stones, encircled the principal buildings, remained.

Pizarro had issued a proclamation forbidding the molestation of private dwellings, but public buildings were regarded as objects of plunder, and their interior decorations supplied them with considerable booty. They stripped off the jewels and rich ornaments that garnished the royal mummies in the temple of Coricancha. No place was left unexplored, and many of the natives were tortured to make them reveal the hiding-places of their treasure. In a cavern near the city they found a number of vases of pure gold, richly embossed with the figures of serpents, locusts, and other animals. Among the spoil were four golden llamas and ten or twelve statues of women, some of pure gold, others of silver, all figures being life-size. Several of these were reserved for the royal fifth and sent to Spain in their original form, where they are preserved to this day in the royal museum. In one place they found ten silver planks or bars, each being twenty feet in length, one foot wide and two and three inches in thickness. The possession of this enormous wealth brought about a spirit of gambling among the soldiers, and with it a spirit of improvidence, to which the Spaniards owed much of the misery and trouble that followed.

A short season of rest and peace, very grateful

to Estevan and Nicosia after toilsome marches and conflicts, followed the entrance into Cuzco. Estevan had noticed that the spirits of Nicosia were drooping. Hardship, excitement, and bloodshed were too much for his young and tender nerves; he gave way to nervous prostration, and for days was unable to leave his cot. While the soldiers were gambling away their share of the booty, Estevan remained at the side of his young friend to nurse him back to health. One day when Nicosia was convalescent, De Soto came to the apartment.

"I have news for you," said the cavalier. "Manco is to be crowned on the day after to-morrow."

"And become another tool in the hands of Pizarro," put in Estevan.

"You speak truly, Estevan. I have become so thoroughly disgusted with the perfidious conduct of Pizarro, that I have resolved to quit Peru and return to Spain."

"You have some object in view, De Soto?"

"I will admit that I have. With Pizarro we have both won gold; but perhaps we have incurred the ill will of the general by stubbornly opposing his inhumanity. Why may not we lead the hosts of Spain to new conquests as well as Pizarro? I do not mean to usurp his power; but there are other fields as rich or perhaps richer than Peru or Mexico."

"Where?"

"Have you not heard of Florida, discovered by Ponce de Leon nearly twenty years ago, and which Panfilo de Narvaez sought to conquer, but failed?"

"Yes; but neither found cities nor gold in large quantities."

"But a soldier under Narvaez said they heard of a vast hill of pure gold. That hill or mountain in the north is worth more than Mexico or Peru. I shall leave the army as soon as practicable, hasten to Spain, and, with my wealth and influence, procure a commission to conquer that part of the new world called Florida. I want to be an explorer, a conqueror, and a colonizer. It is to the north and not the south of the New World that all Europe will one day turn their eyes."

"May I go with you, De Soto?" asked Estevan.

"You shall."

"And I too?" put in Nicosia.

"Alas, poor boy, have you not already had enough of hardship and toil?"

"If he goes, I also will go," was Nicosia's answer.

"It shall be as you say."

For a moment Estevan was silent, his eyes fixed on the strange youth; then, turning to De Soto, he said, "De Soto, I have one favor to ask. When you go to Spain, intercede for me that the hatred

of Velasquez may no longer keep me from those I
love in Cuba."

Nicosia started up from his seat and clasped his
hand over his heart, as if in pain.   Both gazed after
him as he averted his face and left the apartment.
De Soto promised to intercede for Estevan; but his
mind recurred to the Indian youth.

"He is no Indian; dark as is his skin, I believe
there flows the purest Castilian blood in his veins."

"He is a mystery," Estevan answered.

They were, at this point of their conversation,
interrupted by wild yells and rejoicings.   On looking out to determine the cause, they discovered .
that the natives were making all the hubbub over:
the announcement that Manco, the legitimate son
of Huana Capac, was to be crowned Inca.

"Everything will be done to maintain the illu-
sion with the Indian population," remarked De
Soto, as he viewed their antics of joy.   "Poor
fools, they are only tightening the shackles about
their wrists."

The young prince kept the prescribed fasts and
vigils; and on the appointed day the nobles, people, and all the Spanish soldiery assembled in the
great square to witness the concluding ceremonies.

"What hollow mockery!" thought Estevan, as
Father Valverde performed mass, and gave to Manco
Capac the fringed diadem of Peru.   The Indian

lords now tendered their obeisance in the customary
form, after which the royal notary read aloud the
instrument asserting the supremacy of the Castilian
crown, and requiring the homage of all present to
its authority, which ceremony was performed by
Inca and nobles, each waving the royal banner
twice or thrice with his hands. Manco next pledged
the Spanish commander in a golden goblet of
sparkling *chicha*, and the trumpets announced the
conclusion of the ceremony.

There followed another, far more interesting to
Estevan on account of its novelty. The accession
of the young monarch was greeted with all the
usual fêtes and rejoicings. The mummies of his
royal ancestors, with such ornaments as were still
left them, were paraded in the great square or *plaza
de royal*. They were attended each by his numerous retinue, who performed all the menial offices,
as if the object of them were alive and could feel
their import. Each ghastly form was seated at the
banquet-table—now, alas, stripped of the magnificent service with which it was wont to blaze at
these high festivities—and the guests drank deep
to the illustrious dead. Dancing succeeded the
banquet, and the festivities, prolonged to a late
hour, were continued night after night by the giddy
population, as if their conquerors were not en-
trenched in the capital.

With the seizure of Cuzco and the coronation of Manco, the subjugation of Peru was practically completed. That determined old warrior, Quizquiz, and a few followers continued to hold out in the mountains. Almagro, with a force in which were Estevan and Nicosia, was sent to disperse them.

Near Xauxa a terrible battle was fought, in which the Indians were routed and the brave old Quizquiz slain by his own warriors, which put an end to further resistance. During the hottest of the fight Estevan, with visor down and lance couched, charged into the thickest of the conflict, Nicosia riding at his side.

Suddenly the youth's light charger was seen to rear in the air, and Estevan heard a wild shriek, which, now undisguised, had to him a familiar sound. Nicosia's horse dropped dead, and he fell heavily on the ground. His casque, becoming loose, rolled from his head. In a moment Estevan dismounted and raised the insensible youth in his arms. The wave of battle swept on and left him alone with the insensible lad. He carried him to a brooklet, bathed his face, took off his breast-plate and tore open the doublette to give him air. Then he started back with a cry of astonishment.

Nicosia was a woman.

Estevan had always noticed something familiar in the manner and voice of the lad; but the shorn locks and slight disguise had imposed on him, as a stranger, his foster sister Christoval Balboa. The sounds of conflict rolled still farther away, leaving them alone in the forest. He proceeded to bathe her face and restore her to consciousness. When at last she opened her eyes, he spoke to her:

"Christoval, sister, I recognize you at last. Why did you disguise yourself and go with the army?"

"To be with you," she answered, no longer disguising her voice.

"You must return to Cuba at once."

"And you?"

"I dare not go until my pardon is obtained. Meanwhile I will wait at Panama or Darien."

"Cannot I go there also?"

"No, you have been too long from our parents; go to them with my blessing."

He kept her secret; at the first opportunity she was sent to Cuba; and a week later he sailed for Panama.

CHAPTER XXI.

THE SECRET MARRIAGE.

WITH a strange feeling of fear and hope, Christopher Estevan saw the town of Panama come in sight. Would he find Inez there? Was she still true to him, or had some other won her in his absence? Bay and shore loomed up to view; then fort and castle, and finally, rounding a point of headland, the whole town lay before them.

The deafening boom of cannon announced their approach, and from the fort came, in response, a succession of heavy shots, awakening the echoes of all the surrounding hills. The ship came to anchor, and cheer after cheer rang out on the air from ship and shore. There was the excitement and confusion usual on the arrival of a vessel, and boats put off from shore to learn the very latest from Peru.

Estevan landed among the first and was surrounded by scores of people eager to learn full particulars of that remarkable conquest of which they had only heard the wildest rumors. As soon as possible he rid himself of the questioners, and made his way to a small public-house, where he ordered food. The proprietor, a fat old Spaniard, as anxious to impart the information he had as to gain more, brought the refreshments, and, seating himself by the side of his guest, began a fire of questions.

"Where do you live?" was the first one.

"In St. Jago, Cuba," Estevan answered.

"Are you going there at once?"

"No."

"To Spain?"

"I do not know yet."

"Your plans have not been formed?"

"Not yet."

Then came a silence. The fat Spaniard poured for himself a mug of wine, and, drinking it off, resumed:

"Well, of course you know your business; but I should go to Peru."

"You have an excellent opportunity to go," Estevan answered.

"Ah, not at my age; but if I were a young fellow and not quite so stout, you know, I should enjoy nothing better than the land where so much wealth abounds."

"How long have you lived here?" Estevan

asked, to change the subject, and gain the information he so much desired.

"Nine years ago, señor, I came from old Spain. I was born and reared at Truxillo; yes, señor, right in the same town with Pizarro. I knew the rogue when a lad. He was naught but a swine-herd then; but, St. Anthony! see to what he has arisen."

Estevan cared nothing for the early life of his host, nor was he interested in the biography of Pizarro. His wish was to gain some information from the garrulous fellow without exposing his design.

"You must know almost every one in Panama?"

"Verily, señor, I do, and I saw Pizarro and Almagro both when they were here. Many is the time that they drank and ate at this board."

"Do you know Oviedo?"

"The chronicler who came with Ojeda to Darien, you mean? I know him right well, señor."

"I don't mean him, but his brother, Don Oviedo," explained Estevan.

"You refer to the rich hidalgo who came from Spain three or four years ago?"

"I do."

"I have seen him."

"Does he live here?"

"That he does."

"Where?"

"Come with me to this door, señor, and I will show you. Look at the castle upon the hill and you will see his place of abode."

He led Estevan to the door of the house and pointed out a castle which stood on a considerable eminence. Estevan returned to the table and the garrulous old Spaniard followed him, keeping up a lively conversation on every subject except that which interested his auditor. Without abandoning hope, Estevan continued to ply him with questions whenever he had an opportunity to do so.

"Does the old Don live alone?" he asked.

"Yes, alone."

"Quite alone?"

"Quite alone, señor, with no one but his servants and daughter, the Doña Inez; but if all rumors be true, I suppose they will not long live a lonely life."

"Why?" asked Estevan, his heart beating wildly within his breast.

"Why, I have heard that he is soon to have a son-in-law, the gallant Antonio Velasquez, nephew to the governor of Cuba."

Estevan bounded to his feet, as if his flesh had been pricked by a lance. He could not utter a word, and, to conceal his emotion, he hastened out into open air.

21

"Can it be true?—oh, can it be true?" he asked himself, as he hurried from the town. Reaching the outer gate he ran from it to the woods, and, sinking down upon a stone, covered his face with his hands. "What are all the honors and all the wealth won in Peru to me, now?" he groaned. "She for whom this treasure was earned and these laurels won is false. Inez, the only being whose love and esteem I crave, has changed with time. But, no, I will not upbraid her. There was, perhaps, a father's influence against me; and, doubtless, she did not know that I lived. Saint Anthony forgive me if I have wronged her!"

He turned his eyes upon the great, gloomy castle which stood near the summit of a cliff overlooking the sea, forming one of the impregnable strongholds of Panama. Perhaps Velasquez, his bitterest enemy, was even then at her side. The distracted lover wandered up the hill nearer to the castle, then returned to the town and sought, by mingling with the people, to forget. Why had fate played such cruel pranks with him? Why was he destined to meet her only to be plunged in misery forever after? Why was he not slain in the many hard-fought battles in Peru, or why had he not returned broken in health or impoverished in purse, as so many others had done? His vast riches and robust health seemed only to add to his misery. It was many days before he dared venture again up to the hill, or even beyond the walls of Panama.

A caravan was coming from Darien, and from the top of an eminence he made out the man riding farthest in the rear to be his enemy, Antonio Velasquez. He was coming, no doubt, to claim his bride. Estevan, hardly knowing what he did, ran down the hill to intercept his rival, who rode some distance in the rear of his companions. The cavalcade had disappeared over the brow of the hill when they met, and there was no eye but God's to witness the fierce encounter. A few wild words, and then the ready blades leaped from their scabbards; but Antonio was no match for one of Pizarro's battle-trained conquerors. His sword whirled from his hand, and his rival felled him by a blow. Estevan raised his sword to plunge it into Antonio's body; but, too proud to stab a fallen foe, he turned away, not knowing whether his rival was slain or only stunned.

An hour later a man, pale and covered with blood, made his way to a road-side cottage. He was too weak to explain how he had received the gash on his head. It was the wretched Antonio. The peasant who took him in knew him not; but, finding him weak and delirious, sent for a doctor of medicine to come and heal his wounds. Velasquez was near to death's door, and it was weeks before he could speak the name of his assailant.

When the first burst of passion was over, Estevan felt guilty of murder, for he had provoked the quarrel. Like a lost spirit, he wandered through the hills and forests seeking to excuse himself by the loose code of morals of that day for the assault, and, perhaps, the death of Antonio.

One day as he wandered through the forest, he came face to face with a Spaniard whom he recognized at a glance as his guide from Salamanca to Seville. The recognition was mutual, and the men advanced to greet each other.

"Many years have elapsed, and many great events transpired, friend, since we met; but I have not forgotten you, and once more allow me to thank you, good fellow!" cried Estevan, seizing the man's hand.

"Nay, nay, señor!—thank not me, for I but did the bidding of my mistress, the Doña Inez Oviedo."

Estevan started at the name as if he felt a sudden throb of pain; then, hardly knowing why, he asked, eagerly:

"Is she in yonder castle?"

"She is, señor."

"I would that I could see her! Does she know I am at Panama?"

"She heard of your arrival."

"Then she cares naught for me, or she would have sent me some word of welcome. What can she care for me? She is to wed my rival and bitterest enemy." He turned away to put an end to it all by returning to Peru, or sailing for Mexico. But, seized by some strange impulse, he wheeled about.

"Can I see her?" he asked.

"Does the señor wish it?"

"Yes."

"Then he can."

"When?"

"What time would suit the señor best?"

"Let it be at the earliest possible moment."

Despite all that had passed, he felt within his breast a strange hope arising.

"If the señor will be at the large stone called the Shadow Rock, at moonrise to-night, Doña Inez will join him there," said the servant.

Of course he would. There was something so friendly in the attendant's manner that Estevan grasped his hand, called him a good fellow, and went away, buoyant with unreasoning hope. As the moon was climbing the eastern mountains Estevan hastened to the Shadow Rock. He had not long to wait. Footsteps were heard approaching, and, with palpitating heart and trembling form, he stood

in the deeper shadows until he saw a slender figure,
enveloped in a dark cloak, coming, followed at a
respectful distance by a male and female servant.
He started along the path with outstretched hand, ·
murmuring the single word—

"Inez!"

"Christopher!"

He started, and stopped. She did the same.
Both hesitated for a moment, and gazed at each
other in the full gleam of the moonlight, and then,
casting aside reserve, jealousy, and everything
which had made life miserable, he sprang toward .
her, and clasped her in his arms. Before they:
were aware of it themselves, they were in the dense
shadow of the rock, where, free from the gaze of
others, they plighted anew their vows. She told
how she had all these years pined for him; she had
learned of his arrival; but, as he seemed cold and
indifferent, her pride would not permit her to say
that she was dying to see him. Why had she not
answered the letter left for her on his departure for
Panama? She knew nothing of his ever having
written such a letter. Some one had intercepted it.
Was it her father? No, he was not a cruel parent.
He had forbidden their marriage until Estevan's
trouble with the governor of Cuba was settled to
the young Spaniard's credit; but he was not a
personal enemy of her lover, and he would not

stoop to such mean actions as intercepting letters.

"Are you to marry Velasquez?" Estevan asked.

"No! How did such an absurd story ever reach
your ears?"

He blushed to admit that his credulity had no
other foundation than the report of a gossiping old
inn-keeper. Velasquez had been an occasional
caller at the castle on one pretence or another, which
had probably given rise to the rumor that they were
betrothed. She had never thought of him as a
suitor.

The meeting at the Shadow Rock was productive
of so much happiness that it was repeated again
and again, until the lovers scarce missed a night.
Estevan saw the old Don once, and urged him to
give his consent to their union. The hidalgo
listened to him until he had finished.

"Dare you return to Cuba?" he asked.

"No, señor, for I am unjustly charged with
treason."

"Then remove that charge and I will interpose
no further objection to your marriage with my
daughter."

"Father is unjust," said Inez, when Estevan
gave his answer. "Had he my happiness at heart
he would go to Cuba and investigate the matter
himself; then I know he would give his consent."

Estevan, finding the parent inexorable, began to urge her to consent to a secret marriage. He knew a priest who would perform the marriage rites and keep their secret. They might wait for long, weary years before the stain of treason was removed from his name, though he hoped that De Soto, who was now in Spain, would effect his vindication. But royal favors come slowly, and one as obscure as the young cavalier might wait long before his pardon came.

"If De Soto does not succeed, I will myself go to Spain and plead my own cause. Meanwhile, you need a stronger protector than your father, who grows more feeble every year. Give me the right as your husband to defend you!"

She yielded at last to his urgent entreaty. With only her trusty servants and two faithful friends, all sworn to secresy, they went to the small monastery at midnight, where Inez became the wife of Estevan. Then followed a long, sweet honeymoon in secret. Occasionally he was permitted to come to the castle; but they usually stole away for days together, and passed the time at the house of a mutual friend, or took short voyages in Estevan's caravel.

Thus more than a year glided by in blissful joy. Cheerful tidings came from Spain, calculated to inspire the hope that De Soto would yet succeed in restoring to the young husband all his ancient rights and privileges in Cuba. The marriage was still kept a secret, for neither of them dared brave the wrath of an angry father.

One evening, as Estevan strolled about Panama in the full glory of a southern moon, he saw a horseman riding a tired steed at a furious pace up the hill. Stopping his reeking horse directly before the young cavalier, he asked:

"Do you know one Estevan from Cuba?"

"I am he; what will you with me?" he asked.

"I have sad news for you, señor. Your father lies at death's door, and I am sent to fetch you secretly to Cuba. A caravel with a picked crew awaits at Darien and, by taking the nearest route, with good horses, and God and the saints willing it, we may cross the isthmus before another sun sets."

Dared he venture to Cuba? His father was dying. His mother and brother had sent for him, and he would brave all danger. While a servant was sent to bring fresh horses for the overland journey to Darien, Estevan wrote a letter to his wife explaining his sudden departure, and assuring her he would return as soon as possible. This letter was placed in the hands of their friend the priest, and, as the horses were ready, they hastened on their long, dark ride.

The isthmus was crossed, the caravel found, and,

boarding it, they sailed away to Cuba. Estevan landed in disguise on a wild shore, and was conducted by his younger brother to the home of his parents. His father was suffering and dying from the effect of old wounds received in Mexico. Hardship, wounds, and long exposure had undermined his vigorous constitution, and he was rapidly sinking. He yet had strength enough left to seize the hand of his son.

"Christopher, my son," he said, gazing into his face, "I leave you to complete the conquest!" He was too weak to say more.

His parents and relatives had heard good reports of his bravery in Peru. Christoval's adventures were known, also, to all the family, but were kept a secret. Estevan told no one of his secret marriage; for, until his wife gave him permission, no one was to know of it.

While at home, he was more strongly than ever impressed with the tender watchfulness of his foster sister Christoval. She became a self-constituted spy, always on the lookout for some of the governor's officials. Antonio had returned from Panama as soon as he was able, and spread a wild report of an attempted robbery and murder of himself by Estevan, whom he so maligned that all Cuba came to look upon him as an outlaw.

The father sank rapidly, and, four weeks after

the arrival of his son, died and was buried near the town of St. Jago. When the funeral obsequies were over, Christopher, who had lived all the while in concealment, took leave of his relatives and secretly departed for Panama. It was a dark night when he left his childhood's home. Christoval and his brother accompanied him to the shore where he was to embark. As he stood on the rocky beach, awaiting the boat which was to convey him to the vessel, he was left alone for a few moments with Christoval Balboa.

"Will you ever come back to Cuba to live again?" she asked in a voice which betrayed more bitter grief than if it had been drowned in tears.

"The saints grant that I may soon return, Christoval, and never be forced to leave you again!" he answered, clasping her to his breast, and imprinting a brotherly kiss on her lips.

Heavens! how she starts! how her heart gives one wild throb, and then seems to stand still! The rich, hot blood mantles her neck and face, while, gasping for breath, she seems about to swoon.

"Holy Virgin! Christoval, are you ill?"

"No, no, no; it is gone now. I am better—much better.

The boat ran up alongside the rocks at this moment, and the boatmen called to him to come aboard. He tore himself away from the brave girl who had risked life, health, and honor for him, was rowed away to the caravel, and taken back to Panama.

De Soto had meanwhile made his way to Spain, and, repairing to Valladolid, laid before the king his plans for the conquest of Florida. Charles V. granted his request, and the commission was given him. Being dissatisfied with the governor of Cuba, the ruling incumbent was removed, and Hernando De Soto appointed in his stead. The cavalier was already rich and powerful, but he longed for fame. While in Spain he married a lady of noble family. Mustering the finest army at Seville which had ever started for conquest in the New World, he sailed for Cuba, where he arrived late in the year 1538. Learning that Estevan, for whom he had obtained a pardon, was still at Panama, he dispatched a messenger for him.

Estevan was not informed by the messenger that a full pardon had been granted him by the king, nor did he know that he had received an appointment in the army of the new governor. The fact that he was invited to Cuba by De Soto was sufficient inducement for him to obey at once. He had a secret meeting with his wife, told her all, and hoped for the best. Then he bid her an affectionate farewell, little dreaming that months and years of toil, danger, and privation would elapse before he saw her again.

De Soto was at Havana, and thither Estevan repaired, where all his good fortune was explained to him, and he was urged to take a command in the two vessels to be sent out at once to explore the harbors of Florida. He was so grateful to his friend for having procured his pardon, and so anxious to engage again in an adventurous career, that he accepted the command. The vessels were to sail the next day, and De Soto declared that much of their future success depended on Estevan's immediate departure. That night Estevan wrote two letters; one to his wife, telling her of his pardon and restoration to good citizenship in Cuba, of his command in the army, and his immediate departure for Florida, a new conquest and the founding of a new empire. The other letter was to his mother. He told her of his first meeting with Inez in Spain, of their betrothal, of Velasquez, his own adventures in Peru, and lastly of his secret marriage. He concluded as follows:

"Don Oviedo will probably forgive us and accept me as his son; but whether he does or not, invite this new daughter to your home and care for her as you would your own. She will be lonely while I am gone; but I hope soon to return, laden with riches and honors as my father before me came from Mexico. Adieu!

"Your son,
"CHRISTOPHER ESTEVAN."

CHAPTER XXII.

AN INDIAN GIRL'S LOVE.

ESTEVAN'S ships reached Florida, and after coasting along the low shores and through waters that were safe enough for them to venture in, he, with a dozen men, went on land. They saw a few natives, who watched them shyly from the woods, but did not venture to come near them. Perhaps they had some recollection of the former visit of Narvaez, ten years before, and were suspicious. After some considerable trouble, Estevan managed to capture two of the natives, whom he sent back to Cuba in one of the ships, while he remained in the other at an island.

The Indian captives, on reaching Havana, were taken to De Soto, who conversed with them by signs, and interpreted their replies as affirming that Florida abounded in gold. De Soto and his troops were roused to the highest pitch of excitement, and all were eager to begin the voyage of discovery. The infection spread throughout Cuba, and volunteers came by the score from all parts of the island to engage in the enterprise. One Vasco Porcullo, an aged and wealthy man, lavished his fortune in magnificent outlay for the expedition.

Estevan still lay at the island, awaiting the arrival of the fleet, when De Soto, on the 14th day of May, 1539, sailed from Havana with nine ships, large and small, a thousand followers and many horses, cattle, mules, and a herd of swine, leaving public affairs at home in charge of his young wife. The parting was very affecting; for she seemed to realize that they were never to meet again; but De Soto, whose lofty mind was filled with ambition to become a Cortez or Pizarro, saw nothing but imperial cities and golden conquests in the future. Cortez had conquered Mexico; Pizarro, Peru; and he would seize the rich cities and wonderful mines in Florida.

Estevan had grown weary awaiting the arrival of the fleet when it hove in sight. He fired a gun and his crew shouted themselves hoarse. The entire fleet now sailed to Florida, and came to anchor in Tampa Bay, where the air was burdened with the most delicious perfumes, which came from the shores; for all Florida was in bloom. Such magnificent foliage, such rare exotics growing wild, such everglades and such wonders and delights of the floral world, had never before greeted the eyes of the Spaniards.

Next morning the disembarkation commenced. Estevan was first to go ashore. He had not met De Soto yet; but soon after he landed he saw the governor coming ashore with a boat's crew and a dozen soldiers, while three more boats, loaded down with armed cavaliers, were landing. Estevan went to a hillock where grew a tall palmetto-tree, and beneath its branches awaited the arrival of De Soto.

Having landed, the governor advanced to greet Estevan and gain the full particulars of all the information the officer had obtained. It was little the young cavalier had to impart.

"I found but few natives, governor, and those I did see fled before us. There is something decidedly menacing in their manner, and I fear they will make trouble for us."

"How can they, Estevan?"

"These deep, almost impenetrable everglades will afford many excellent hiding-places for them. There they can lie in wait and pick off our soldiers with their arrows; for they are expert archers."

"I will make it so terrible for them with our blood-hounds, that they will not dare to attack us."

"I pray you to forbear any act of cruelty," said Estevan, whose early training under the pious old Las Casas had a wonderful effect on his morals. "It is not only inhuman, but unwise, to attack the natives."

"One of the chief objects of this colonization scheme is to procure slaves, for the supply at Cuba and San Domingo is almost exhausted," replied De Soto. Estevan was about to enter a further remonstrance when De Soto suddenly led his mind to a more absorbing topic. "I have a surprise in store for you, Señor Estevan," he said.

"A surprise? What can it be?"

"As I was mustering my forces at Havana to embark, a new recruit presented himself, an old friend of yours. Can you not guess his name?"

"I cannot."

"The Indian boy, Nicosia."

"Mother of Jesus!" and Estevan staggered as if he had been dealt a blow. De Soto was amazed at his strange emotion; but not understanding the cause, he concluded that it must be the result of surprise. After a few moments, during which he regained his composure, Estevan asked where Nicosia was, and if he could be assigned to his command.

"Certainly," De Soto answered. "I expected you would make this request, and had already decided on the arrangement. You were inseparable in Peru, and I supposed you would be the same in Florida. Where has the Indian boy been since his return from Peru?"

"In Cuba, I believe."

"He has not been with you?"

22

Estevan shook his head in the negative.

"There is some deep mystery about this young fellow which I cannot solve."

"No more can I, governor. Let me have Nicosia with me as soon as possible."

Estevan had grown suddenly pale, and his form, never known to quake in battle, was now trembling like an aspen-leaf. Walking apart to himself, he thought over the strange matter.

"There is something strange and incomprehensible in this Indian blood. A race the origin of which is unknown, with thought, manner and passions all new to us, is bound to be a mystery."

Nicosia joined him. The same sweet, humble, loving face which had been his guardian angel in Peru had come to follow him through the wilds of Florida. Once more he felt the magic spell of those dark, watchful eyes, and her sympathetic care. The troops were landing their horses, cattle, mules, hogs and effects, and Estevan had a few moments' leisure.

"Come with me," he said.

Nicosia, with downcast eyes, and olive cheek much paler than usual, followed him down the path, through tropical forests, into the dense everglades, where he paused and turned suddenly on Nicosia.

"Christoval!"

"No! not Christoval. Remember that I am Nicosia," she answered. "Nicosia, the Indian boy."

"While in that garb you are to be known to all others as Nicosia; but to me you are Christoval."

A glad, happy light dawned on her face, and she gave utterance to an almost suppressed cry of joy.

"You must to others be Nicosia, the Indian boy, but I will not forget that you are my dearly beloved sister. Why did you come, Christoval?"

Turning those great, soft eyes, all beaming with impassioned, overmastering love, to him, she answered:

"I learned you had joined De Soto and knew you would be in danger, so I followed to be ever near. Were you hard pressed, my hand could defend you, and if you were wounded or sick, I might be at hand to nurse you back to life and health."

For a moment Estevan stood gazing at her, an expression of pain and wonder on his face.

"Did my mother tell you she had received a letter from me?" he asked, after a pause.

"She did not."

"Know you nothing of what that letter contained?"

"Nothing," answered the disguised girl, her

beautiful eyes wide opened in wonder. "Perhaps she received your letter after I disappeared to join De Soto at Havana. Did you write of me?"

"Yes," he answered, with a bitter sigh. "I could not forget my poor sister, who had dared so much to follow me through the wilds of Peru." He did not tell her all that letter contained; of his secret marriage to Inez, for some reason, he had not the power to tell her. "What am I to do with you now?"

"Nothing," she quickly answered. "Allow me to accompany you, and the army will not know but that I am an Indian boy. But for Nicosia, your body would have found interment in Peru."

"I owe my life to you, Christoval, and would be happy to grant any request you would make; but I cannot consent to your going on this dangerous crusade. De Soto will soon send the ships back to Cuba, and you must go with them."

She shook her head; but he was firm in his command, and, fearing that he might force her to return, she stole away the night before the ships sailed on their return to Cuba, and could not be found, having secreted herself in one of the deepest everglades. Estevan, though the only one who surmised the correct cause of her disappearance, was much alarmed, fearing she had been captured by some band of Indians. He asked De Soto's per-

mission to take a small party and go in search of
the supposed Indian boy. His request was granted,
and with a score of horsemen he set out on the
search, which was as dangerous as it was futile.
About a league from the camp of the Europeans,
a large party of Indians was discovered. At sight
of the steel-clad warriors mounted on those strange
awe-inspiring beasts, they let fly a shower of arrows
at them, one of which struck the breast-plate of
Estevan.

"Lower visors—charge!" cried Estevan. With
visors down and lances couched, they bore down
on the Indians, all of whom save one fled in terror.
That single savage fell on his knees imploring the
cavaliers by gestures and piteous cries to spare him.
Estevan's keen lance was almost at his breast,
when, suddenly, to the amazement of all, he cried
in the Castilian tongue:

"I am a Christian! I am a Christian! Slay
me not!"

"Saints be praised! Can it be true?" cried
Estevan, dropping his lance, leaping from his
saddle and seizing the hand of the poor wretch.
"Who are you?" he asked.

"I am Jean Ortiz, a native of Seville, and for
ten years I have been a slave or a wanderer in the
forest."

"How came you here?"

"I was one of the unfortunate Narvaez expedition."

"Have you learned the Indian tongue?" asked the young trooper.

"I have."

"Then you will be of incalculable value to Governor De Soto," and Estevan lifted him on his own horse, and, together, they returned to the camp.

While De Soto was interviewing the rescued captive, whose wild adventures would make a larger volume than this, Estevan went among the troopers enquiring after the missing Nicosia. To his joy, he found him in the camp. Now that the ships were gone and Christoval had no fear of being sent back to Cuba, she returned to become the guardian angel of him whom she so passionately, yet secretly, loved.

De Soto was ready to enter upon the conquest of Florida in earnest. His troops were clad in coats of mail to repel the arrows of the native archers, and they had, in addition, strong shields, swords, lances, arquebuses with match-locks, crossbows, and one falconet or small cannon. The cavaliers were mounted on one hundred and thirteen horses. Savage bloodhounds from Cuba were the allies of the Spaniards, and the Castilians were plentifully supplied with iron neck-collars, handcuffs, and chains for their captives. With these instruments of cruelty, a drove of swine, many cattle and mules, and accompanied by mechanics, priests, inferior clergy and monks, with sacerdotal robes, holy relics, images of the Virgin, and sacramental bread and wine wherewith to make Christians of the conquered Pagans, De Soto began his march, in June, 1539.

Estevan was given command of the advance-guard, and Nicosia, at his own urgent request, was permitted to ride at his side.

"We both would be much safer if you were in the rear," said Estevan, as the army pushed its way into the vast, unknown wilderness. "My anxiety for you will make me less careful for myself."

"No, no, no!" answered Nicosia with a vigorous shake of the head. "I cannot consent to go back to the rear. The anxieties and torments would drive me mad. At each halt I would think you unhorsed, or that some harm had befallen you. At each clash of arms borne by the wind to my ears I would believe you slain. No, no, if you would not drive me mad, allow me to ride by your side."

He interposed no further objections, and, side by side, they rode in the van. With so large an army and so many animals, their movements through a wilderness like Florida were necessarily very slow.

On the third day of their march, a few Indians were seen flitting about in the forest, which aroused the suspicion of Estevan. They pressed on, however, until they began to enter a narrow defile, when the Indians were seen in considerable numbers among the trees and rocks.

Estevan halted his small command, but before the advance could form, a shower of arrows was poured upon them. So sudden was the attack, that one poor fellow was wounded in the face before he could lower his visor, or cover himself with his buckler.

An arrow would doubtless have wounded Estevan, had not Nicosia interposed his own buckler and saved him. So sudden and unexpected was the attack, that for a moment the Spanish advance-guard was thrown into confusion, and, unable immediately to recover, fell back before the yelling foe. Discharging arrows and brandishing war-clubs, they pressed on the strange, steel-clad invaders. The confusion of the Spaniards was but momentary. Their leader had been trained on the battle-fields of Peru under such an indomitable spirit as Francisco Pizarro, and, giving utterance to the terrible war-cry of the Spaniards, he charged down on the Indians, with Nicosia at his side and his followers close in his rear. The plunging, snorting, neighing war-horses struck terror to the hearts of the savages, who fled in dismay. The natives, having been made intensely revengeful by the cruelties of Narvaez, ten years before, resolved to fight these new invaders until not one should remain on their soil. The law of retaliation, universal among savage and civilized people, was enforced to the uttermost. A Spaniard, when captured, was mercilessly tortured to death. The captured Indians were loaded with chains, without regard to age or sex, and made to bear burdens so large that they frequently fainted beneath them. Estevan, in the hope of ameliorating the condition of the invaders and Indians, interposed his advice for a more lenient policy; but De Soto had become hardened to scenes of cruelty under such infamous tutorage as Pizarro, and at first would not heed the wise counsel of his officer.

"They are treacherous, ungodly heathen," he replied. "They can be conquered in no other way than by extermination."

"But they are retaliating, governor, and are from everywhere concentrating against us. Follow the wise course of your predecessors in the conquests of the New World. Cortez and Pizarro, while they fought one tribe of natives, made another their friends and allies, thus dividing the enemy against themselves."

Moved by this sound advice, the governor decided

to try and form a treaty with Acuera, a powerful
Muscogee or Creek chief, whose territory he had
entered.   Estevan and Jean Ortiz were sent to invite
the cacique to a friendly interview.

With becoming dignity, the grim old warrior
met the embassy, and, after listening to their proposal, indignantly refused the overtures.

"No!   Others of your accursed race have, in the
years past, disturbed our peaceful shores.   They
have taught me what you are.   What is your em-
ployment?   To wander about like vagabonds from
land to land, to rob the poor, to betray the confiding, to murder the defenceless in cold blood.   No!
With such people I want neither peace nor friendship.   War—never-ending, exterminating war, is
all I ask.   You boast yourselves to be valiant, and
so you may be; but my faithful warriors are not
less brave, and of this you shall one day have
proof, for I have sworn to maintain an unsparing
conflict while one white man remains on my borders—not openly in the battle-field, though even
thus we fear not to meet you, but by stratagem,
ambush, and surprise."

"You do not comprehend the object of our visit.
Estevan returned.   "We are not come to extermi-
nate you, to enslave you, nor overturn your kingdom, but to ask you to yield obedience to the king
of Spain, and become his vassal."

At this, the haughty cacique became still more indignant.

"I am king in my own land," he exclaimed, "and will not become the vassal of a mortal like myself and no better. Small of soul and coward by nature must be one who submits to the yoke of another, when he may be free. As for me and my people, we prefer death to the loss of our liberty and the subjugation of our country."

"It is useless to try to make peace with him," said Estevan on his return to De Soto. "Acuera is prejudiced against the Spaniards, and will listen to nothing but war to the hilt."

Nicosia took Estevan aside and pleaded with him.

"Do not go to the cacique again! He may assassinate you, and then what would become of me, alone in this dreadful wilderness?"

For twenty days De Soto remained in the vicinity of the cacique, hoping to patch up some sort of a truce. Again and again he sent his ambassadors to the cacique with propositions for a treaty.

"Keep on! robbers and traitors!" cried Acuera. "In my province and in Apalachee you will be treated as you deserve. We will quarter and hang every captive on the highest tree."

The chief kept his word. Fourteen Spaniards were slain while in his province, and some who were taken captive were horribly mutilated.

"I will begin the war of extermination at once," declared De Soto, one morning, on finding a sentry dead. "It has grown so that we hardly dare post a sentry anywhere. The treacherous, cunning savages creep upon the unwary soldier and slay him when he least expects a foe near."

"They can beat us at extermination," Estevan answered.

"Why so? Have they better arms?"

"No; we are superior to them in arms, discipline, and courage, but they have the advantage in numbers. While we cannot afford to spare half a score, they can lose half a million."

"We cannot make a treaty; then we must fight," said De Soto.

Cutting their way through hostile tribes, the Spaniards reached the fertile region of Tallahasse, where they encamped for the winter. Estevan erected a small log hut for Christoval. Her sex was, of course, kept a secret from all. While he loved and respected her as a very dear sister, her gentle bosom was stirred by a stronger and deeper emotion.

"Sister, if you would let me send you away out of this danger, I could pursue the journey through the trackless wilderness with actual pleasure."

"I would be miserable anywhere else," she answered.

There was such a look of meek appeal in those tender eyes, such an expression of consuming love, that the awful truth began at last to dawn upon the foster brother, and, turning aside, he groaned in pain.

"Saint Anthony preserve me! am I responsible for this?"

An expedition sailing westward in De Soto's ships to explore the coasts, returned in February to report that the skeletons of the men and horses of the Narvaez party had been discovered. The commander was ordered to return to Cuba and bring supplies to Pensacola, whilst De Soto should march across the country to the same point. De Soto was about to break up winter camp and go in that direction, when a rumor of gold in the north reached him. He also heard of a beautiful Indian maiden who ruled over a large country, and he decided to await her visit before leaving his present location.

CHAPTER XXIII.

THE FATHER OF WATERS.

DE SOTO had suffered so sorely from the continued attacks of the Indians, that he was anxious to make any sort of a treaty which promised to secure him an ally. The friendly visit of the queen's embassadors filled him with hope, and on the morning she was expected, he had his troops drawn up in military order to receive her.

"She comes! she comes!"

A whisper ran through the camp, and all eyes were turned eagerly toward the river from whence the dusky friend, who was expected to share their toils and dangers, was to come.

In a richly wrought canoe, filled with shawls and skins and other presents for the wonderful men who had come to their shores, the dusky cacia glided across the river.

Leaping ashore with a nimble grace, she advanced toward the governor, who came to meet her. She was no doubt amazed at the great man, clothed in shining steel producing a hollow clanking sound at every tread.

"I come to welcome the great pale men from the far-off country," she said. To this, De Soto, through his interpreter, answered:

"I come from my monarch, who is a great king living across the ocean, to offer you my services, and to assure you, if you will but become his vassal, he will protect and defend you against all your enemies."

After this formal greeting, presents were exchanged. Those she had brought in her canoe were fetched and laid at the feet of the conqueror.

"SHE COMES!"

She wore about her neck a magnificent string of pearls. Drawing this off over her head, she timidly advanced toward the great governor and hung it about his neck, saying, as she did so, "Wear this, great warrior, in token of your regard for me."

That he promised to do, and then she invited him and his followers to cross the river to her village. Estevan was in another part of the camp when news reached him that the army was going to cross the river and accept the bounteous hospitality of the Indian queen. Every canoe and raft was already secured, and he found that he and Nicosia would have to remain on this side unless their ingenuity could devise some means of crossing.

"Can you swim?" he asked her.

"I cannot," she answered.

"Are you afraid to trust yourself with me?"

"I am not."

"Then we will seize a floating log. You get on the log with our arms and armor, and I will swim and push it along before me to the other side." He procured the log and Christoval Balboa took her place upon it with weapons and armor, and he began propelling it across the stream. Their horses swam over, led by the bridles by cavaliers who were fortunate enough to secure canoes.

Having crossed the stream, the Spaniards encamped in a beautiful valley in the shadows of some mulberry trees, where they received a bountiful supply of turkeys, venison and maize. The Indian queen became very much attached to the Spaniards; but De Soto, disappointed and angry at finding no great cities or gold, ill repaid her kindness. Estevan grew disgusted with his commander, and could not but contrast his conduct as a governor-general with his gentle manner as a subaltern.

"Men who make agreeable soldiers may become tyrants as rulers."

Early in May, the Spaniards determined to leave

the new territories, and De Soto seized the gentle queen.

"Why have you done this wicked act?" Estevan asked.

"I am in command," was his answer.

"Your conduct will make her our enemy."

"The Indians are already our enemies, and their queen I shall retain as a hostage for the good behavior of her people toward the Spaniards."

Day by day Nicosia watched the beautiful queen and noted how sad she looked. Too proud to weep over her afflictions, she traveled in silence, keeping her eyes on her captors in a savage, defiant manner. Nicosia, who had learned something of the Indian tongue, went to the unfortunate captive one evening after the army had halted.

"Beautiful queen, are you so unhappy that you fade like a flower plucked from its stem?

"Who could be happy when a captive, borne far away from people and friends?"

"I will give you your liberty if you will be very cautious."

"I know the meaning of the word. Who are you? You are not a white lad, and yet you are too fair to be an Indian."

"My mother was an Indian, my father a Spaniard."

That evening while all the camp, save the sen-

23

tries, were buried in slumber, Nicosia released the queen and, carefully conducting her beyond the lines of her enemies, bade her go to her home, which she did, and was ever after a bitter enemy of the white people.

The direction of the march was to the north; to the country of the Cherokees, where gold is now found, but which was then unknown in that region. It is seldom that the heart of man is thoroughly attuned to the circumstances of the scenery around him. How often do we need to struggle with ourselves to enjoy the rich and beautiful landscape that lies smiling in all its freshness before us! How frequently does the blue sky and calm air look down upon a soul darkened and shadowed with affliction! And, on the other hand, how often have we felt the discrepancy between the lowering look of winter and the glad sunshine of our hearts! The outward world in harmony with our inward thoughts is the purest as well as one of the greatest sources of human happiness. Estevan had seen the grandeur of the Andes, the floral wonders of Florida, and was now to behold the Alleghanies in all their grandeur; yet he was out of tune with nature, and not calculated to enjoy the feast of beauty spread before him. His thoughts and anxieties were divided with the wife at home, whom he had so suddenly left, and the sister who had more than a sister's affection and anxiety for him.

Though reason acquitted him of any wrong to Christoval Balboa, yet he felt within his breast an accusing spirit rise. "I might have foreseen it all. I might have been more discreet, and yet I never regarded her as other than a sister." Never did a brother more tenderly and conscientiously watch over and care for a sister than did he. She occupied almost as much of his thoughts as the beautiful wife from whom he was wandering, day by day, further and further into an unknown wilderness.

De Soto did not cross the mountains so as to enter the basin of the Tennessee, but passed from the head waters of the Chattahoochee to the head of the Coosa River. Then, for long months, the Spaniards wandered about in the valleys which send their waters to the Bay of Mobile. No gold had been discovered in any great quantities; but the Indian guides continued to point in various directions where it might be. Being aggravated by continual disappointments, De Soto at last turned the guides over to be torn to death by the dogs.

Estevan was sent with an exploring party to the north; but they halted, appalled by the aspect of the Apalachian chain, and many who were along declared the mountain impassable.

"What can lie beyond?" Estevan asked, as he gazed on the mighty range.

"Don't try to discover it," whispered. Nicosia, who had a mysterious, superstitious dread of those great walls of stone reared like barriers to heaven.

"Why?"

"It seems as if hell would be only across those rocks."

The party sent to discover mines and gold came back with a buffalo-robe as their only trophy.

In the latter part of July, the Spaniards reached Coosa. In the course of the season, they had occasion to praise the wild grape of the country, which grew in the fertile plains of Alabama, and has since been thought worthy of cultivation. A southerly direction led the train to Tuscaloosa, and in October the wanderers reached a considerable town on the Alabama, above the junction of the Tombigbee, and about one hundred miles, or six days' journey above Pensacola. Here, one of the most bloody Indian battles that was ever fought on the soil of the present United States occurred, and but for a timely charge of Estevan's cavalry, De Soto would have been slain. Eighteen Spaniards and twelve horses were killed, and one hundred and fifty men and seventy steeds wounded; while almost all the Spaniards' baggage was destroyed by fire.

Ships from Cuba soon after arrived at Ochus; and

the governor could have returned in them; but, although no tempting stores of gold or silver had been accumulated, the stern old Spaniard determined to wander north in quest of that hill of gold of which the natives had told him. Winter came on them, when the Chickasaw territory, now Mississippi, was reached, and they went into winter quarters on the west bank of the Yazoo River in the small town of Chicaca.

At the approach of the whites, the Indians deserted their cabins, leaving a wealth of maize standing in the fields, and an abundance of dried venison and turkeys.

Through the severe winter of 1540 and 1541 Estevan devoted his spare time to looking after the comfort of Nicosia, so much so that his affection for the Indian boy became a matter of comment among the soldiers. Even the stern old governor, who had become moody and silent from disappointment, could not but mark the attention of the young cavalier. The best apartment possible was secured for the young Indian, and Estevan insisted on cutting his wood and making his fires.

Gloomy, despondent and disappointed, the Spanish governor sat in his quarters, day after day, during the long winter. Within his soul he felt creeping the shadow of failure. While Cortez and Pizarro were enjoying the fruits of their conquests, he had as yet met nothing but hard blows. No city, no rich country, no gold! The winter was severe, and the Spaniards did well to find such excellent shelter as they had. When March came, De Soto determined to push on, and demanded of the Chickasaw chief two hundred men to carry the burdens of his company. The Indians hesitated. Human nature is the same the world over. Like the inhabitants of Athens in the days of Themistocles, or the Russians of Moscow, the Indians determined to destroy their own dwellings, hoping by the act to forever rid themselves of a dangerous and powerful enemy, who threatened their liberties. At least they would not permit the hated whites to occupy their homes.

It was midnight, and Estevan, unable to sleep, sat by the side of his cot. His coat of mail, with greaves and buckler, hung from a peg on the wall near by. Suddenly there came on his ears a strange crackling sound, while to his nostrils was borne the odor of burning wood. Starting to his feet he donned his armor and seized his sword as if impressed that he was soon to undergo some trying ordeal. At this moment a yell as if ten thousand devils had suddenly been turned loose made the earth tremble.

"The Indians! the Indians!" he cried, beating wildly on the door of Nicosia's room. "Awake,

Nicosia!—Christoval, awake! The Indians have attacked us!" he cried.

He heard her, bewildered and terrified, running about in her room. The wild yells and the roar of flames were now accompanied by the thundering strokes of Castilian halberds. The battle raged hot without and the smoke and flames made it suffocating within. Estevan broke down the door, burst into the apartment, and seized the affrighted girl in his arms.

"Christopher, we will die together," she calmly and sweetly said, turning her dark eyes in proud defiance upon the raging flames which enveloped the house. No thought or hope of escape was entertained by Christoval, and she welcomed death if it would unite her with him whom she loved with all her passionate soul.

"Don't despair, Christoval; we can escape," he cried.

"No, no, no! I can die happy if I die in your arms," she answered wildly.

"Sister, this is folly. You must, you shall live!"

Then, in the wildest desperation, he kicked down the front door, and, with his left arm about her slender waist, his good Toledo blade in his right hand, he literally hewed his way through the masses of enemy to a slight eminence where the Spaniards were assembling. Had the Indians acted with calmness and bravery, they might have gained a decided victory, for the Spaniards were taken completely by surprise; but the wretched Chickasaws, trembling at their own success, dreaded the unequal combat against weapons of steel. Many of the horses had broken loose; these, terrified, without riders, roamed through the forest, and seemed to the ignorant natives the gathering of hostile squadrons.

Estevan, reaching the rallying Spaniards, left Christoval in a place of security and caught and mounted one of the loose horses.

"Ho! Estevan!" cried De Soto. "Rally the scattered forces; sound our battle-cry, and at them!"

The Indians, appalled at a foe which seemed to rise phœnix-like from the flames, fled in dismay.

Several horses and eleven Spaniards, including a soldier's wife, with most of the hogs, perished in the flames, and, what was equally unfortunate to the Spaniards, most of their clothing was destroyed, and the bleak, chilly winds of March penetrated the thin covering they wore.

"Let us turn back," said one cavalier, who stood with chattering teeth and shivering form, clothed only with an Indian robe.

"Never go back!" the indefatigable governor

answered. "I will find a land the equal of Peru or perish in the wilderness."

From some captives, the Spaniards had heard of a vast river to the west, but like all other stories, they had come to doubt the truth of it.

"They seem the incarnation of lies," De Soto declared, "and one can believe nothing they say."

"Let us go in the direction of the river for a few days," Estevan suggested.

"Why so? Why explore for rivers?" demanded De Soto. "It is not rivers but gold we came to seek."

De Soto little dreamed that he was to make a discovery of far greater importance in the future than either Cortez or Pizarro—men whom he died envying. His discovery would last when theirs' had in a measure passed away. The glory of the Montezumas and Incas has faded forever, their vast wealth in gold and silver has disappeared, and Mexico and Peru have dwindled to insignificant powers; while the great discovery of De Soto sweeps majestically on to the sea, and will to the end of time.

The remainder of the inclement season was passed by the Spaniards in wretchedness. Cold, hunger and grievous wounds tortured them, and the Indians fell on them night after night, like fierce tigers. Estevan, in the sudden flight from the burning camp, had only been able to snatch a few articles of clothing for Christoval, and she had not enough to keep her from suffering.

"Take my doublette," he said, giving it to the shivering girl, who trembled with cold at his side."

"No, no! Keep it for yourself!"

"My coat-of-mail will keep me warm," he answered. "If it should not, the exercise of fighting day and night will not allow me to freeze."

"Heaven grant that warmer days and more peaceful scenes may dawn for us soon," she murmured.

It was with difficulty that he persuaded her to accept his doublette. March passed away, and with it the cold, bleak winds and distressing rains. April came, warmer and brighter, to alleviate the sufferings of the Spaniards, who moved in a northwestern direction, in search of the land of gold of which they had dreamed so long. The trees, lately bare, were clothed with verdant foliage, while shoots of tender green from out the sodden ground bore evidence that the queen of the spring was spreading her carpet over the earth and breathing her breath on the gale.

The march might have been pleasant, but for the constant harassing assaults of the Indians. At an Indian town called Alibona they found a large body of natives drawn up to dispute their progress.

A desperate battle was the result, which, for a short time, seemed doubtful. The Spaniards were astounded at their own weakness, and, although De Soto gained the victory, he was unfavorably impressed with the increasing stubbornness of the Indians. Of a captive taken in this battle he asked the oft-repeated question for gold. The Indian pointed to the northwest.

"Not three days' journey from here," he said, "you will come to a mighty river. By crossing that river, the white men, after a great many days' journey, will come to much gold." The Spanish governor was now as anxious as he had formerly been indifferent to reach the wonderful river. It was about the 17th of May, 1541, that the army, wending their

DE SOTO.

way out from the hills just below the Chickasaw bluffs, came in full view of the great Mississippi, the Father of Waters. After gazing on the river, Estevan turned to De Soto and said:

"Next to Balboa, you are the greatest discoverer Spain has sent to the New World. Here is a river which drains a mighty continent."

The Spaniards were guided by the natives to the usual crossing, the lower Chickasaw Bluffs. A vast multitude of savages turned out to gaze upon the strangers of whom they had heard so much. At first they showed some inclination to resist; but, aware of their own weakness, they brought loaves of bread made of the persimmon, and dried fish for the strangers.

De Soto took great precaution to guard against surprise. His forces had been so considerably reduced, that he no longer felt an abiding confidence in his army. At night Estevan went to the tent of the governor and found him gloomy and despondent. He was making a map of the country, and writing a journal of their daily progress.

"I am glad you came, Estevan," he said, "for I want to talk with you."

When his visitor had seated himself on a buffalo-robe, the governor continued: "I feel very much discouraged to-night."

"Why should you be discouraged, governor?" Estevan asked.

"Why should I be discouraged? Saint Anthony! friend, can you realize that my expedition is going to prove a failure?"

"I cannot, as it is already a success."

De Soto shook his head.

"No, it is a failure. While Cortez and Pizarro

have discovered rich cities, I have found nothing but Indian hamlets filled with a cunning, treacherous foe. They gained priceless riches, but no gold has come to my coffers. Cortez found Mexico and her wealth; Pizarro conquered Peru and her gold; but what have I discovered to perpetuate my fame?"

"A vaster country than theirs." Estevan answered. "A land that will some day be the richest and greatest nation on earth, and a river capable of floating the navies of the world."

The eyes of De Soto gleamed for a moment with hope; but the light slowly faded away as his mind interposed objections to the glory with which Estevan's predictions would crown him; and, with a sad shake of the head, he resumed:

"No, the success of the Spaniard can only be measured in gold."

"It is not so with other parts of the world," Estevan asserted. "It may not be so in the future, when everything may be valued according to actual benefit to man. The forests and plains we have traversed will some day be fields of waving vegetation, and the bread for the world may grow in this land. Then the name of De Soto will be perpetuated long after Pizarro and Cortez are forgotten."

CHAPTER XXIV.

THE WANDERER FINDS REST.

THE natives at this point of the Mississippi were quite friendly, and when they learned that the white men wished to cross the great river, they offered their boats and personal services. The canoes of the natives were too small and frail to transport the horses, and the river too broad to think of swimming them; so almost a month expired before barges large enough to hold three horsemen each were constructed for crossing the river. At last the Spaniards embarked, and were borne to the western bank of the Mississippi.

The country southwest of the Missouri was then occupied by the Dacota tribes. De Soto had heard the country so much praised, that he supposed it the vicinity of mineral wealth, so he resolved to visit its towns. With longing eyes they pressed on and on in the delusive hope of catching a glimpse of some Caxamalca, and day by day hoped that the rising or setting sun might throw its rays on the glittering spires and towers of a Cuzco with temples to despoil and altars to desecrate; but, alas, they were ever doomed to disappointment. "Hope deferred maketh the heart sick," and as day after day and week after week went by with only the long, endless stretches of prairie and woodland in view, De Soto's heart sank within him. He grew more silent, and, in his despair, pressed on, as if determined to make some great discovery, or carry his decreasing band beyond human reach.

In ascending the Mississippi, they were often obliged to wade through morasses. At length they came, as it would seem, upon the district of Little Prairie, and the dry and elevated lands which extend toward New Madrid in Missouri. Here the Spaniards were worshipped as children of the sun, and the blind were brought in their presence to be healed by these sons of light. "Pray only to God for whatever you need," De Soto told them.

The pecan nut, the mulberry, and several species of wild plum furnished food for the wanderers. At a place called Pocaha,* somewhere in the State of Missouri or Kansas, the Spaniards halted forty-five days. This marked the extent of their northward

---

* This place was evidently in Livingston County, Missouri. In 1889 Mr. Goben, near Spring Hill in Livingston County, Missouri, found, in the ledge of a cliff, some images and plates with inscriptions on them, which, by good authority, were supposed to have been the property of De Soto's missionaries.

march.   Estevan, with a small party, went a little
further northwest, to find only endless stretches of
prairie, but thinly populated and with the bisons
roaming over the plains.   Then came long, weary
months of wandering over the plains in every direction which the imagination of the Spaniards or
caprice of their leader would indicate that gold was
to be found.   Estevan and Nicosia had but one
horse between them, which carried their arms and
baggage, while they trudged along on foot, close
behind the grim chieftain, who walked at the head
of his diminished army.   Their numbers were
constantly reduced by sickness and famine.   Some
favored returning; others were for pressing on to
Mexico and joining Cortez.   They found the natives a little further advanced in civilization than
on the eastern side of the river.   They were an
agricultural people, with fixed places of abode,
subsisting on the products of the field rather than
the chase.

The condition of the Spaniards was now growing
desperate.   The sixth of March, 1542, found De
Soto on the Washita River, in what is now known
as Paul's Valley, Chickasaw Nation, Indian Territory, north of Red River.*   By following Red

---

* There is a species of wild swine in this part of the
Indian Territory, said to be descended from the herd of
De Soto, some of which escaped him at this place.

"THEN CAME LONG, WEARY MONTHS OF WANDERING O'ER THE PLAINS."

River, on the 17th of April they came to the Mississippi River. On asking if there were settlements below, De Soto was told that the lower banks of the Mississippi were an uninhabited waste. Unwilling to believe such disheartening news, he sent Estevan, with eight of his horsemen, to descend the banks of the Mississippi and explore the country. For eight days Estevan pressed on through bayous and almost impassable cane-brakes, being able to advance only about thirty miles. The report was received by De Soto with anxiety. His horses and men were dying around him, and the natives day by day became more bold in proportion to the weakening of his ranks. At Natches, the governor tried to overcome the chief by claiming a supernatural birth and demanding obedience and tribute.

"You say you are a child of the sun," the undaunted chief replied. "Dry up this river and I will believe you. Do you desire to see me? Visit the town where I dwell. If you come in peace, I will receive you in good faith; if in war, I will not shrink from you."

"Alas, I am no longer able to punish the temerity of these savages," De Soto groaned, on receiving this insulting reply. The governor's stubborn pride was changed by long disappointments into a wasting melancholy, and only a few evenings later Es-

24

tevan found him in his quarters burning with a malignant fever.

"Governor, you are ill! What do you wish?" he asked.

"To return to New Spain, to see my wife again; but that can never be."

"Cheer up, governor; you must not despair."

"Estevan, my friend, I thank you for the encouragement you try to give; but it is of no use. We have fought our last battle, conquered our last nation, and made our last discovery together. I want all who can to return to Cuba and report this country as boundless. As for me, I shall not live to advance a single league. Bring my officers to me for a last council."

They came, and he named Moscoso as his successor. All night long Estevan and Nicosia watched by his bedside. He became delirious, raving of cities of gold, mountains of pearls, and rivers of blood. When he called the name of his young and beautiful wife, in his more lucid intervals, his watchers were melted to tears. Shortly after sunrise he sank into a comatose state from which he never rallied, dying at noon on the 21st day of May, 1542. His death was kept a secret from the Indians, and for a long time it was a serious question how they were to dispose of the body. Moscoso ordered him to be buried secretly

at the gateway in the camp, and gave it out that
he had gone up to Heaven, but would soon return.
The suspicions of the Indians, who had seen him
sick, were aroused, and Moscoso ordered him to be
disinterred at midnight. He was taken in a boat,
wrapped in his finest robe, and sunk in the great
river which he had discovered.

The enterprise was now in its fourth year, and
nothing but disaster had followed it from the beginning. It was decided to seek Mexico by land,
rather than reach Cuba by such wretched vessels as
they could procure; but after another half a year
spent in wandering through wilderness and prairie,
they returned once more to the Mississippi, reaching it a few leagues below the mouth of Red River,
where they erected forges, and, with every bit of
available iron, proceeded to make brigantines.
Horses and hogs were killed, and the flesh dried
for food, and in July, 1543, they were ready to
begin the voyage home.

Going home! What a world of joy the thought
brought to Estevan! In the last terrible three and
a half years he had expended his ambition to become a great explorer. Away from home and
wife, from mother and scenes of peace, with Christoval a constant care upon him, no wonder he
longed to go home!

Christoval had borne up well under the hardships

of the long and fatiguing march. During the tedious voyage of over five hundred miles down the Mississippi she maintained the same wonderful fortitude. She was gay and sad at intervals, as hope and despair caused her spirits to rise and fall. Estevan would watch her for hours, studying the varied emotions stirring the gentle soul of the Indian girl, asking himself how this was to end. He dreaded the awful fate to which they seemed helplessly drifting. Often she detected his gaze and read its meaning by his sighs and silence. At such times she would press her hands across her breast as if to keep back the bitter, jealous thoughts, and turn away, afraid to trust herself longer.

The Gulf of Mexico was reached, and the brigantines carefully hugged the shore, dreading to launch out on the voyage to Cuba. One evening, as Estevan, wearied with the toils and anxieties of the day, reclined upon some skins in the forecastle, gazing at the stars and moon just rising o'er the deep, he heard a light footfall, and Christoval, with whom he had not been able to speak for three days, stood at his side. Turning his eyes upon the sad, sweet face, he bade her be seated, at the same time making room for her at his side. All the while he felt a strange premonition that something he had all along dreaded would result from this interview. For a moment the girl's face beamed with hope and joy.

"Sister," he whispered, "we will soon be home again, and the joy at my own safe return will be insignificant compared to the knowledge that I shall be able to restore you to our mother."

"To your mother, not mine," she quickly interrupted, with a sigh of pain. "O Christopher, Christopher!" she gasped in uncontrollable agony, "I must speak, or my heart will break. Why keep up this miserable farce longer? I am not your sister, and the same blood flows not in our veins; but I love you," she whispered hysterically.

The avowal almost took away her breath, and Estevan trembled. She regained her speech, and with her southern blood on fire resumed:

"For three days I have been banished from your presence. I know not during that period if the sun has shone, or the sky smiled. My sky and sun were hidden from me, for I live only in the light of your eyes. Am I too bold? Do I breathe that secret which the modesty of my sex should keep locked in my heart? Alas, I must, for in you alone can I find sympathy and hope. We have traversed mountain wilds and forest glades together. Side by side, we never faltered or failed each other in the thickest of the battle. It is no ordinary affair, but one of happiness or misery which prompts me to speak."

"Speak boldly, Christoval, and I can promise

you my sympathy," he sadly answered. Though
not much encouraged, she continued:

"Even were I of the humblest mould, the spirit
of your nature has entered my soul to ennoble, to
sanctify, to inspire. But I am not one for whom
you should blush. In my veins flows the gentlest
blood of two proud races. My mother was a princess and my father a Spanish cavalier of the best
blood of old Castile; am I one of whom any one
should be ashamed?"

"The Holy Virgin can testify that you are not,
Christoval. You are one of whom the greatest in
the world might well feel proud."

As his trembling hand seized hers, Christoval's
heart gave a joyous bound, and she felt as by a
sudden revelation that those feelings which she had
so long and innocently cherished were love. Alas,
there was only a brotherly touch in that grasp, and
even as she trembled with hope, her heart grew
heavy. For a moment her maidenly modesty was
crowded into the background by the wild prompt-
ings of her heart, and in a voice almost choked
with emotion she went on:

"Forgive me, Christopher, for this bold, unseemly avowal. Have you been so blind all along?
Will the scales never fall from your eyes, that you
may see me as I am, and as I should be? It may
be wrong in an Indian girl to love one as great as

you, but how could I help it? From the hour I was snatched from the fangs of the bloodhound I learned to admire you and look on you as my protector. My happiest childhood days were spent wandering hand in hand about the coast and forest with you. When you left for Spain I experienced my greatest heartache, and on your return my most supreme joy. When you went to the strange, far-off southern land, infested by foes on earth and in air, I followed you. You remember well that no battle ever raged too hot, and death and danger were never too near, to keep me from your side. My own breast was often bared to the darts of the foe, that my buckler might screen you from danger. And when you went to the unknown land of the north, I was at your side, with no higher wish than to die for you. Estevan! Estevan! are you so blind as to not know what motive impelled me to deeds so unbecoming one of my sex?"

Her breath was exhausted, and she paused to await his answer. He was under the gunwale in the deeper shadow, so that his features could not be seen. What would Christoval not have given at that moment for a ray of light upon his face, to have watched the effect of her speech, to have seen the sudden burst of ripened love, to have worshipped with more than Persian adoration the rising of that sun which her credulous soul believed was to break upon her dreary night?

Estevan's heart was full, and for a few moments the bitterness of his soul checked the utterance of his speech. Never did a sympathizing judge announce the sentence of a condemned prisoner with more bitter regret than he replied to the girl whom he loved as a dearest sister.

"I have known for some time, Christoval, that no sisterly love, however great, could prompt one to undergo the trials and hardships which you cheerfully assume. No Castilian maiden of this modern age, be her love ever so great, would don the buskin, sword, and buckler, and march to the field of battle. Such events belong to the ages of the past. Your conduct has been unbecoming, yet, knowing, as I do, what prompted it, I am happy to freely forgive you. Nor have I forgotten that you have in your veins the blood of this aboriginal race, whose thoughts and emotions are all strange to us; but you are an angel, Christoval, the dearest sister man ever had. For your happiness I would willingly lay down my life; but you can never be more than a dear sister to me—I—I—have a wife at Panama."

She neither shrieked nor swooned. She leaned for support against the gunwale, and her cheek, flushed to scarlet but a moment before, was now of the color of death, while her slender fingers were convulsively entwined about each other, her eyes were on the deck, and she scarce seemed to breathe. Doomed to return to Cuba—doomed to take shelter under his roof—doomed to breathe the same air—and doomed, in the first rush of an awakening hope, to learn that he loved another, to realize that she was of a race far below him, to feel all at once the utter nothingness which she was—which she ever must be, but which, till then, her young mind had never realized. What wonder that, in her wild and passionate soul, all the elements jarred discordantly; that, if love reigned over the whole, it was charred and blackened by a heated blast of despair.

Estevan was shocked at her silence, at the awful pallor of her face, and the glassy stare of her eyes. He sprang to his feet, and, seizing her in his arms, breathed her name three or four times in his low, impassioned tones without receiving any answer.

"Christoval, sweet sister! your misery makes my existence a hell," he murmured. "Won't you, for my sake, speak. Only one word, say you forgive me."

It was a hard struggle for her to appear calm; but her stoical Indian nature came to her aid, although she was not able to entirely repress the fluttering of her heart.

"Christoval, you shall always be my sister, and,

next to my wife, receive my warmest love and sympathy. Listen, I am rich, and all that I have shall be shared with you, and all that can be done shall be done to make you happy."

At last she grew quite calm and sat at his side a long time, making him tell her of Inez, as if she were interested in her. She had him narrate his romantic career in Spain and his secret marriage in Panama over and over, as if she took pleasure in the story. Then he persuaded her to retire to the little cabin which he had prepared for her in the after part of the brigantine.

It was all over, and Estevan felt a sense of relief. She had borne the blow much better than he had feared she would. Then his mind wandered away to other scenes, and Christoval was, for the time being, forgotten. The cavalier lay on his back gazing at the moon soaring high in the heavens, and thought that the same moon shone on loved ones at home. Almost four years had elapsed since he sailed from Cuba. What changes might have come in that time? Were his wife and mother still living? Had the proud old don forgiven them for the secret marriage which had brought so much misery to poor Christoval? Despite all reasoning to the contrary, he felt guilty at not having told her of that marriage. Had he done so all this misery might have been averted;

but he hoped for the best, and, as he lay gazing at
the moon and far-off stars, he began weaving happiness for his beloved Christoval. He could, he
would yet make her happy.

Care and sleepless toil overcame him. His eyes
grew heavy and closed; he slept, while the brigantine glided slowly on amid the calm and silence of
a peaceful night. When all save the drowsy helmsman were hushed in sleep, Christoval silently rose
from her berth, and, softly stealing to the little
door, opened it and glanced out on the deck. No
one was in sight, and she emerged silently, and,
gliding to where Estevan lay, bent timidly over
him and kissed his brow and lips, while a tear fell
on his cheek. Brushing it gently away, she fell
on her knees, and, with her great, dark eyes up-
turned to Heaven, prayed:

"Holy Virgin, thou mother of Jesus, who doeth
all things well, bless Estevan in his sacred love!
Dear, dear Estevan, may you ever be happy with
your beloved one! And may you sometimes have
a tender thought for the poor, unfortunate Indian
girl, who, like her despised race, is of no further
use on earth."

She rose and stole away along the deck, keeping
under the shadow of the gunwale that the eyes of
the man at the helm might not see her. Then, in
the darker shadow of that cabin which had been

erected by him she loved, she paused and leaned
far over the side of the vessel. The glad waves
leaped upward as if eager to kiss her heated brow,
and the gentle breeze played with her hair. She
carefully put back those silken tresses, and, raising
her eyes to God, murmured in her tenderest ac-
cents:

"Thou great, divine Ruler, forgive me. It is

"Estevan—Farewell!"

better thus! I could not
endure it; this jealous
madness would destroy
my soul and his happi-
ness. I cannot see him
caressed by another,
him, whom I was so fool-
ish as to believe all my
own. How calm and
peaceful those waters
look! how inviting, O
placid sea, are your dim-
pled waves! When they
roll above the troubled
breast of poor Christo-

val, then will she be at peace. Estevan, earth,
sky, moon and stars, a last farewell!"

The helmsman heard a splash, and, looking out
across the side of the vessel, he saw a ripple in the
waves fast drifting astern. There was no cry, no

struggle, and, supposing it but the splash of a playful dolphin, he made no investigation of the incident. The craft sped merrily on, while the beautiful daughter of Vasco Nuñez de Balboa sank beneath the waves forever.

CHAPTER XXV.

ONCE more to St. Jago we must invite the reader. A brigantine has entered the peaceful harbor and dropped anchor. There are few demonstrations of joy as the battle-scarred, gray-visaged veterans land and make their way from the seashore to the town. Their haggard visages and weather-beaten features tell a frightful story of suffering and hardships in the wilderness. The news had reached Cuba of the death and strange burial of De Soto. Wild stories had been borne on the breeze, as it were, of battles with all manner and form of man and beast in the wilderness. Tales of suffering and heroic devotion, which would have harrowed the soul of the bravest and brought tears to the eyes of the strongest, were recounted.

One of these strange stories which soon became current, not only in New Spain, but all over the civilized world, was the narrative of a young Indian boy named Nicosia, who was strangely attached to Estevan, one of De Soto's favorite officers. Those

382

who had known the quiet youth never tired relating his heroism and devotion to the man whom he loved, and how he had often saved his life at the risk of his own. The story-tellers went on to relate that one night on the voyage across the gulf, Nicosia mysteriously fell overboard and perished. The captain over whom he had so long been a guardian angel knew nothing of his death until next morning, when he wrung his hands in the bitterness of his grief and wept for the lost one. That was all. Nicosia's secret was securely kept, and no one ever thought of connecting the lost Indian boy with Christoval Balboa.

Estevan was one of the crew of the brigantine. As he ascended the hill, he seemed a score of years older than when, four years before, he bade adieu to wife and relatives, to depart with the governor to the subjugation of Florida. A settled melancholy had come over his face, and he felt as one who knew that his race had been run, as one whose life had been clouded with some deep sorrow. He had but just landed, and, as yet, had heard nothing from home. He knew not who would greet him in that beautiful mansion where he had left his loved ones.

Tidings of the arrival of the returned explorers spread like wildfire through the town soon after their disembarkation, and people everywhere turned out to gaze upon the wildly-clad, half-starved survivors, as they wandered about the streets in quest of friends and relatives whom they once had known. Estevan had passed the limits of the little city when he met the first face familiar to him. It was his brother Philip, now grown to a great, stout man.

He called to him; but it was several moments before Philip could recognize in the sun-browned, battle-hardened, weather-beaten veteran, the handsome brother of a few years ago.

"Brother! Christopher!" Philip cried at last, rushing to his brother and clasping him in his arms.

"Does mother live?" he asked as soon as he could command his voice.

"Yes."

"I must see her at once, brother—only to bid her adieu, however, for I must hasten to Panama."

Philip gazed at him for a moment with a look of sorrow and amazement. He began to say something, to interpose some objection to his brother returning only to take his leave, when Estevan put an end to it all by commanding him to lead the way to his mother at once. Philip went before him, and, on reaching the portals of the old-fashioned Spanish house, called to his mother who was within, and announced the welcome news, the arrival of his brother.

"Christopher! Christopher!" cried a matronly

woman, rushing to the front apartment, to meet him, and clasping the battle-scarred wanderer in her arms.

Her cry of joy, and the name "brother," "Christopher," had reached other ears. A heart, beating more fondly than a mother's, leaped with joy at the glad news, "Christopher has returned." There was a joyous cry, and a moment later the portières of another apartment were thrown aside, and a young and beautiful woman sprang forward to entwine her arms about his neck, and, in a voice brimming over with love, to exclaim:

"Christopher! Husband! The Holy Virgin be praised that you are once more restored to me."

Amazed at this wholly unexpected reception, the cavalier was for a moment dazed; but after an effort he gasped:

"Inez!"

"It is I, your wife."

She gently drew his bearded face down to her and pressed kiss after kiss upon it.

"I—I only stopped here to learn of you from mother. I was to stay but a moment and then hasten to Panama. I—I little dreamed I would find you here!" he stammered.

"Then it is indeed a glad surprise for you," said his mother, who stood smiling at the happy bewilderment of her son.

25

"A glorious surprise, indeed, mother. This is the greatest hour of my life. But how did it all come about? I can scarce believe that it is not a dream from which I will awake to find myself back in the wilderness of Florida. Come, explain, for I am all eagerness."

The wife and mother vied with each other in ministering to his wants. They made him take the most comfortable seat, and with one on either side he listened to the explanation he had so eagerly demanded. The mother, on receiving his letter informing her of his secret marriage, made a visit to Panama to this new daughter and assured her of her love and sympathy. The old don was terribly enraged at first on learning of the secret marriage; but in a few months he became reconciled to it. A year and a half later the father died and Inez was easily persuaded to take up her residence with her husband's mother at Cuba until her husband returned. Here she had lived ever since, as happy as she well could be while his fate was unknown. At times they had given him up for dead; but when they began to mourn him as no more, a rumor reached them from that mysterious, far-off land that he still lived and would return. With an abiding trust in a kind and all-wise Providence they waited and lived in hope, reconciled to the inevitable.

When the story was finished and they had listened in part to his wild adventures, the mother, seeking an opportunity to speak with her son alone, asked:

"Where is Christoval?"

"Alas, mother, she is no more. The sea has claimed her, and I pray you to never again mention the name of that noble but unhappy girl."

His mother understood him better than any other could, and kept his secret. Never afterward was the name of Christoval mentioned. Her life and mysterious fate was the only secret which Estevan never shared with his beloved wife. Through the long, happy years that followed, he was at times haunted by that sweet face, and often sighed in silence, or brushed a tell-tale moisture from his eye as memory recalled that last sad night at sea.

When the mother had been informed of the fate of Christoval, the wife once more came to claim her husband, and, with her arm lovingly about his neck, she whispered in his ear:

"I have still another surprise for you."

"What greater surprise can you have than I have already enjoyed."

"Come with me and you shall see that this one is the most happy of all."

She led him softly through the cool, darkened

rooms, where tapestried curtains, gently rustled by the breeze, seemed to hint at sweetest slumber. At last they paused in a dainty chamber, where stood a bed hung about by the finest of curtains. With a happy smile on her face Inez advanced and parted the curtains.

"Behold your son!"

Before Estevan's vision there appeared the daintiest, downiest bed he had ever seen, on which was a sleeping child, three and a half years of age. For a moment Estevan, who had never before dreamed that he was a father, gazed like one entranced upon that sweet young face, and asked himself if it was reality or some pleasant dream; while the happy wife and mother smiled in her joy upon his confusion.

In the noble features and brown, curly hair, clustering about the chubby face, Estevan saw the reproduction of his own image. It was several minutes before he had recovered from the surprise sufficiently to speak or move. But soon he regained himself and clasped his wife in his arms, tears raining down his weather-beaten cheeks.

"Inez, why did you not tell me of this before?"

"The surprise was too pleasant to be revealed by others. I wanted you to make the discovery."

"This joy is too great; my cup of happiness is full to the brim."

"BEHOLD YOUR SON!"

Stooping over the sleeping infant, he pressed on its soft young cheek the first fatherly kiss. Within his heart there was born a new emotion, a new love, to which every one but a parent is a stranger His voice was low and husky, his eyes moist, and the stern warrior was all tenderness and joy. As he gazed on the sweet young face of his sleeping babe, did his prophetic soul read the future of a long line of noble Americans who were to occupy conspicuous places in the future history of an unborn nation?

THE END.

HISTORICAL INDEX.

	PAGE
Alcalde Mayor, Encisco as.	25
Arms of Balboa's army.	36
America, how named.	55
Arrest of Cortez.	66
Arbolancha, Pedro de, sent by Balboa to Spain.	72
Acla, Balboa at.	81
Armament of Cortez.	105
Aguilar found by Cortez.	105
Artist of Montezuma.	130
Ahualco, Sierra of.	151
Ajotzinco, halt at.	155
Approach of Montezuma.	161
Ayllon arrested by Narvaez.	170
Andes, Spaniards crossing the.	269
Atahualpa receives Pizarro's envoys.	279
Atahualpa enters the plaza.	285
Attack on the Inca.	288
Atahualpa seized by the Spaniards.	290
Atahualpa's offer of ransom.	292
Atahualpa's trial.	295
Atahualpa executed.	297
Arms and armament of De Soto.	343
Attack on De Soto's advance.	344
Acuera and De Soto's embassadors.	346
Apalachian chain reached by Spaniards.	355
Albonia, battle of.	362

391

PAGE

Bovadilla's plots to ruin Columbus...................   3
Balboa, Vasco Nuñez de...........................   4
Bachelor Encisco lends Ojeda money for expedition..   7
Balboa arrested for debt..........................   12
Balboa in the cask...............................   18
Balboa discovered................................   20
Balboa deposes Encisco...........................   26
Balboa deposes Nicuesa March 1, 1511.............   29
Balboa at Coyba..................................   30
Balboa departs for conquest of Ponca.............   37
Balboa sets out for Comagre......................   39
Balboa learns of the great South Sea.............   41
Balboa's search for the "Golden Temple."...   43
Balboa's commission..............................   47
Balboa sets out to find the unknown ocean...........   48
Balboa's conduct inquired into...................   75
Balboa arrested by Pedrarias.....................   77
Balboa recalled to Acla..........................   85
Balboa arrested by Pizarro.......................   86
Balboa executed.....   90
Bachelor Encisco has Pizarro arrested at Seville...... 225
Battle at Xauxa.................................. 304
Battle at Tuscaloosa............................. 356
Burial of De Soto................................ 371
Castilla del Oro.................................   1
Columbus, Don Diego..............................   2
Cortez, Hernando.................................   4
Carthagena, Encisco touches at...................   21
Colmenares.......................................   26
Carrol favors dispossessing Nicuesa..............   27
Careta, chief of Coyba...........................   30
Coyba, conquest of...............................   31
Careta captured..................................   31
Comagre's dwelling...............................   40
Comagre and his sons baptized....................   42

PAGE

Commission sent to Spain to report South Sea....... 47
Cuba, conquest of by Velasquez..................... 57
Cortez a conspirator............................... 64
Cortez captured at the church...................... 67
Cortez conciliates the governor.................... 71
Codro Micer, astrologer............................ 83
Cortez married..................................... 91
Cortez a planter................................... 92
Cortez appointed to the conquest of Mexico......... 96
Cortez, hearing of the governor's double dealing, re-
    solves to sail at once........................ 100
Cortez, description of, at the time of the conquest.... 104
Cortez at Cozumel.................................. 105
Cortez enters the valley of Mexico................. 151
Chinampas (floating gardens)........................ 157
Cuitlahuac, halt at................................ 157
Cuitlahua, Montezuma's brother..................... 157
Cortez at the gateway.............................. 160
Cortez meets Montezuma............................. 162
Cortez sends a friendly message to Narvaez......... 173
Cortez's speech to army at the "River of Canoes".... 176
Cortez attacks Narvaez............................. 180
Caleza discovered and rescued...................... 211
Cortez meets Pizarro in Toledo..................... 228
Charles V. affected to tears by Pizarro's story........ 231
Cordilleras, the................................... 269
Condor, the, of the Andes.......................... 278
Caxamalca, city of................................. 278
Cuzco, march to.................................... 302
Challcuchima and men accompany Spaniards to Cuzco 302
Challcuchima suspected............................. 308
Challcuchima burned at the stake................... 309
Cuzco, Spaniards enter............................. 310
Coricaucha, temple of.............................. 311
Coosa, Spaniards at................................ 356

PAGE

Chickasaws defeated by De Soto..................... 360
Darien, Encisco at................................. 25
Dobayba, tradition of............................... 43
Dobayba conquest of............................... 44
Discovery of the Pacific Ocean...................... 52
Duero de Andres 94
De Soto, Hernando................................. 264
De Soto meets the envoy at Caxas.... 273
De Soto sent to Huamachuco........................ 294
De Soto attacked on the mountain pass............. 305
De Soto appointed governor of Cuba................ 332
De Soto sails from Havana for Florida............. 335
De Soto and the Indian queen...................... 351
De Soto hears of the Mississippi................... 361
De Soto discovers the Mississippi.................. 363
De Soto at Pocaha................................. 367
De Soto on the plains.............................. 368
De Soto's illness and death........................ 370
Embarkation of Ojeda.............................. 11
Encisco beats up for recruits....................... 14
Encisco, Bachelor, sails for Darien................. 18
Encisco's, Bachelor, rage at Balboa................ 20
Encisco returns to San Domingo.................... 26
Embarkation of Cortez............................. 101
Escudero hung.................................... 134
Epidemic in Pizarro's army........................ 258
Envoys to Atahualpa.............................. 279
Fulvia, Careta's daughter and Balboa's Indian wife.. 32
Fulvia's influence over Balboa..................... 34
Florida, discovery of.............................. 55
Fitting out an expedition to bring back Cortez from
     Mexico....................................... 168
Florida, Narvaez in............................... 211
Fray Vincente de Valverde and Atahualpa.......... 286
Gold, division of, at Comagre's dwelling........... 40

PAGE

Garabito Andres arrives from Cuba................. 76
Garabito Andres betrays Balboa..................... 83
Golden hill, Narvaez's search for................... 211
Guayaquil, Gulf of................................ 261
Hatuey, cacique of Cuba burned.................... 58
Hurtado Bartolome supersedes Balboa.............. 87
Huayna Capac first hears of white men............ 250
Huascar assassinated............................. 293
Internal quarrels at Darien.....................· 47
Indian slaves, cruelty to......................... 112
Indian legends of Peru........................... 117
Iztapalapan...................................... 157
Inca's reply to the Dominican friar............... 287
Inca Toparca dies at Xauxa....................... 308
Indian captives sent to De Soto at Havana.......... 334
Indians attack De Soto's troops................... 341
Indian queen seized by De Soto................... 353
Juan de la Cosa settles a quarrel between Ojeda and
    Nicuesa..................................... 2
Jamaica, dispute settled... 2
Juan de Esquibel first governor of Jamaica......... 2
Jester of Governor Velasquez..................... 97
Juan Diaz, conspiracy of......................... 134
King of Tezcuco interviews Cortez................ 155
Leoncico, Balboa's bloodhound.................... 37
Lares de Amador................................. 94
Lake Chalco..................................... 156
La Villa Rica.................................... 171
Llama, the only beast of burden in the New World.. 231
"Little Philip"... 251
Morales and Pizarro at the Island of Pearls......... 78
Mexico.. 122
Marina, Doña, Cortez's interpreter................ 125
Marina's story................................... 126
Montezuma hears of Cortez....................... 127

PAGE

Mexico, Valley of.................................... 151
Montezuma's forebodings........................... 154
Montezuma under Spanish protection............... 171
March to Cuzco..................................... 302
Manco Capac claims the throne of Peru............. 309
Manco Capac crowned Inca.......................... 314
Manco Capac pledges allegiance to Spain........... 315
Midnight attack at Chicaca......................... 357
Mississippi, discovery of........................... 363
Moscoso chosen in place of De Soto................. 370
Nicuesa settles his dispute with Ojeda.............. 6
Nombre de Dios..................................... 27
Nicuesa forced to fly to the woods................. 28
Nicuesa perishes at sea............................ 29
Negroes brought from Spain 63
Narvaez sets sail to capture Cortez................ 170
Narvaez at Cempoallo.............................. 178
Narvaez wounded in the teocalis................... 181
Narvaez and officers captured..................... 182
Narvaez obtains commission from Charles V. to ex-
    plore Florida... 210
Narvaez, fate of.............................. 211
Ojeda sails.. 13
Ojeda leaves Darien with Bernardino de Talavera.... 23
Ojeda, death of.................................... 55
Oviedo, notary and historian...................... 74
Olmedo, priest.................................... 123
Ortiz, Jean, rescued by Spaniards.................. 341
Ochus, De Soto's ships at.......................... 356
Pizarro, Francisco................................. 4
Pizarro arrives at Carthagena...................... 22
Ponca, conquest of................................. 38
Ponca won over to Balboa.......................... 49
Pacific Ocean, the discovery of.................... 52
Ponce de Leon, search for the fountain of youth...... 55

PAGE

Pedrarias, governor of Darien...................... 72
Pizarro first hears of Peru.......................... 79
Panama, town of, founded......................... 82
Palm Sunday service............................... 122
Pedro de Alvarado left in command at Mexico....... 174
Pizarro chooses to go to Peru....... 211
Pedro de Candia........................... 212
Pizarro arrested at Seville (1528)............... ... 226
Pizarro on being released goes to Toledo............. 228
Pizarro and Cortez, before Charles V............... 230
Pizarro granted commission by the queen, to conquer
        Peru, July, 1529...... 232
Pizarro visits his birthplace. 233
Pizarro's four brothers enlist in the enterprise....... 233
Peruvian superstitious and warnings................ 250
Pizarro's army.................................... 256
Pizarro sails for Tumbez........................... 257
Pizarro's march by land 257-258
Puna, island of.................................... 260
Puna, conflict at.................................. 261
Peruvian scenery.................................. 265
Pizarro's march from San Miguel.................... 268
Piura, Spaniards crossing the...................... 269
Pizarro addresses his soldiers...................... 271
Peruvian roads.................................... 276
Plaza, or public square in Caxamalca............... 283
Pizarro preparing to seize the Inca................. 284
Pizarro wounded.................................. 289
Pizarro and Almagro come to De Soto's relief........ 308
Pizarro entering Cuzco............................ 310
Pizarro's proclamation............................. 311
Peruvian festivities............................... 315
Quaraqua defeated................................ 49
Quetzalcoatl, popular tradition of.................. 131
Quizquiz slain.................................... 316

PAGE

Regidor Valdivia's return...................... 43
Reporter for Montezuma...................... 130
Royal audience of San Domingo seek to prevent Velasquez................................. 170
River of Canoes, Cortez at.................... 175
Ruiz, Pizarro's pilot......................... 212
Rumor of uprising at Huamachuco 293
Road of the Incas to Cuzco.... 302
San Domingo........ 1
Santa Maria de la Antigua del Darien............. 25
South Sea heard of...................... 41
St. Antonio, Cortez at.................... 105
San Juan de Ulua, Cortez arrives at........... 123
Spaniards land at Vera Cruz.................. 128
Soldiers of Cortez falter..... 153
Sandoval commander at La Villa Rica.......... 171
Salvatierra's boast....................... 174
Spanish conquerors, character of.............. 243
St. Mathew Bay, Pizarro at.................. 257
San Miguel, founding of.................... 265
Spaniards grow discontented................. 270
Spaniards suffer crossing the Andes........... 277
Silver, Spanish horses shod with............. 294
Silver bars of Peru...................... 311
Seville, mustering of De Soto's army at..... 332
Spanish barbarity....................... 345
Spaniards at Tallahasse..................... 348
Truxillo, birthplace of Pizarro............... 4
Tubanama, dominion of.................... 42
Trinidad, Cortez at...................... 103
Tobascan tribe.......................... 121
Teuhtlile, Mexican cacique 127
Teuhtlile's interview with Cortez.............. 128
Tierra Caliente, plain of........ 175
Tumbez, Pizarro landing at.................. 261

PAGE

Tumbez, fight at........ 262
Tangarala 265
Treasures brought to ransom the Inca......... 294
Toparca succeeds Atahualpa as Inca................. 301
Tampa Bay, De Soto at.............................. 335
Uraba, Gulf of...................................... 43
Valenzuela and brigantine lost at sea............. 24
Velasquez, governor of Cuba.... 57
Velasquez urged to recall the commission of Cortez... 99
Velasquez orders Cortez to return.................. 102
Vera Cruz, city of, laid out...................... ... 134
Velasquez decides to send Narvaez to bring back
    Cortez.. 167
Vilcacauga, Sierra of............................. ... 304
Valladolid, De Soto at............................. 332
Vasco Porcullo...................................... 335
Voyage down the Mississippi 372
Wandering of De Soto.............................. 355
Washita River, De Soto on... 368
Xeres de los Caballeros, the birthplace of Balboa.... 4
Xuarez sisters...................................... 59
Xochialco Lake....... 156
Xauxa, Pizarro halts at............................ 304
Xaquixaguana, in the vale of...................... 308
Yazoo River, Spaniards at......................... .. 357
Zenu, province of.................................. 24
Zemaco warns cacique of Dobayba.................. 44
Zemaco's plot to destroy the Spaniards............. 45
Zemaco surprised and slain....... 46
Zaran, Pizarro at.................................. 272

CHRONOLOGY.

PERIOD II.—AGE OF CONQUEST.

FROM A.D. 1509 TO A.D. 1542.

1509. ACCESSION OF HENRY VIII. to the throne of England,—April 21.

OJEDA sailed from San Domingo to conquer Darien,—Nov. 10.

1510. BALBOA by a strategy evaded his creditors and sailed with Encisco.

1511. CUBA conquered by Velasquez.

1512. PONCE DE LEON discovered and named Florida,—March 27.

BALBOA supplanted Encisco as Governor of Darien.

1513. BALBOA discovered Pacific Ocean,—Called it the South Sea.

1514. BALBOA superseded by Pedrarias.

1517. BALBOA executed by order of Pedrarias.

CORDOVA discovered Mexico.

1519. CORTEZ, with a land and naval force, sailed from Cuba to conquer Mexico.

1520. MAGELLAN, a Portuguese, in the service of Spain, explored Straits of Magellan.—He named the Pacific Ocean.

NARVAEZ, sent to bring back Cortez, defeated and captured in Mexico.

THIS YEAR DE AYALLON led an expedition to Carolina,—called it Chicora.

1521. CORTEZ CONQUERED MONTEZUMA in Mexico—which he called New Spain. Montezuma died of wounds received from his own subjects.

1522. FIRST CIRCUMNAVIGATION of the globe by Magellan's ship.

1524. VERRAZANO explored the coast from Carolina to New Foundland,—Called it New France.

1528. NARVAEZ attempted to conquer Florida. His fate is unknown. Four survivors reached Mexico.

1530. PIZARRO sailed with fleet and army to conquer Peru.

1531. PIZARRO CONQUERED PERU.—Inca put to death. City of Lima founded.

1534. CARTIER, a Frenchman, under Roberval, explored Gulf and River of St. Lawrence.

1539. DE SOTO WITH TEN VESSELS and 600 men sailed from Havana, Cuba, to conquer Florida,—May 14.

1540. DE SOTO wandering in the wilderness in Florida.

1541. DE SOTO DISCOVERED THE MISSISSIPPI RIVER,—May 17.

1542. CABRILLO, a Portuguese in the service of Spain, explored the coast of California.

1542. HERNANDO DE SOTO DIED AT NOON and was buried in the river he discovered. A few of his followers under Mascoso afterward found their way back to Cuba,—May 21.